By Chance

Kerry Love and Jill Cammack

To best friends everywhere

By choice or by chance
By chance or by choice
We wait for fate
Or use our voice
Either/or it seems to be
Is life our plans or destiny
But say the sage
All things are true
So maybe it's
A blend of two
We chance the choice
Or choose the chance
But shake your ass
'Cause life's a dance

1

None of them look like a movie star to me, Beth thought as she looked out at her new class. It was the first day of the fall semester and the room was filled with the same mix of students she saw every year. There were frat guys, goth kids, surfers, and preps. Several of the students had the classic California-girl look with long blonde hair and sun kissed skin that sometimes made them hard to tell apart until she got to know them better. The boys seemed to be more varied—everything from the slim, awkward computer programmers who didn't look old enough to drive to the hulking, bearded athletes who looked closer to middle age than college-aged. And then there were the ones who had cherubic boy faces atop hairy man bodies. They reminded Beth of centaurs, the mythical half man, half horse.

"Good morning," she said. "This is Creative Writing. Is everyone in the right place?" The students looked around at each other but remained silent. "Am I in the right place?" she added. A few of them nodded but most just stared at her.

"Well, that's a relief because I have totally gone to the wrong classroom on the first day of school before and that's really embarrassing." Finally, a couple of students laughed.

"I believe in easy first days so we're just going to go over the syllabus and introduce ourselves. I'll start," she said, smiling warmly at them. "I'm Beth Grant. I grew up in a little town in Florida called New Smyrna Beach. Anyone heard of it?" The students stared at her blankly and she laughed. "No? I didn't think so." The students continued to stare at her and she marveled at how this class of strangers, in just a few short weeks, would all become her 'kids.' It was her favorite part about teaching.

"Okay, now, I'd like to know about you. Tell me your name, where you're from, and your favorite thing to eat." The students looked confused again. "Imagine it's your birthday and you can have any meal you want. What is it? Roscoe's chicken and waffles? Grandma's meatloaf? In and Out Burger? And be specific. Don't just tell me pizza. What kind of pizza? Thin crust? Deep dish? Lots of cheese? What's on it? What makes it so good? Remember this is *creative* writing. Now," Beth paused and grinned, "who wants to start?"

Most of the students looked down at their desks. Finally, a small, pale girl raised her hand. The pixie cut of her dark hair gave her an elvish quality Beth found charming. Her name was Michelle and she said her favorite meal was sushi and a gallon of Dr. Pepper. As the students shared about themselves, the awkward, first-day tension dissipated. When it was the last student's turn, a centaur named Caleb who was describing the best fish tacos he'd ever had, the door opened and a tall, broad-shouldered guy slipped into the room. He took a seat in the back and Beth knew without looking exactly who he was. When Caleb finished, she turned to the newcomer.

"Hi, welcome. We're doing introductions, so please tell us your name, where you're from, and your birthday meal."

He took off his sunglasses and she noticed something vaguely familiar about him. "Uh, birthday meal?" The class stirred as they began to recognize him. On the spectrum of the male college student, this guy was firmly in the full-grown man category. It wasn't just that he was tall or muscular, though he was both. It was more than that. Something about him dwarfed everyone else in the room. Even the tattered baseball hat he wore couldn't hide it. Beth's heart stopped beating for a moment but she barely noticed. *And that must be what a movie star looks like.*

"Yes, the meal you'd eat if it was your birthday. Or just your favorite thing to eat. And be specific." She smiled at him encouragingly.

"Uh, okay. I'm Todd. I'm from Miami. And I, um, really like breakfast."

"That's good," Beth said as a few of the students began to whisper. "I like breakfast, too. But are you a waffles kind of guy? Or bacon and eggs? Biscuits and gravy? What exactly would you have?"

"Uh, I guess…" Just then a phone began to ring.

"Shit," he said, digging in his pants pocket. Beth had expected him to take the phone out and silence it. So she was shocked when he looked at the screen, mumbled an apology, and left the classroom.

She closed her gaping mouth when she realized the class was watching her for a reaction. "Well, I guess we'll never know. All right, let's take a look at the course syllabus." Somewhere between her attendance policy and assignment breakdown, Todd returned to his seat at the back of the class.

"Now, you did a pretty good job with your meals today. But," she paused and looked around the room. "I think you can do better. So for next class, you'll need to expand on that and write out a detailed description of your favorite meal, how it tastes, what it smells like, the texture, and even the memory you associate with it. What makes that meal so special to you? Just a couple of paragraphs, no more than a page. Okay?" A few of them nodded. "Are there any questions about this assignment or anything we've talked about today?"

She was about to dismiss them when a hand shot up. It was the girl with the pixie cut. Beth nodded at her. "Michelle, right?"

She nodded. "Professor Grant, I was wondering, what is your birthday meal?"

Beth laughed, a big happy sound that bubbled up from deep in her stomach. "Well, I guess it would have to be a vat of Pancho's guacamole and a margarita on the rocks." Michelle nodded in appreciation, and someone in the back of the class said, "Oooh, I love Pancho's!"

Someone else called out. "Class field trip!"

Beth laughed again. "I'll think about it but I'm pretty sure the administration would frown on that." There were a few dramatic groans of disappointment and she couldn't help but smile at the energy of the class. If they were this open and responsive on the first day, it was going to be a good semester, despite celebrity interruptions.

* * *

The day before, Beth had been sitting in her tiny office wondering where the summer had gone when there was a knock. The door opened before she could reply and she knew this little lack of courtesy could only mean one thing: Gene Walker.

"Hi, Gene," she said and bit back the same snicker she did every time she greeted the head of her department. The battered chair across from her creaked and sighed loudly as he sat down. As the last faculty member hired, she had the smallest office of anyone in the English department, maybe even the whole college. When colleagues would stop by and ask how she could work in a space barely bigger than a closet, she would sigh and shrug and put on her "make the best of it" face. But secretly she loved it. It was cozy, it had a window, and it was more of an office than she had ever had before. Even if it was outfitted with orphaned and discarded furniture including the olive green chair where Gene now sat. The chair was probably older than she was and the wooden legs were uneven, causing the occupant to tilt awkwardly forward. She had meant to bring in a saw and even up the legs until she noticed that the uncomfortable chair seemed to keep visitors from lingering. Except for Gene.

"Hello, Beth. How was your summer?" He crossed his ankle over his knee, displaying a swath of hairless white flesh.

"Good, but too short. You?"

"Yep. Same thing every year. I can't believe how quickly the time goes by," Gene said. "We took the RV back to Alabama to visit family. Little Jean got to spend time with her sisters shopping and gossiping and all those things you ladies like to do." Gene's wife was also named Jean and Beth found her to be equally unpleasant.

Seriously, dude? Beth inwardly cringed but bit back a snarky response.

He continued, folding his hands on his soft belly. "But enough about the summer, I want to talk to you about something. I gave a student an override for your creative writing class."

Even though it was rare to give a student an override for a writing class, it seemed odd that Gene would want to discuss it with her in person. *Why didn't he just email me?* "Okay. Is that all?"

"Yes, yes, but you should know, this student is different."

"How so?" Beth felt the smallest flash of dread.

"Well, he's an actor. A fairly popular one, from what I

gather. He's decided to go back to school in between films."

"Really?" She hadn't expected that. "Who is it?"

"Todd Allman. The young man who played He-Man."

"Todd Allman?" The name didn't even sound familiar. Despite living in southern California for the last year, Beth hadn't caught the Hollywood bug. She couldn't even remember the last movie she'd seen, let alone who was in it. "I don't think I know who that is."

"No matter. You just need to make sure you provide him with any accommodations he may need."

"Sure. I don't see why that would be a problem." She was trying to figure out what Gene wasn't saying, why the tone of the conversation seemed so strange.

"Well, I did recommend that he take his first class from a more tenured professor. You know, someone with a little more experience to help guide him but..."

And there it is... "Wait, this is his first class? He hasn't taken the prerequisites?" Her Creative Writing class was not just a random elective. It was an upper level course and required at least two prior English classes.

"The dean has decided to make an exception. I really don't think it will be an issue, Beth. His people have assured us that he is quite serious about this class."

"His *people*?" The thought popped out of her mouth before she could stop it and she hoped it didn't sound as snarky out loud as it did in her head. Gene didn't seem to notice.

"I told them that because you are a more junior faculty member, I will personally oversee his progress in your class."

"Oh." Again, Beth wasn't sure what to say. The thought of Gene looking over her shoulder all semester made her eye twitch.

"So, I expect you to make sure that he is happy here. I don't think I have to remind you how precarious funding is for our department."

"Funding?" All the reading between the lines was giving her a headache.

Gene sighed heavily. "I'd really prefer to handle it myself but since that's not an option, I need you to work with me on this. The dean is keenly aware of the exposure and potential income that this student can generate for the department. If you don't think you can get on board with that..." His voice trailed off, an unspoken threat.

She forced a smile. "Of course, Gene. I'm just trying to make sure I understand you."

"Listen, this is his first class and we want to make sure he feels at home here. I'm only asking you to make sure that he has what he needs to be successful, which may mean going above and beyond as his instructor."

Beth nodded. "Okay. I'll be happy to work with him on his schedule or whatever. But what if he... well, what if he doesn't do the work? You don't want me to just give him a pass on the writing, do you?"

"If his work in your class becomes an issue, I will take over the management of his grades. Are we clear?"

Oh, you'll take over the grading? That way he passes the class even if he doesn't deserve to? She wanted to protest. Students who thought they were the exception to every rule were the only thing Beth hated about teaching. Now a celebrity was going to be in her class demanding special treatment all semester long, with Gene standing over her making sure he received it. It pained her to do so but she just nodded, "Yes, I understand."

"Thanks Beth. I'll let you get back to your course prep," Gene said as heaved himself out of the chair with a puff of stale coffee breath.

Before he could close her office door she called out. "Wait, Gene! Why did you put him in my class?"

"His people requested it."

* * *

Beth had just walked into her house and dropped her bag on the kitchen table when the phone rang.

"Hi, Jenna," she said. Jenna was her best friend and the main reason she had moved to Los Angeles the year before.

"Tell me all about Todd Allman! How did it go?"

"Ugh," Beth groaned. "He showed up 20 minutes late. Which I don't usually mind on the first day, except his phone went off in the middle of class and then instead of turning it off, he left to take the call!"

"Okay but what was he like? Was he as hot in person? He used to date that Victoria's Secret model Missy DeVida but they broke up."

"I have no idea who that is. And who cares what he looks like if he's an ass?"

"He was probably just nervous. I read an interview with him in GQ and he seemed cool. I bet he's actually really nice," Jenna said.

"Oh, well if a magazine article says he's cool..."

Jenna ignored her. "Hey, Asha is getting back this weekend so I told her we would meet her out on Saturday." Asha was Jenna's college roommate. She had been on tour all summer with her husband Levi, the lead singer of the rock band, Dipping Bear.

"Okay, want to grab dinner at Pancho's?"

"No! We're not going Pancho's. We go there all the time. We're going to their new place, The Meat Shed."

"Whose new place? What's a Meat Shed?"

"It's *The* Meat Shed. And Levi and Asha are part owners."

"I don't know, Jen. You know how the first few weeks of

school go. I'm pretty beat. Maybe I'll just sit this one out."

"You are not sitting this one out!" Jenna was practically shouting. "When was the last time you went out? When was the last time you even flirted with anyone?"

"Actually, you'd be proud of me. I hit on some guy at the gas station last week."

"What? Who? At a gas station? Why didn't you tell me?"

"I don't know," Beth said. "I never heard from him so I forgot."

"Well, did you give him your number?"

"I gave him my business card."

Jenna sighed, exasperated. "Beth, no one *calls*. No wonder you haven't heard from him. He probably tried to text your office phone."

"Well, whatever. My email address was on there, too."

"Email address! Ha!" Jenna began to laugh. "You have no game."

2

The following day when she checked her email, Beth found 47 override requests from students trying to get into her creative writing class. While she was trying to decide whether to mass delete the emails or respond to each, there was a knock on her office door.

"Come in!"

A young woman with breasts too artificially full for her slender frame entered the office carrying a form.

"Can I help you?" Beth asked, already guessing what she wanted.

"Um, I just talked to Dr. Walker, and he said that you could, like, maybe give me an override into your creative writing class."

Like hell, Beth thought. "I'm sorry. That class is full."

"Right, but I like need that class to graduate," the young woman said, flipping her long, straight hair over her shoulder, her tiny tank top riding up to expose a flat, tanned stomach.

Beth sighed and took the form, looking it over. "Bentley, is it? It says here that you're a business major."

"Right, but I want to be in the *movie* business and I need your class so I can graduate in December," Bentley said.

Beth bit her lip to keep from laughing. If this young lady

10

weren't so ridiculous, such a complete cliche, she might actually admire her moxie.

"You can take any elective in any department to satisfy your requirements for graduation," Beth said as patiently as she could. "And as a business major, you haven't taken the prerequisites for this course."

"You don't understand. I've always wanted to be, like, a writer. It's my dream and I'm graduating in December. This is my last chance to take your class."

"If you're really interested in writing, I can see if I have an opening in my intro class," Beth said, turning to her computer to pull up the course information.

Bentley stopped, visibly changing gears. "Listen, Professor, um..." she looked down at the nameplate on Beth's desk. "Grant. I know Todd Allman is in your class. I need to be in class with him so he can help me like, get discovered. I'm totally serious about getting into the business and this could be my big break. You have to let me into your class."

Beth shook her head. "I'm sorry. That class is full. I'm not giving any overrides this semester." *Honestly, I do not have time for this shit!*

"But you don't understand. This might be my only chance." She sounded close to tears.

Maybe she'll make it as an actress after all. "Listen, I'm sure it will all work out. But I can't give you an override into that class. I've had 47 requests already today and no one else is getting in. Not even actual English majors."

Bentley snatched the form out of Beth's hand and turned on her heel. As she left, Beth thought she heard the girl mutter "bitch" under her breath.

Fucking Todd Allman, she thought as she closed her laptop and headed to class.

* * *

A flock of people, mostly young women, stood chattering and primping outside of the classroom. *Good lord, am I going to have to deal with this all semester?*

"Excuse me, please," Beth said in her stern teacher voice as she tried to squeeze by them.

One of the women, a pretty brunette in very small, lacy shorts glared at her. "We're all waiting for Todd. You don't need to just push your way through."

"Push my way through? This is *my* classroom!" Beth said, gritting her teeth. "And you are blocking the door."

"Oh," the woman said, without apology. "You're his teacher? Tell us, what he's like!"

Beth ignored her and punched the code into the keypad on the classroom door. "You all need to move. My class starts in ten minutes and you cannot stand here. It's disruptive and it's a fire hazard." Some of them shuffled away but most didn't move.

In the classroom, she set up her presentation while her students whispered to one another and glanced at the door. Todd Allman was noticeably absent. She tried to start class but the noise in the hallway had only gotten worse. *Time to pull up my bitch pants and lay the smack down.*

"Just a minute," she said to the class and strode purposefully down the aisle. Beth opened the door into a flutter of hair flipping and eyelash batting. In the middle of the commotion was Todd. He was smiling politely and posing for a selfie with two of the young women.

"Excuse me," Beth interrupted. "I am trying to hold class in here. You all need to take this circus elsewhere." Todd looked up at her and she thought she saw him cringe. The crowd reluctantly started to disperse. A few moments later, Todd slipped in and sat at a desk in the back of the room.

After class, as Todd turned to leave with the other students,

Beth called out to him. "Mr. Allman, do you have a moment?"

"Uh, yeah. Sure."

"Join me in my office, would you?"

He followed her down the hallway to a door with a small rectangular window. She unlocked it and ushered him in. He was an imposing figure in her office and she had to squeeze behind him to get to her desk. "Sit," she said gesturing to the green chair. He slouched like a disobedient child across from her. "I understand that your situation is different from my other students. That you have certain..." She paused, searching for the right word. "Constraints."

"Yes, ma'am," he said.

The "ma'am" caught her off guard and she raised an eyebrow trying to decide whether he was messing with her or not. He continued, "I appreciate your understanding. I didn't mean to be an interruption."

"Yes, well, you were an interruption," she said brusquely. "I know it must be tricky for you, but I have a class full of students that I have to think about, many of whom are getting through school by working multiple jobs so they can pay for tuition. I can't let you interfere with their learning." Then before she could help herself, she added, "They actually deserve special treatment more than you do."

"Special treatment?" Todd raised his head and met her eyes defiantly. "I didn't ask for special treatment."

Beth crossed her arms over her chest. "Didn't you? As I understand it, you haven't even taken the prerequisites for the this class, have you?"

"Well, no but I don't want any other special treatment," he stammered.

"I told Dr. Walker and Dean Hatton that I would make allowances for your schedule and other things beyond your control, but getting to class on time is well within your control, is it not?"

"I was here on time," Todd protested. "You think it's my fault that people wait for me in the hallway? You think I enjoy the extra attention?"

The force of his response surprised her. But she wasn't backing down. "Mr. Allman, you made a *choice* to join my class. My students did not choose to have a class with you. I can appreciate that the lifestyle you have *chosen* makes certain things difficult for you. However, getting here late and interrupting my class by causing a scene in the hallway is unacceptable."

"You have no idea what my life is like," Todd muttered.

"Excuse me?" Her temper was about to get the better of her. Then she remembered her conversation with Gene and what it would mean if Todd complained about her, if she didn't work with him, keep him happy. Taking a deep breath, she was going to try to back-pedal when he spoke.

"Sorry," he said, looking down at his hands. "It's just hard to get away, sometimes." He pushed the brim of his hat up, rubbing his forehead. "I have to try really hard not to be a dick… um, sorry, I mean jerk."

Is he blushing? Beth sighed, the exasperation draining from her, replaced with something softer. "Hey, I get that it's tricky for you." There was empathy in her voice now. "Please just do the best you can to keep the ruckus in the hallway to a minimum and to get to class on time." The office darkened as Todd met her eyes and again she felt there was something familiar about him. *Maybe I have seen one of his movies?* Unsettled, she looked away from him, over her shoulder out the window. Thick gray clouds were rolling in. *What the heck?*

When she turned back he was nodding. "Okay."

"Though I'm not sure how you'll do that. Those ladies seem very persistent." She smiled at him and he hesitated before returning his own million dollar grin.

"You have no idea."

"Well, oddly enough, it looks like it's about to pour so get out of here before you get soaked. I'll see you on Tuesday." He stood up and walked to the door.

"And Todd?"

"Yeah."

"Sometimes it works best to come in the back way, around the psych building. Whenever I want to slip out, I go that way. I'll email you the code to the classroom so if you want to get there early to avoid the crowd, you can."

"Okay. Thanks, Professor Grant."

Beth looked back out her office window. *If I hurry, maybe I can make it home before Homer freaks out.* Homer was her eighty pound chicken dressed up like a dog who was afraid of thunderstorms. Whenever it rained, he would make a nest in the shower with anything he could find. She felt terrible coming home to him hunched in the bathroom shaking in terror. It was something she almost never had to worry since they had moved to California.

She grabbed her bag and headed out to the parking lot. It was deserted, all the students in class or having taken shelter from the incoming storm. It was dark and windy and the air seemed to crackle with energy. She had never seen a sky like that in Los Angeles. It looked like a summer afternoon in Florida.

Beth dug through her bag for her keys as she stepped off the curb. But the storm was moving faster than she thought and halfway through the parking lot the sky opened up. *Shit!* She broke into a run. The rain was so heavy she felt like someone was dousing her with a hose. Streaks of water ran down her face into her eyes making it impossible to see the crack in the uneven pavement. Her heel caught and she tumbled to the ground, her bag flying out in front of her, her shoe flying off behind her.

"Ow! Shit!" she shouted, then pounded the ground with her fist, laughing at her own ridiculousness. *Stupid!* She sat back on her butt, the water soaking through her jeans and underwear. There was no sense in hurrying now. She pulled off her other heel and got to her feet as the rain started to let up. If she had just waited two minutes, she wouldn't have been caught in the downpour, at least not the worst of it. Gathering her bag and shoes, she plodded toward her truck, the wet pants chafing her legs with each step.

The parking lot had become a maze of puddles. At first, Beth tried to avoid them. *Why am I bothering?* she wondered. She couldn't be any wetter if she had jumped in a pool. So she slogged right through the next puddle, kicking up a spray, leaving a wake behind her. It was surprisingly satisfying. She glanced around to make sure she was alone, then, just for a minute, Beth jumped in the puddle, laughing, splashing, and stomping like when she was a little girl.

When she got to her truck, she flung the door open and threw her stuff on the passenger seat. She stepped one bare foot onto the edge of the truck to hoist herself in and felt the water oozing out of her pants. The idea of making her commute in wet jeans stopped her. She looked around. The parking lot was still empty, a good half hour before the next wave of classes ended. There was an empty van parked next to her and her open truck door would block the view of anyone in the building. She turned around and squinted at the row of cars behind her. Seeing no one, she hastily unbuttoned her pants and shimmied out of them, flinging them into the truck and hopping in after them.

3

Jenna flopped down on her couch. "So tell me. How was your second class with Todd Allman?"

"Eh, it's just annoying really. There were all of these people waiting for him in the hall before class. And do you know how many stupid kids tried to get an override just to be in class with him?"

Jenna laughed. "I know I would have. Have you seen his spread in GQ?"

"I haven't seen his anything anywhere," Beth said. "What movie was he even in?"

"Movies, Beth. Plural. I told you, he was in the He-Man franchise. How do you not know this? I thought you were going to google him."

"I forgot." Beth shrugged and took a sip of her wine. "And honestly, I really don't care. He's just a pain in the ass. I'll be glad when this semester is over."

Jenna rolled her eyes. "I am going to show you what the big deal is. Maybe then you'll understand." She set down her wine and grabbed her laptop off the coffee table. "Come here."

Beth sat down next to Jenna and looked at the screen. There were dozens of pictures of Todd Allman. Jenna clicked on a GQ cover of Todd in a dark gray suit with a bright blue tie. His broad shoulders looked like they were spilling off the sides of the magazine. The corner of his mouth turned up in just a hint of a smile. He had a faint scar running through his left eyebrow that seemed to punctuate his eyes. *How have I not noticed how dark his eyes are?* Beth wondered. The deep brown, nearly black was a startling contrast to his sun-bleached hair.

Jenna clicked on the slideshow and Beth watched as the screen filled with a picture of Todd in a wetsuit, holding a surfboard. His blond hair wet, his grin wide. Jenna kept clicking and picture after picture flashed before them. Todd with his chin on his steepled fingertips, looking serious. Todd walking backward down the street laughing, his arms wide. Todd in a laundromat wearing only a pair of unbuttoned jeans, leaning over a sexy, young woman backed up against an industrial dryer.

"See?" Jenna said. "You have to admit he's good looking."

Beth took another sip of her wine. "Well, yeah, in those pictures. But he doesn't look like that in real life. He's always wearing a ratty old baseball hat."

"I think he looks like a young, Paul Newman. But bigger, with the body of a... oh I don't know... of..."

"An Olympic swimmer," Beth finished, unable to look away from the screen filled with shirtless Todd Allman.

"Exactly!" Jenna was triumphant. "You should hit that. What a story to tell your grandkids!"

"Jenna! I'm not going to 'hit that.' He's my student!"

"I know it may scuff up your goodie-two-shoes, but you could break the rules just this once." Beth rolled her eyes and Jenna continued. "Okay, maybe not him but you do need to have sex with someone. How long has it been?"

"Um." Beth tried but she couldn't remember.

"And that's my point," Jenna said and shut the laptop.

* * *

"I thought the Meat Shed was a restaurant." Beth was looking at the line of shiny, polished people that snaked around the corner of a large industrial-looking, red brick warehouse.

"It is, but only until 11, then it turns into a nightclub."

"Why don't we just come back for dinner, instead?"

"Get out, Beth," Jenna said, as she handed her keys to the valet. "And stop tugging at the dress. You look great. I wish I had your boobs."

Beth realized that she had been simultaneously trying to pull the dress up to cover her breasts and down to cover her knees, bruised from her fall in the parking lot. *Fuck it,* she thought, pulling her shoulders back, holding her head high. *If I've got them, I might as well flaunt them.*

Elizabeth Grant did not have the type of look that stopped men in their tracks. At least not in Southern California. She was not blond, tan, or leggy. Her breasts were her own, round and full, and like many natural breasts, they were balanced by an equally round and full backside. She was not large by any normal standard but Los Angeles is not a place of normal standards. And her short, curvy frame would never be a sample size.

She had never tried Botox or even considered plastic surgery. She didn't get spray tans or fake nails. The only thing artificial about Beth was her hair color- a dark auburn that brought out her green eyes. It was a color that her stylist, Rene, had told her she was "born to have." Because she loved him and because she loved the touch of red, she didn't point out that if she was "born to have" auburn hair, she would have *actually* been born with it.

In any other part of the country, she would have been considered cute or even pretty. In Southern California, she was practically invisible. Until she smiled. Beth's smile was brilliant, and like sunlight, it warmed every place it touched. It transformed her face from the girl-next-door into something truly stunning and sometimes caused her students to fall just a little bit in love with her.

She followed Jenna past the line of people. Jenna kissed the bouncer on the cheek and they were inside. The club was already packed, warm with bodies pushing past each other, vying for a spot at the bar. Beth imagined this was exactly how cattle must have felt in a real meatpacking facility. For the hundredth time, she considered becoming a vegetarian. Jenna grabbed her arm and they squeezed through the crowd to a circular staircase at the far side of the room. Their heels clacked on the metal stairs as they made their way to the rooftop terrace.

It was a little quieter on the roof and Beth took a deep breath of the warm, dry air. They ordered drinks from a lanky bartender with a handlebar mustache. Jenna turned to her with a mischievous grin. "Maybe we'll see Todd Allman here tonight." She leaned her back against the bar and scanned the room hopefully.

Beth rolled her eyes. "God, I hope not. I've seen him enough this week." Just then, the woman next to Jenna turned to look at them. She had a deep orange spray tan and thick dark bangs that framed her round face. Her thin eyebrows arched high above bright white eyeshadow, giving her a look of perpetual surprise. When she saw Beth, she pulled a face like she had tasted something sour.

"You know Todd Allman?" she asked, skeptically.

"Um, no," Beth coughed, startled. She stared at the girl for a moment trying make sense of her. "I was, uh, making a joke."

"Oh," the orange woman sniffed, giving her a once-over. "I didn't think so."

When she turned back around Jenna began to giggle. "She looked like a jack-o-lantern," she whispered.

"Let's sit down," Beth said. "What's that over there?"

"They call that 'the eye.'"

In the center of the terrace was an enormous domed glass atrium that was surrounded by a low wooden bench. They walked up to the dome's railing and looked down. Although it was dark inside, Beth could make out the people below. She felt like a voyeur while at the same time exposed, and tugged on her dress again, wondering what someone might see if they did happen to look up.

Jenna held up her drink "To getting you laid!" Beth laughed and they clinked glasses. She took a gulp and immediately began to relax, finding it much easier not to fidget now that she had a drink in her hand. When their drinks were gone, Jenna headed back to the bar and Beth closed her eyes and inhaled deeply. She barely had a moment to herself when she felt someone sit down next to her.

"Geez, I leave you alone for 5 minutes and you get hit on! Did you run him off or what?" Jenna handed a drink to Beth.

"No, not really. Well, kind of I guess."

"What did he say?"

"He asked if he was interrupting my nap," Beth laughed.

Jenna scrunched her nose. "He said what?"

"When you went to the bar, I closed my eyes for a second, you know, just trying to be present. And he happened to walk up just as I was doing that."

"Well, is he getting you a drink?"

"He offered but I told him you were getting me one."

"What is wrong with you? You should have let *him* buy you a drink! You have zero chance of getting any action from me."

Beth laughed. "That's true. I just wasn't… I don't know. I

always feel weird taking a drink from some random guy."

Jenna checked her cell phone. "Oooh, Asha texted. She's waiting for us downstairs. Come on, we've had enough fresh air for now." Jenna grabbed Beth's hand and they crossed the terrace and descended the spiral staircase. She lead them to the raised section of the club that overlooked the dance floor. Small booths and tables dotted the plush red carpet that led to a private bar tucked in the back corner.

Beth leaned in to her. "VIP? Really?"

"This is Levi and Asha's place, of course we're going to the VIP section."

"Oh, right." Beth studied the club more closely. The Meat Shed was a big place but she kept being drawn back to the eye. Looking up through the same greenish glass she had just looked down from gave her a strange feeling of deja vu. "How did they manage that while they were out on tour?"

"Um, they have some other partners."

Beth heard a happy squeal and turned to see Asha rushing toward them. Jenna shrieked in delight and the big man at the entrance to the VIP section moved the velvet rope aside just in time for them to embrace each other. Physically, Asha and Jenna were opposites. Jenna was petite and fair with curly blond hair and a big bubbly smile under a smattering of freckles. Asha was tall with mocha skin, sleek black hair, and a serious face that belied her mischievous nature. She was a model for a few years but now spent her time designing for Levi's clothing line.

"Asha, I'm glad you're here because I need help. Tonight is operation G-B-L," Jenna announced. "Get Beth Laid!"

Beth rolled her eyes. "Jenna!"

"Well, finish your drinks and let's go dance," Asha said. "There are some hot men on the dance floor tonight. Oh, and mark your calendars, Levi and I are having a Halloween party and you have to come!"

Beth's attention wandered as Asha and Jenna tried to talk over the loud, pulsating music. There was something about The Meat Shed that was warmer than most clubs. She turned back to her friends and saw Asha smile, whisper to Jenna, then get up and stalk through the VIP area.

"What was that all about?" Jenna just shrugged, but a few moments later Asha returned followed by a guy with dark hair. They were each holding two shots. He was wearing a sheer white shirt unbuttoned a little too far, displaying his muscular chest.

"Ladies! This is George. He's the rep for Thrasher. You know, the energy drink that sponsored Levi's tour?" Asha shouted over the music. "George, this is my friend Jenna. And *this* is Beth!" She realized with horror that Asha was holding her arms out like Beth was part of the Showcase Showdown on *The Price Is Right*. "Doesn't she look hot tonight?"

"She sure does," George said. "But we actually met earlier." He took Beth's hand but instead of shaking it, he bent down and brought it to his lips. While his head bowed, Beth shot Asha an "are you kidding me?" look. When he stood back up, she saw that he did have a handsome face. His lips were on the thin side but he had a sweet smile and soft brown eyes.

"Can I buy you a drink now, Beth?" George asked. "I have a table in the corner."

"You don't need to. We already have a tab," Beth said awkwardly. George looked confused and she felt Jenna pinch the back of her arm. "I mean, um... Yes, thanks."

"Great!" he said, taking her by the hand to lead her to his table. Uncomfortable with touching a stranger, Beth slipped out of his grasp.

"I'll be right there," she called after him.

"I can't believe you sent him away before!" Jenna shouted.

Asha nodded. "He's *really* cute."

"If you can get past the shirt," Jenna added.

"I didn't even know they made see-through shirts for men," Beth said with more curiosity than snark.

"Okay, enough talk. It's time to put your game face on." She fluffed Beth's hair out over her shoulders and turned her in George's direction. "You're going in!" Jenna said, smacking her on the ass.

Sipping her drink, Beth tried to keep up with what George was saying as he shouted over the loud music to tell her about working at Thrasher. She politely nodded her head and smiled, but conversation was difficult and now three drinks in, Beth was itching to dance.

"George, it really was so nice to meet you. Twice now," Beth said loudly, putting her empty drink glass down. "And thank you for the drink. But I'm supposed to be having a ladies' night with my friends and I feel like I'm ditching them right now. Can I give you my number and maybe we can grab a drink some time, some place quieter?"

"Of course, of course," George said and gestured to the dance floor. "Maybe dinner too?"

Beth smiled instinctively and said, "I'd like that," before realizing that she actually meant it.

4

Beth was in her office prepping for class when George texted her a few days later, "hi beth it's george."

Oh boy, here we go, she thought. *What do I do? Do I text back right away or am I supposed to wait a little while?* But she didn't have it in her to play games. If that's what he wanted, she figured she wasn't right for him anyway.

BETH: Good morning. How are you?

GEORGE: just got back from the gym

Hmmm… how to respond?

BETH: Wow. You're really committed.

GEORGE: yep. gotta stick to my schedule

Okay. So… I guess…

BETH: Thanks again for the drink the other night.

GEORGE: yeah - no problem. hey would you like to get dinner this week?

BETH: Sure. What did you have in mind?

GEORGE: do you like flavor

Huh?

BETH: The flavor of what?

GEORGE: lol i meant the restaurant called flavor

BETH: I've never been there. But "flavor" sounds delicious. *Hahaha… I'm so funny.*

GEORGE: it's OK we can go there. i'm sure you will like it
Did he get my joke?
BETH: I'm sure it's great.
GEORGE: Friday work? give me your address
Um… no. Even if Ashsa can vouch for him…
BETH: I can meet you there. What time?
GEORGE: how about 8

Beth had left the house feeling confident but now that she was walking up to the restaurant, she was surprised by how her heart thudded in her chest. *I wonder if I've dressed up enough?* Beth had gone to Flavor's website and she could tell it was too swanky for jeans. But first dates were awkward enough without wearing something uncomfortable just to impress. So she settled on a black maxi dress, what Jenna called the "yoga pants of real clothes." Taking a deep breath, she stepped into the restaurant and found George waiting for her at the hostess stand. His smile when he saw her seemed so genuine that she relaxed a little.

"Right on time," he said, and gave her a quick peck on the cheek. "You look great, Beth."

"Thanks. You do, too."

Jenna and Asha were right. He *was* good-looking. George's clothes were perfectly tailored and highlighted his broad shoulders and narrow waist. The sleeves of his black shirt were rolled up to show off his tanned, muscular forearms. And his cologne smelled good, if a little strong. He placed his hand on the small of Beth's back and they followed the hostess through the main dining area. The restaurant had walls of natural stone and dark wood. Brightly-colored stained-glass light fixtures were hanging above each table and architectural artwork adorned the walls. The hostess led them out to the patio and sat them at a modern, candle-lit table.

"I hope it's okay, I requested a table outside."

Beth nodded. "It's fine."

The waiter appeared and set out two water goblets that he filled with a glass carafe.

"Have either of you dined with us before?"

"I'm a regular," George said.

"Fantastic! I'll give you a moment to look at the menu and then..."

"Actually, we'll start with a trois champignon flatbread and a glass each of the Santenay pinot to accompany. That is, if it's okay with you, Beth?"

"Sure. I don't know much about wine but I'm up for anything."

"I'm a bit of a wine expert so I won't steer you wrong," George said with a smile. "The Santenay is from Burgundy—that's in France."

"I didn't realize this was a French restaurant," Beth said.

"Oh, it's not. The trois champignon is just their mushroom flatbread. And I wouldn't normally start out with a red, but it really pairs well with mushrooms."

"Like I said, I'm up for anything. It's all Greek to me... or French rather." Beth grimaced inwardly and chastised herself for saying something so corny. Then she wondered how she would casually choke down an appetizer covered in her least favorite pizza topping. *Maybe this is why I don't date.*

"Are you in the mood for fish? Chicken? A salad? The entire menu here really is wonderful. It's all seasonal and really healthy."

How about a nice juicy steak? Beth looked down at the menu. Steak did not appear to be in season tonight at Flavor. She wanted to ask when exactly beef was in season but she bit her tongue. "Um... I'm not sure yet. Everything does look delicious."

When the waiter returned, they ordered and George picked out more wine. Then George asked, "So, Beth. What do you like to do when you're not teaching?"

"Well, I really enjoy paddle boarding. And also yoga. Jenna, my friend that knows Asha? She opened a studio back in March so I go there a lot."

"I love yoga."

"Really?" Beth was not great at small talk so she was relieved to find some common ground. And because her last two relationships, really her only two relationships, had begun as friendships, she had almost no experience with the "interview round" that seemed to be the protocol on first dates.

He continued, "Have you ever tried hot yoga? It's incredible. I think it's a great supplement to the gym."

"I did try that once. It wasn't really my thing." The only time she had tried hot yoga, she felt like she was being tortured inside a car in the Florida sun. In August. *But for people who really love to work up a sweat, it's probably great...*

The waiter brought their appetizer and Beth stared down at the piece of flatbread George had put on her plate. It was completely covered in mushrooms. There wasn't even any crusty edge. *Where exactly is the bread?*

"So how's a girl like you still single?" George asked, taking a large bite of his piece of flatbread.

Well, first, I am a woman not a girl... "Exactly what kind would that be?" She asked before she could help herself. *So much for small talk, Beth...* He looked a little flustered. *Whoops!*

"Oh, well... um, I don't know. I mean, like, someone pretty..." *Pretty? Because that's the most important thing about me...* But she bit her tongue this time. And while he stammered, she took the opportunity to pick up her flatbread at just the right angle to dump the top layer of mushrooms onto her plate.

She smiled at him and shrugged. "I've had a couple of serious relationships but I guess I just haven't ever thought of settling down as a goal." Which was true, even if she had been settled once. She wasn't going to share that with George. On a first date. She never shared Jeremy with anyone new. She had learned from experience that their responses were always awkward and often even painful. She didn't blame them. No one ever knew what to say to you about that kind of loss. She took a bite of the flatbread, forcing her teeth to slice through the slick, chewy fungi. *How do people enjoy something with this texture?* When George asked her if she liked it, she nodded politely and took a gulp of wine.

"So, how about you, George? What's your story?"

The rest of the evening went as most first dates go, a comparison of resumes and small talk. But the food was nice and the wine was nicer, and even the small talk got a little less small and a little more interesting. Halfway into the second glasses of wine, with George's handsome face smiling back at her from the other side of the candlelit table, Beth found she had relaxed enough to actually enjoy herself.

After the plates had been cleared, the waiter returned to ask about dessert.

"Nah," George said with a wave of his hand. "I think we're good."

What do you mean no dessert? The wine made her bold. "Actually, I'd like to look at the dessert menu, please."

"Of course." He smiled down at her and handed her a small menu. "I'll give you a moment to look it over."

"Uh, sorry. I didn't realize you wanted dessert." George said.

"I'm not sure I do," Beth smiled. "But I always like to see what they have. Don't you?" She was searching for something chocolate. But like beef, it seemed that chocolate too was not in season at Flavor.

"No, not really. I don't have much of a sweet tooth and I try to watch my carbs in the evening. It messes up my training."

"What are you training for?"

"Oh, I'm not training for anything in particular. I just try keep my body fat at 10% or less." Beth must have looked confused because he added, "I like to keep in shape."

"Yes, I can see that." She grinned at him flirtatiously over the menu and he visibly relaxed. When the waiter returned, Beth declined dessert, so he brought the check. And with that, all the first-date awkwardness was back. She hated this part of the date the most, maybe even more than small talk. *Is he going to pay? Should I offer to pay?*

"Let me just get my wallet," she said and dug through her purse. Before she could find it, George had already handed the waiter his credit card.

"Beth, please," George said, touching her hand across the table.

"Are you sure? I'm happy to split it or pay the tip or something?"

"No, I'm sure."

"Well, thank you." Beth breathed a silent sigh of relief. She had no idea how much those glasses of wine were but guessed they might be way over a college teacher's budget.

"My pleasure." He smiled at her, his hand still on hers. She waited a moment before slipping it out from under his. "Well, shall we?"

He walked her to the parking garage and looked at his watch. "It's still early, would you like to grab a drink somewhere?"

"I would but I'm driving. And it's been kind of a long week. Another time?"

"Sure," George said. "This is you?" He sounded surprised

as he took in the big, yellow truck.

"Yep."

"Well, that's not what I was expecting." He laughed. "I would have thought you'd drive something more…"

She raised an eyebrow. "More what?"

George laughed again. "Smaller, I guess. What is it? An old Jeep?"

"It's a '77 Landcruiser. I know it's not practical but I'm loyal and probably too sentimental and we have a history."

She opened the door and threw her purse in, then turned to face him, not sure what to do next. This was definitely in the top three awkward moments of a first date—to kiss or not to kiss? "Thank you for dinner," she said holding her hand out to him. He took her hand in his but instead of shaking it, he used it to pull her to him. Then in one swift motion, George put his other hand against the side of her face and kissed her gently. She felt herself instinctively lean in to him, putting her hands on his chest, kissing him back. His lips were strange and firmer than she expected, but nice. After a moment she pulled away. "Very smooth, Mr. Verrano."

"Come home with me?" She threw her head back and laughed. George grinned. "Can't blame a guy for trying."

"No, I guess not. Well, thank you again for dinner." Beth gave him a quick peck on the lips, then turned and stepped up into her truck.

5

Her eyes sparkled as she stood in front of the classroom. The caffeine was kicking in but it was more than just a coffee buzz. Beth loved teaching. Though she had never planned to go into education, it was truly her calling. And after Jeremy, teaching became more than her calling. It became her whole world. Behind her, the presentation screen was lit with an image of an ancient text, opened to the middle, smoke and stars pouring from its pages.

"Good morning class," she said looking out at the faces, some still half asleep. "Today I want to talk to you about," she paused and then spread her arms wide, "magic!" They stared at her blankly and she dropped her hands to her hips. "Come on! Who doesn't love magic?" A kid in the back yawned but at least had the decency to look embarrassed when she met his eyes. Beth was undeterred, confident she'd get them to engage. She almost always did. "Writing," she said, pausing for effect. "Is magic! What do I mean by that?"

The small young woman with short dark hair raised her hand. Beth nodded to her.

"Go ahead, Michelle."

"Um, like Harry Potter?"

Beth laughed. "Well yes, of course Harry Potter. That's literally magical. But the magic I'm talking about is more figurative." She changed the slide to a quote from Yeats.

The world is full of magic things, patiently waiting for our senses to grow sharper.

"What does Yeats mean by this?" Beth waited, watching the wheels turn. She had found that one of the hardest things to do while teaching was to pause and give the students space to come up with the answers.

Another young woman, this one with long blond hair and perfectly tanned skin raised her hand. Beth tried to remember her name *Kristy? No, Kelsey?* She nodded at the young woman who said, "That we need to look at the beauty of things?" Then Kristy/Kelsey glanced over at Todd self-consciously.

"Yes, that's definitely on the right track. Can anyone expand on that?" Half of the class looked blank and the other half looked at their laps, and probably their phones. Beth waited again. This time the lanky guy in the back of the class wearing a Sex Pistols shirt raised his hand. She nodded to him.

"Yeats is saying we are not observant enough to see the magic in the world around us."

"Good. Good. And can you tell me why I would pick that quote to start with?"

"Because to be good writers, we have to be good observers?" Sex Pistols stole a glance at Todd. *Seriously, people? He's just some guy.*

"Exactly! Thank you! But even more than just observers, we need to be explorers and discoverers. We need to hone our senses so that we can discover magic everywhere, in the extraordinary and, even more importantly, in the mundane. It's writing that's filled with magic that we remember. That kind of writing changes us. And I'm not just talking about Harry Potter, or Narnia, or Middle Earth. I'm talking about writing so vivid that it has the power to transport your reader—whether it's to Hogwarts to learn spells or to the floor of a gas station restroom where your character is having a meltdown. Writers who can harness that magic touch something deep inside of us."

She grinned at her students, some smiled back, some still looked asleep. Beth continued undeterred.

"You must be able to find magic in the world around you—and I don't just mean in sunsets and fields of tulips—I mean in the ugly, dirty parts of life, too. If you can't see the magic everywhere, you will never be able to put words together in a truly meaningful way. I try to see the magic in the everyday stuff—in a really great cup of tea, in a warm but not too hot day when I can roll the windows down in my truck and crank the music, in watching my dog sleep—especially if he's dreaming about chasing a squirrel and his paws are doing that twitching thing." She stopped and smiled at them, a few were actually smiling back. "But also in things like cleaning out my fridge or emptying the trash. There can be a magic in the satisfaction that you get from making more space in your world. Does that make sense?"

A few students nodded. "So now I want to ask you, who here has experienced some magic recently?"

The girl sitting next to Sex Pistols raised her hand timidly. "Yes Denice?"

She smiled shyly. "I got to go with my sister to her ultrasound yesterday. We found out she's having a baby girl."

"Denice, that's wonderful! You can't really get more magical than new life, can you?" Denice beamed and her eyes darted briefly to Todd Allman. Beth suppressed an urge to cringe. "Is this her first baby?" Denice nodded. "And your first time being an aunt?" She nodded again. "And how did that make you feel?"

"Gosh," she stammered, pink rising up her neck. "It was really cool. I could see her little heart beating. My whole family is just so excited."

Beth smiled and addressed the class. "The magic of new life will always be a great topic to write about. Especially if Denice can put into words the excitement and the emotion a family feels when they find out their world is about to be rocked by a little baby girl. But magic doesn't just have to be in those big moments where you discover that your life is expanding by a whole other person. It can also be in the little things. Who else has experienced some magic today?"

"The vending machine gave me two bags of chips when I only paid for one," Michelle said. Beth laughed.

"Okay, that's a good start Michelle. Now, what made that feel so special?"

"Well, I was running late to class and didn't have time to grab breakfast. And I was really hungry but I only had a dollar. So when two bags of chips dropped from that little spinny wheel in the vending machine, that sort of felt like magic." She looked directly at Beth without the hint of a peek in the movie star's direction. And for that, as well as her wit, Beth liked her very much.

"Good, good. That's exactly what I'm talking about. It's so simple and some people might just call it coincidence and not think twice about it but who can relate to Michelle's story?" She waited a moment as students raised their hands. "Right! Most of us can totally relate to the magical feeling when the universe hands us a little surprise! Even if it's as simple as an extra bag of chips—which can mean a lot when you're hungry. Am I right?" Some of the class nodded. "And Michelle may want to write an entire story based on the vending machine experience." The class laughed. "Hey, stories have been written about less. Or maybe Michelle just wants to remember that feeling of 'huzzah! double chips!' and incorporate that into a much larger story."

Beth changed the slide again.

"Words and magic were in the beginning one and the same thing, and even today words retain much of their magical power." - Sigmund Freud

"Words *are* magic. Which means writers are magicians. But it's not always the way you think. Sometimes the magic of words is just something so true, so honest and vulnerable, that we wonder 'huh, how can I have never thought that before?' Or maybe it's the opposite. Maybe the author puts into words something you never stop thinking about and you wonder, 'how did they know exactly what my heart feels?' Either way, they touch you with their magic. If you want to be a good writer, you need to get in harmony with the magic you see in the world around you and the magic you don't see but you know is there."

Beth clicked to the final slide.

"Magic is believing in yourself, if you can do that, you can make anything happen."- Johann Wolfgang von Goethe

"But most importantly, you need to get in touch with the magic you have inside you. You need to really believe that you have the power to put the magic you find around you onto the page. That your words are powerful enough to connect with your audience, no matter the topic. So this week, I want you to write about some magic but in a place where we don't normally find magic. Someplace mundane. For Denice, that might be a doctor's office. For Michelle, it might be a vending machine on a college campus. You can create a scene from personal experience or you can pluck something from thin air. It's your choice. But I want the location to be the center of the story. Don't focus on dialogue, we'll get to dialogue later. For now, I want the magic to be in the location or what's happening in the location. Any questions?"

Beth waited for the students to pack up their belongings and shuffle out before pulling her phone out to check for messages. When she looked up, she was surprised to see Todd Allman standing in front of her.

"Oh hi, Todd. What can I do for you?"

"Hi, uh. I have to go to Japan." He had shoved his hands into his pockets and was rocking back and forth on his heels.

Is he nervous? She wondered. And then with a twinge of guilt, *Maybe I shouldn't have been so hard on him the other day.* "Okay," she said slowly. "Right now?"

He laughed and stood up a little straighter. "No, no. I'm leaving on Monday, but I know the assignment is due next Thursday so I didn't know if you wanted me to turn it in early, before I leave, or email it to you or what."

The classroom door opened and a perky, young woman peered in at them.

Beth summoned her most teacherly voice. "Can I help you?" The girl didn't even answer, just popped back into the hall, letting the door close with a bang. Todd sighed. It was clear that she was waiting for him. And it was clear he didn't know her. *Jesus, how can you stand it?* She thought briefly of asking him but instead said, "Business or pleasure?"

"What?" He looked startled, his raised eyebrows almost disappearing under his baseball hat.

"Are you going to Japan for business or pleasure?" She clarified.

"Oh, for work. I have to go for work."

"All right," she said, "I don't usually accept work via email. It's just easier for me to grade hard copies, but in your case, it's fine. Do you think you can get it to me by Friday?"

He nodded. "Thanks Ms. Grant. I'll be back next week and I shouldn't have to miss any more classes this semester... well, maybe one…"

She waved her hand at him, half dismissing his absences, half shooing him out of the classroom. "That's fine. I'll see you when you get back." She gathered her things and followed him out of the classroom. In the hallway there were several people waiting, and as Beth left Todd and the gaggle behind, she almost felt sorry for him.

* * *

Later that week, Beth was in her office grading papers when her phone buzzed.

GEORGE: in your area, can you meet for coffee?

She flipped through the stack of assignments in front of her that she had planned to finish… *I guess they can wait.* As she shut down her computer with a little thrill of excitement, there was a knock. *Damn it!*

"Come in!"

Gene opened the door and sat down. Beth sighed in unison with the cushion of the chair. "I'm glad I caught you. How is your semester going so far?"

"Great," she said hesitantly, certain this was not the real reason for his visit, but not sure how to hurry him along. "But I'm actually just getting ready to leave for… an appointment."

"Good, good. Well, this won't take too long," he said, taking his glasses off and cleaning them on his shirt. "We just need to touch base about our star pupil. So how is Todd Allman doing?"

Of course… "He's fine. Why do you ask?"

"I was thinking we need to come up with an action plan on how to handle his education. That way you and I are on the same page. How have you been helping him get acclimated? Have there been any problems that I need to know about?"

What the hell is an action plan? Beth was confused. *Was I too harsh when I met with him the other day? Did he complain?* She had thought they ended on a positive note but now she wasn't so sure. "Um, just some groupies crowding the hallway but I suppose that's to be expected." She hadn't actually paid much attention to Todd, other than brushing off the annoyances of having a celebrity in her classroom. Hastily going back over their interactions for something else to add, she said, "And I offered to let him into the classroom early to avoid them. I don't anticipate it continuing to be a problem."

"Okay. What about his work? Are you providing him with whatever he needs?"

"Actually, he's on his way out of town for work but I told him he can turn his assignment in via email. And I gave him extra time on it since he'll be traveling." She silently thanked Todd for telling to her about his trip to Japan.

"Okay, good. Well, I'm counting on you to make sure he's comfortable. Don't forget, he's not a regular student. The same rules don't apply to him."

She rubbed her forehead to keep from rolling her eyes. "Of course, Gene. Whatever he needs." Beth was going to have to keep better tabs on Todd if these little meetings with Gene were going to be a regular thing. She looked at her watch. Now she was going to be late. *Fucking Todd Allman!*

"All right, good," he said rubbing his hands together. His nails were cut, or maybe bitten, to the quick making his chubby, pink fingers look like little sausages. "Well, I've got to be off." She was already shutting down her computer as he hefted himself out of the chair.

* * *

Vroom! The big engine of the 4x4 roared satisfyingly. Beth rolled down both windows, wound her hair into a bun and slipped on her sunglasses. She cranked up the volume and put the old truck in gear. The sun was shining, a breeze was blowing, and as Ludacris began to pump through her speakers, she was thinking of nothing but leaving work behind and meeting George. And just maybe, kissing him again.

Beth bobbed her head and sang along at the stoplight, waiting to turn out of campus. She was about to grab her phone and text George that she was running late when she saw movement out of the corner of her eye. Someone in the car next to her was waving. She looked over to see familiar dark eyes peering up at her from under a tattered baseball cap. Todd Allman was leaning out of the passenger window of a shiny black Porsche. She felt a hot flush creep across her cheeks and turned down the music.

"Professor Grant!" He grinned up at her, waving one muscular arm out the window.

"Hey Todd," she said, laughing at herself. "I thought you were in Japan."

"We're on our way to the airport right now," he said, gesturing to the guy next to him, who was now leaning forward and looking her over through his designer sunglasses. "This is my manager, Danny."

She waved. "Hi Danny."

"I just wanted to stop by and give you my paper but you weren't in your office," Todd continued. "I slid it under your door. I hope that's okay."

"That's fine," she said, wondering why he hadn't just emailed it to her. "When do you get back?"

"Not until next week."

The traffic light turned green and she shifted into gear. "Okay, see you then!"

6

"George, I'm sorry I'm late," Beth said, finding him at a table in the back. "My boss came in right as I was getting ready to walk out the door."

"Don't worry about it. I'm just glad you could meet me on such short notice." He stood up and gave her a quick hug. Beth caught a whiff of his cologne and felt her heartbeat faster. He smelled good and he looked good and she was glad she had agreed to meet him.

"So, was it a tough day on the job? What did your boss want?"

"Ugh, I have this 'special' student…"

She was interrupted by George's phone. "Oh," he said, frowning at his phone. "I'm so sorry. This is work. Let me just send them a quick text."

"No worries," Beth said.

George slid his phone back into his pocket. "So what were you saying about your boss?"

"Oh, it was nothing. Tell me, what brings you to this side of town?"

"There was a production meeting for the new commercial we're shooting. Nothing too stressful. What are you doing this weekend?"

"Oh probably just catching up on grading, maybe going to the beach. Watching football. The usual. What about you?"

"You like football?" George looked skeptical.

Beth shrugged. "Doesn't everyone?"

He laughed. "No, actually. I've never dated a girl who liked football."

"Well," she said, unable to stop herself. "I'm not a girl. I'm a woman."

"Yes, I noticed." George grinned at her over his coffee cup. "So who's your team?"

"Unfortunately," she groaned, "I'm a Dolphins fan. But I play fantasy too so at least my team wins sometimes."

"You play fantasy football?"

"You didn't know you were having coffee with the league champ, did you?" She smiled flirtatiously at him.

He laughed. "No, I did not. But I'm honored."

"So what about you? What are you up to this weekend?"

"I'm headed out of town. I've got to go to New York for work."

Beth was surprised to find she was a little disappointed. "Oh, cool. Jenna and I used to live in New York."

"Really? What did you do there?"

She and Jenna had moved to New York after college. She told him about doing her graduate work at NYU and getting a job as a copy editor. What she didn't tell him was that she took the copy editor job to keep her afloat while she pursued a writing career. Beth had stopped telling people about that dream. In Los Angeles, telling people you were an aspiring writer was as common and pitiable as telling people you were an aspiring actor. Plus, then she'd have to admit to herself how long it had been since she'd actually written anything. She also stopped short of telling him about losing her job in the recession, moving back home, and all that happened after.

"Jenna married her now ex Kent and moved out to Los Angeles. I left New York and taught in South Carolina for a while before moving here," Beth said. "What about you? Where are you from originally?"

"Here," George said and he told her about growing up in Los Angeles. He told her about being raised by a single mother—*we have that in common*—and about trying to keep his younger brothers out of trouble. And before she knew it, nearly two hours had passed.

Outside the coffee shop, he took her hand. "Can I see you when I get back?"

"Sure," she said, giving his hand a squeeze. "Just give me a call." Before she could feel awkward or make it awkward, she leaned in and kissed him. She liked the way it felt to be kissing someone and she was looking forward to his return from New York.

* * *

"You sound like you're in a box. Where are you?" Jenna asked.

Beth adjusted the phone in her lap. "You're on speaker because I'm driving."

"Where are you going?"

"I'm actually going to the Dolphins' game." She paused. "Guess who with?"

"Todd Allman!" Jenna's voice shouted excitedly from the phone.

"What? No! I can't believe you would even say that. Why are you so obsessed with him?"

"Um, I dunno… maybe because he's hot!"

Beth rolled her eyes.

"I can hear you rolling your eyes, Beth Grant." Beth laughed. "You were, weren't you? I know you so well. Okay, so are you going with George?"

"Yeah, it turns out Thrasher has some sort of private box at the stadium."

"Oooh, fancy! So do you like him?"

Beth thought for a moment. "Um, yeah. I think. He seems nice."

"Whoa, don't get carried away," Jenna laughed.

"It's nice to be with him. But I'm not sure if it's George or if it's just nice to be with *someone*."

"Well, does it matter at this point? You don't have to have it all figured out right now on your second date."

"Third date, if you count coffee last week."

"Okay, third date. Do you have to know if he's the one by your third date?"

"Jen, you know there isn't a 'one' for me. By the very definition of the 'one,' there can't be."

Jenna sighed, uncharacteristically serious. "Beth, do you honestly think that just because Jeremy died, that's it for you? That you are somehow destined to be alone?"

"No, no, that's not what I mean. I'm not trying to be melodramatic or anything. But I also know that I won't find what I had with Jeremy with anyone else. I just don't think there is someone else out there with that spark. That connection that makes you feel all heart-fluttery but at the same time calm and safe. Like you're home. Do you know what I mean?"

"I get what you're saying but I don't agree with you."

"No?"

"Every relationship is different. Just because you don't feel that spark with George right now doesn't mean you never will. We're not school girls anymore. Maybe mature relationships are more like a slow burn. Ya know?" Jenna said. And then burped. Loudly.

Beth began to laugh, "Oh yeah, we're really mature."

They hung up and Beth dropped her phone into her lap. The next turn sent it flying onto the floorboard. She pulled into the condominium complex and stopped at the gate. Fumbling under her seat to get the phone and find the text from George with the access code, she didn't notice the car that pulled up behind her. The driver honked and she sat up to see a guy in a convertible Audi gesturing at her impatiently. He had opened the gate with his remote and continued to honk. Once she pulled through the gate, he revved his engine and whipped the sports car furiously past her.

Lovely, she thought and considered giving him the finger. The encounter with Mr. Audi explained why George had given her very specific parking instructions. If everyone in the complex had that kind of attitude, she didn't dare park in the wrong spot. By the time she found an empty spot marked "Guest" she was five minutes late. Beth grabbed her purse and rushed around the corner to George's building where he was waiting for her by his car.

"Hi George," she said.

"Wow Beth—You look ready for the game!" he said and kissed her on each cheek, leaving a wake of cologne behind when he pulled away.

She gestured to her Dan Marino jersey. "I really hope it's not poor form to wear this. I brought a different shirt just in case."

"Nah, it's fine as long as you don't mind being the only Dolphins fan there." He grinned as he opened the car door for her.

"I think I'm the only fan in the state, so I'm used to it."

Beth slid into his glossy, silver BMW with low-profile rims. She looked around George's car, searching for some hint of who he was, what he liked. But the car was immaculate. Even the music was non-descript electronica. *Okay, so he takes good care of his things and he likes things neat. There's nothing wrong with that. God, what would he think of my car? Old and covered in dog hair and sand. What does that say about me?*

They arrived right before kickoff and George led her up to a most impressive skybox. The room was wide with leather couches and high-topped tables. Sliding doors opened to a private section of extra plush stadium seats that overlooked the 50 yard line. Along the wall were tables with sandwiches, buffalo wings, and chips. Coolers full of Thrasher and beer were stationed around the room and there was a small bar set in the back corner.

George turned to her. "Vodka soda, right?" She nodded, surprised he remembered, and thanked him. He returned with her drink, then took her around the room politely introducing her to various Thrasher co-workers. Many of them ribbed her good-naturedly about her Dolphins' jersey.

After they made the rounds, took a seat to watch the beginning of the game. Beth was disappointed but not surprised that they were losing by the end of the half.

"Can I get you another drink?" he asked, standing up.

"I can get it," Beth volunteered. "I need to stretch my legs and go to the ladies room anyway. Can I bring you something?"

George looked surprised by her offer. "Um, sure. Can you grab me a Corona lite? With a lime?"

When Beth came back from the bar, she saw George talking to a much taller guy in a white T-shirt and dark jeans. His back was to her but there was something familiar about the way the blond hair was tucked under... *Wait! Is that a Dolphins' hat?*

"Beth!" George was waving her over with a huge grin. "There's someone I want you to meet!"

Handing him his beer, she turned to the stranger and found herself face to face with those intense brown eyes.

"Beth," George said. "This is Todd Allman. He's our brand ambassador for Thrasher in Japan. Todd, this is Beth… uh."

It was always surprising to see her students outside of the classroom but running into this semester's disruption, while on a date no less, left her speechless. Todd's old baseball hat was replaced with a slightly less battered Dolphins hat. "Grant," she finally managed to sputter and held out her hand. "Beth Grant." She hoped George would think she was just starstruck, so she added, "Wow, it's nice to meet you."

"He's in from the Japan shoot. I wasn't sure he would be here so I didn't tell you. I didn't want to get your hopes up," he said excitedly. She wondered briefly if she would have skipped the game if she had known he was going to be here. *Probably not…*

"Nice hat," she grinned, still feeling flustered.

"Nice jersey," he said with a chuckle, shaking his head, clearly surprised to see her, too.

"Thanks."

"Todd was just saying that you must like heartbreak as much as he does." Beth's look of confusion prompted George to add, "Because you're both Dolphins' fans?"

"Oh right! Yes, I guess I do," she laughed. "But Gates is my tight end this year, so at least for me there's an upside to this game."

"Your tight end?"

"Fantasy football," George interrupted. "This girl knows her stuff." He beamed with pride and put his arm around her. It was a nice gesture but she couldn't help feeling like a pet who had learned a new trick. Standing bet\ween one of her students and a guy she had just started dating was made her want to bolt. She wasn't yet ready to claim either.

"You play fantasy football?" Todd raised the eyebrow with the scar running through it and she noticed for the first time how much older than 24 he seemed. His presence outside of the classroom was somehow even more commanding. That, along with the way George had introduced them, made her feel like an imposter. The complete role reversal was very unsettling.

She nodded and took a gulp of her drink.

"Hey George," Todd said, slowly shifting his attention away from Beth. "I forgot to mention, Danny wanted me to have you call him ASAP about the Japan campaign. He has some questions about the contract that should probably get cleared up."

"Oh, right now?" George looked surprised and confused. "I, um, I guess I'll give him a call. Sorry, Beth, I'll be right back."

Todd smirked and pulled out his phone as George walked across the room and into the hallway. He typed something into his phone then turned to Beth. "So, a Dolphins fan," he said. "I thought I was the only one."

Beth laughed, "Me, too! I certainly didn't expect to see you here."

"Ditto," he said taking another sip of his beer.

"I thought you were out of town."

"Actually, I should still be in Japan but we wrapped early."

"And you thought after a ten hour flight, you'd just catch a Chargers' game?" She looked up at him. Her heart was pounding but she refused to acknowledge it.

"Fourteen hours, actually. And not a Chargers' game, a Dolphins' game," He grinned. "Where did you get the Marino jersey anyway?"

"This thing?" she laughed. "It's probably older than you are."

"Nah. I remember watching Marino."

They chatted about the woes of being lifelong fans of the Miami Dolphins and other things that only Floridians could appreciate. He seemed much more animated than he was in class and she was glad he was comfortable with her after their rocky start. The last thing she needed was the "star pupil" complaining about her to Gene.

Todd finished his beer and grabbed another one out of a nearby cooler. He opened it, threw the cap back in the cooler, then gave her a piercing look. "So, what are you doing with that guy? He doesn't seem like your type." He took a long pull off the bottle of beer.

"What?" Beth wasn't sure she heard him right.

"That guy isn't your type. What are you doing with him?" He gestured with the beer bottle to the door through which George had left.

"And what would my type be exactly?"

"Not a little guy like that," Todd snickered. He had missed the warning tone in her voice while downing most of his beer. Beth was stunned into silence. *Is he drunk?* "Hey, why don't you let me take you home?"

"Excuse me?" Her dimple and the playful grin were gone, replaced with her no-nonsense teacher face.

"You heard me." He leaned cockily against one of the leather couches.

"You cannot be serious." At some point, confident Todd had morphed into arrogant Todd. *Just add beer…*

"I'm totally serious."

"I'm here as George's guest. I'm not going anywhere with you."

Todd grinned, like he had expected her response. "C'mon, I know you aren't into *that* guy."

"This conversation is inappropriate." She glared up at him. "Are you drunk or something?"

He laughed, unfazed by her anger. "I don't have to be drunk to know you'd have a better time with me."

"I don't know what you're playing at but I'd suggest you choose your words carefully. You don't know anything about me."

Todd looked over her shoulder to the back of the room, then leaned in close to Beth. "I know you have a tattoo on your ass," he whispered, his lips brushing her ear, sending a shiver down her spine. Her eyes widened and her jaw dropped. It seemed that, as an actor, Todd had learned something about dramatic exits because he chose that moment to take his leave.

Her face must have still been a mask of surprise as George came up beside her. "What was that all about?" he asked. "What did he say to you?"

She reached up and rubbed the ear his lips had touched as if that could remove the tingling sensation they left behind. Turning to face George, she forced her face back to a pleasant normal. "Oh, um, he just…" Before Beth could come up with a plausible lie, a woman approached George and tapped him on his arm. She was extremely thin with full lips. Her gold stiletto heels matched her skimpy gold dress that barely concealed anything.

"George, darling," she cooed. "I didn't know you were going to be here." She kissed him on either cheek. Now it was George's turn to look startled.

"Cristal, uh, I didn't know you were going to be here, either." Then more decisively, he added. "This is my date, Beth. Beth, this is Cristal." At first, she thought she had heard him incorrectly but no, George had pronounced her name like the champagne, *krees-tahl.*

"Hi, nice to meet you," Beth said. Cristal slowly and deliberately looked Beth up and down, ignoring her outstretched hand.

"Yeah, whatever," she said, turning back to George. "Georgie, we need to talk."

Beth dropped her hand, more amused than offended. *Georgie?*

"Actually, Cristal, now is not a good time."

"Just one tiny little sec, Georgie, I'm sure she won't mind. Would you, Bessie?" She was slurring her words and Beth was no longer amused.

"It's Beth." George cut her off. "And *I* mind. Now is not the time." His voice was low and Beth saw the muscles in his jaw tighten, but Cristal didn't seem to notice. She grabbed him by the arm and tried to drag him away. George pulled his arm away quickly but that just caused her to stumble into him, and he had to grab her to keep her from falling.

She threw her head back and cackled, clinging to him. "See, you can't stay away from me."

Beth took a step away, anxiety began to spread across her chest. She did not want to be a part of this scene that was starting to attract attention. George gave her a pleading look and Beth mouthed "it's okay" and gestured to the stadium seats. He sat down with Cristal on the couch and Beth went back out to watch the third quarter which had already started. She wondered what George was saying to Cristal. She wondered what would possess Todd to speak to her like that. She wondered if the Dolphins would ever have a winning season.

"I'm so sorry, Beth. I had no idea she was going to be here." George slid into the seat next to her.

"No worries. I wasn't sure if I should try to save you or just let you handle it."

"No, you did the right thing." His jaw was still clenched and he was rubbing his palms on his jeans in nerves or frustration, she couldn't tell which.

"Hey." Beth leaned into him and put a hand on his. "Are you okay?"

"Yeah, yeah, I'm fine." He was looking out at the field but not really watching the game, a muscle in his jaw twitched. Beth looked over his shoulder back into the room where Cristal was talking animatedly to an older guy, her arms flailing wildly. The guy might have been blocking her path but it was hard to tell.

"Hey George, why don't we just go?"

"What?" He looked up surprised. "But don't you want to watch the rest of the game?"

"I have grading to finish for class tomorrow." She shrugged. "Plus, it's not like they're going to win."

George looked over his shoulder at Cristal. "Are you sure? Don't you want to finish your drink? I don't want to let her ruin the game."

Beth held up her glass, only half full, tipped it toward him in a silent toast and finished what was left with one big swallow. "Done," she said and took his hand decisively. It was warm and she liked the feeling of it in hers. They walked hand in hand past Cristal and everyone else in the box. Beth only glanced back briefly, wondering where Todd was.

George opened the car door for her. "Hey," he said. "Thanks for being so cool about leaving."

Feeling impulsive and a little buzzed, she leaned into him. Their lips met awkwardly at first and then with more conviction. He pressed his body against hers and snaked a muscular arm around her waist. It was so nice to be held, she didn't mind how his tongue darted in and out of her mouth a little too aggressively. But when she drew back to get a little space, his weight shifted too far forward and their teeth knocked into each other.

"Ouch," she said, her hand flying up to her mouth. He did the same and they both laughed.

"I guess we'd better get back," he said. She slid into the

passenger seat and he leaned in and kissed her cheek before closing her door.

They didn't say much until George merged onto the interstate. "Do you like jazz?" He pressed a button on the radio.

"Um, sure." Jazz was probably the only kind of music Beth didn't like but she was far more interested in what George was going to say about Cristal than picking the music. She waited, watching him. He looked over at her and smiled. Feeling impatient, she finally asked, "So, what's the deal with her?"

George gripped and released the steering wheel several times and finally sighed. Then he told Beth about Cristal. They had met through his cousin and he got her a job as a Thrasher girl. *Whatever that is,* Beth thought. Cristal had a cocaine habit, as well as a habit of lying and manipulating, which had led to the end of their relationship.

"Oh" was all Beth could think to say to that. She had never even seen cocaine and suddenly felt far out of her element.

"And she's sort of a groupie," George said. "As soon as you went outside, she started hanging all over Todd Allman."

"Really?" *Ew.*

7

When they got back, George jumped out of the car and before Beth could even find the handle, he had opened the door for her. She smiled up at him and let him take her hand.

"Would you like to come up and have a drink? It's early for dinner but we could order takeout in a little bit."

She hesitated for a moment but heard Jenna's voice in her head. "Sure, I'd love to."

The decor was minimalist and modern. George gestured for her to sit on a low gray couch across from a giant, expensive looking television. To Beth's surprise, the couch was much more comfortable than it looked. There was a beige ceramic bowl full of smooth black pebbles on the glass coffee table and a vase with an unlit, white candle in it. The whole living room looked like it was from a design catalog. Even the abstract painting that hung behind the couch seemed staged. Then her eyes fell on a black and white photo in a sleek silver frame on the end table. It was George with his arms around a short, round-faced woman who was laughing.

"Is wine okay?" George called from the kitchen.

"That's fine."

He brought out a bottle of wine and showed it to her. "How's this? It's from Greece. I think their wines are really

54

underrated." Beth had never even heard of Moschofilero and had no idea how to pronounce it, but she nodded with feigned interest. Peter had been interested in wine and had tried his best to teach her. But despite his explanations of the subtleties of Pinots, Bordeaux and the like, she had never developed much interest.

"I'm sure it's great. I really don't know much about wine. I usually just grab whatever looks good from Trader Joe's."

George frowned. "Oh, don't go there. I'll take you to the wine shop I go to. They can hook you up with better stuff than that."

"Um, you know I'm a teacher, right? I don't exactly have a wine shop budget."

"Oh, I didn't mean it like that," he said hastily, filling her glass. "You can get really great wine without spending a lot. Like this one was only about $30."

Beth nodded politely. *I get five bottles of wine at Trader Joe's for $30.* She took a sip as he sat next to her on the couch. "Wow, this is really good!" *Maybe I really should spend more on a bottle of wine.*

He smiled, stretching his arms across the back of the couch. "I'm glad you like it. So, you've heard about my ex. Now tell me, who was the fool that let you get away?"

"Well," Beth started, then took a gulp of wine to stall for time. "I haven't really dated much since I moved here so it's been a little while. But my last relationship was with Peter, when I was living in Charleston." She told George about him, leaving out any mention of Jeremy. That story was always so complicated and painful that she rarely shared it. "Peter was older than me. His wife died about a year before we met so I guess it was probably more of a rebound."

"Really?" George asked, leaning forward to top off her glass. "How did you two meet?"

"Actually, he was my doctor."

"Oh yeah? Don't tell me he was," George gestured to her lap, "that kind of doctor."

"A gynecologist?" Beth laughed. "No, he's an orthopedic surgeon." She didn't tell him about seeing Peter for a sprained ankle and breaking down in his office desperately sad about Jeremy. She didn't tell him about the grief support group Peter recommended where she had run into him again. Or how after the support group they had gone for coffee and had spent hours and hours talking about Jeremy and about his wife, Lillian. She didn't tell him about how sometimes she or Peter would wake in the night crying and how they would cling to each other out of grief and survival.

Instead, she told him about the time they spent on his boat and their shared love of the Charleston food scene. She stopped short of describing how the end of their relationship felt just as natural as the beginning had. How when it was over she felt the same bittersweet feeling she always had when she was done reading a book she had loved. Sad it was over but so grateful to have experienced that world.

When she stopped talking, she realized she was warm and tingly and her wine was gone. "I'm sorry," she said, looking at her empty glass. "Wine makes me so chatty."

"Don't apologize. I like hearing about your life." George leaned forward and took the empty glass from her hand. He set it on the coffee table and wound his fingers through hers, leaning in to kiss her. This time, teeth didn't bump together and quite easily she found herself sinking into the couch under him. When he untucked her shirt and slid his hand underneath, she didn't stop him.

Maybe it was the warmth from the wine or the primal pull deep inside her but when he stood up to lead her to the bedroom, instead of overthinking it, she followed him down the hall. His bedroom was much like the inside of his car—very clean with lots of black leather and expensive looking electronics. The late afternoon light peaked through his dark curtains giving the room a muted, hazy look. She stood before him and unbuttoned his shirt. George pulled his arms out of the sleeves and threw the shirt to the floor. He clearly worked on his body and it was Beth's turn to run her hands over his smooth chest. He grabbed the belt loops of her jeans and pulled her close. The heat from his chest sent a delicious shiver down her spine. Raising her arms above her head, he tugged her jersey off and she let her bra, already unhooked, fall to the floor after it.

"God, you have great tits," he said, and reached greedily for her bare breasts.

She grabbed George's face and kissed him. Then she reached down and unbuttoned his pants. He sighed heavily and guided her over to the bed. When she slid down the zipper, his designer jeans fell to the floor and he stepped out of them, his erection visible through his tight black underwear. He pushed her back onto the bed, then crouched over her while she reached down and stroked him through the silky fabric. He undid her jeans and pulled them off, smiling appreciatively when he saw her black thong. On his knees in front of her, he slid her panties down. Beth sighed in anticipation. But instead of putting his mouth to her, he licked two fingers and pushed them inside her, moving them rapidly in and out. Then, just as quickly, he pulled his hand away, wriggled out of his underwear, and positioned himself atop her.

"Wait!" Beth said, startled by the events, which had fast-forwarded considerably.

George paused. "What's wrong?"

"Um, do you have a condom?"

"Really?" He looked surprised. "Aren't you on the pill or something? Because I'm clean if that's what you're worried about."

"No, actually," she said. "I'm not." Technically, she wasn't on the pill. She had an IUD, but that wasn't the point. There was no way in hell she was having sex with George without protection. She had just met the last woman he had been with and Cristal did not appear to be particularly fastidious where safety was concerned.

He sighed and reached for the drawer of his nightstand. Once he had the condom on, he plunged unceremoniously into her.

"Ooomph," she said, involuntarily. Even though she was turned on and he wasn't particularly well-endowed, she hadn't had sex in a really long time and was feeling tender. George, mistaking her grunt for pleasure, thrust enthusiastically.

"Oooh, you're so fucking tight," he cooed into her ear. *Yeah, that's why it hurts!*

"Wait, wait, wait." She pushed him away from her. "Slow down. I need a second." *I think I've made a mistake.*

He looked down at her, confused. "Are you all right?"

She nodded, shifting beneath him. He began to move again, this time more slowly. "Okay?" he asked again. Again she nodded, feeling her body begin to respond, the excitement slowly building. But George took this as a green light and went back to thrusting away. And before she could really get into it, he grabbed her legs and pushed them into the air, holding them apart in a V. *Good thing I'm flexible!* He was thrusting so hard now, her breasts rocked to and fro almost painfully.

"Come on, baby," he grunted, watching himself go in and out of her.

"I know you aren't into that guy…" Todd's voice came to her

out of nowhere. She pushed it away and tried to focus on George and building up that tingling sensation. But he was so far from her clit now that she wasn't getting any of the delicious friction that usually helped her climax. Suddenly, he pulled out of her. "Why don't you turn over?" His muscular arms flipped her onto all fours before she had a chance to agree. "Oh yeah," he said and smacked her on the ass lightly before entering her. She tried to concentrate on working back up to an orgasm but now George was kneading her butt aggressively. "I like your tattoo," he said, smacking her where the ink stained her skin and thrusting vigorously. Taking matters quite literally into her own hands, she slipped a finger between her legs and lowered her hips slowly to the bed.

"Ohhh, you like it low, baby." The position forced him to slow his thrusts a bit and she gently massaged her clit, feeling the sensation build. She was really starting to enjoy herself when George grabbed her shoulder, "I'm going to come!" he shouted and after one final thrust, he made a strange cooing sound. "Oooohoooohooohooo! Ooohoooohooohoo!" *What the fuck?!?* It was unlike anything Beth had ever heard, a cross between a bird chirping and a giggle. When the noise stopped, he draped his sweaty body on her, the weight of his muscular chest crushing her hand beneath her. The sensation was gone now. George had literally squashed it.

After a moment, he got up and walked to the bathroom. She briefly considered finishing herself while he was gone but he was back before she could even try. George flopped onto the bed beside her, kissing her cheek before rolling to his side, propping himself up on his elbow.

"That was nice." He was grinning at her, so pleased with himself that she couldn't help but smile weakly back. "Come over here," he said and as she shifted toward him, he pulled her close and wrapped his arms around her, nuzzling his face in her hair. "You smell good," he sighed. Her head was on his firm chest which felt a bit like snuggling with a rock. Before long, his breath was shallow and even and Beth found herself wondering what the appropriate amount of time was to let him sleep before she got up. But the low light and the glass of wine worked their magic and soon she was asleep as well.

She woke abruptly from the shadowy mist of a dream, her heart racing. The dark room was disorienting and she felt a brief panic at her naked vulnerability. George snored softly, his arm still wrapped tightly around her. *How long have we been sleeping?* She looked around the room for a clock but found none.

"George," she whispered, shaking him gently. He stirred and when he saw her, he smiled and squeezed her closer, kissing her forehead.

"Man, how long did I sleep?" He looked around the room at the darkness.

"I don't know. What time is it?"

She watched him get up and fish his phone from the pocket of his pants.

"Oh, it's only 7:30," he said, scrolling through his messages.

"Oh wow," Beth said. "I didn't realize it was so late. I should probably get home."

He looked up from his phone. "Really? But what about dinner?"

"Another time, maybe? I really need to feed the dog. And I have that huge pile of grading I have to do."

George looked genuinely disappointed. "That's why I don't have pets."

"Yeah," she said, unsure of what to say to that. She dressed quickly and grabbed her purse.

"Wait, I'll walk you to your car," he said, following her to the front door.

"That's okay. I'm just around the corner from your building."

"Okay, well, I had an awesome time. You're a really great girl," he said, wrapping his arms around her waist. He kissed her softly, then grinned. "Are you sure you don't want to stay for round two?"

She hesitated, wondering how to politely say no. "Um, I really have to get home."

"Okay. I'll text you later?"

"Sure. And thanks for taking me to the game."

* * *

When Beth got home, she took a long, hot shower and sat down with a stack of papers. *Ugh, it is too late to start grading.* She chucked the papers on the coffee table and picked up her phone.

"Hey, Jenna, what are you up to?"

"Well, I just poured myself a glass of wine and I'm channel surfing, so the usual Sunday night excitement. How was the game?"

"Uh, good. And interesting."

"Oooh, how so?"

Beth burst out laughing. "Weird. So fucking weird."

"Oh my god, Beth! Did you sleep with him?" She practically shouted through the phone.

Beth could only laugh.

"You did! I knew it!" she squealed. "Tell me everything."

So Beth told Jenna about the game and Cristal and leaving early.

"Yeah, yeah, okay. Get to the sex."

"Well, it started out okay. But then, he just sort of rushed through it."

"Ah, he was a base-stealer."

"A base-stealer?" Beth was confused.

"Yeah, those guys that rush from first to home without hitting each base."

"Ha! That's exactly what he was. And, I didn't even tell you the best part. When he came, he went 'Ooohhooohhoooo! Oooohoooohooo.'"

"What?!?" Jenna sounded like she had choked on her wine. "That sounds like a demented bird!" She managed to spit out before a fit of coughing and laughter overtook her.

"I know! I've never heard anything like that. It was liked a weird sort of pigeon or something."

"How did you not laugh out loud at him?"

"I was just so shocked that I didn't laugh until I got to my car." Jenna began mimicking the cooing sound and they laughed until Beth had tears in her eyes. "So, thanks for telling me to give him a chance," Beth said sarcastically.

"Oh my god, you are not going to blame this one on me!" Jenna was still laughing. "Every mistake you've ever made. Here we go again."

"Not every mistake. Just the ones from college on. And, did you or did you not encourage me to go out with him? Even after I said I didn't think he was my type?"

"I told you to give him a chance and see where it went. I didn't say you *had* to sleep with him!"

Beth laughed. "I did treat him like a character. And trust me, no one would want to read that sex scene."

"So are you going to see him again?"

"I don't think so. I mean, he's sweet. But there wasn't really any chemistry, so why bother?"

"Well, I don't know. The first time with anyone is awkward," Jenna said. "Maybe you can teach him."

"Is it though?" Beth thought back. "I don't remember it

being awkward with Peter." What she didn't say was that it had *never* been awkward with Jeremy. "Plus, you can't really teach chemistry, can you? The man is 40 years old. If he doesn't know how to even try and please a woman..."

"Maybe he's never been with an *actual* woman. Maybe he's one of those guys that has only dated girls that faked it for him."

"Hmmm..." Beth thought about Cristal. "You're probably right."

"Well, was it cool to see the Dolphins at least?"

"Yeah, it was. And get this, Todd Allman was there."

"What?! Why didn't you start with that instead of birdman George and all the cooing?"

"I don't know. It was really weird seeing him outside of class. I think he was drunk."

"What makes you say that?"

"Well, maybe he was just messing with me or something, but he tried to get me to ditch George and go home with him."

"No shit!" Jenna was really excited now. "He was totally hitting on you!"

"No. I don't think so. He was just drunk."

"Maybe he was, but he was *still* hitting on you. See, sex with George was just punishment for not leaving with Todd Allman when you had the chance. You could have been having sex with He-Man instead."

Beth rolled her eyes. "He's my student, Jenna. And he's like 10 years younger than me. But you want to know the weirdest part? He told me that he knew I had a tattoo on my ass."

"How the hell does he know about that?"

"No idea. He walked off before I could ask him. I've wracked my brain. I even googled myself to make sure no one with my name has a picture online and there was nothing. I think he must have been bluffing."

"Yeah, but why?"

"Who knows? It really was strange."

When they finally got off the phone, Beth was still thinking about the odd interaction with Todd Allman. The stack of papers glared up at her from the coffee table, silently screaming, "Do work!" Without thinking about it, she picked them up and shuffled through them until she found Todd's. She pulled it out and began to read.

"Magic in the Rain"

I didn't expect to find magic in a parking lot. I had never thought about her that way before. She was already on the ground when I finally noticed. She must have slipped in the rain while running to her car. I was about to get out of my car to help her but something caught my eye. Was she crying? I squinted through the downpour. No, she wasn't crying at all. She was laughing hysterically sitting on the black asphalt in the pouring rain. I was mesmerized...

When she finished reading, she put down the paper and picked up her phone to text Jenna.

BETH: I know how he knows about the tattoo

8

The classroom was dark when she opened the door. She had flicked on the lights and was making her way to the front of the room when a low voice came from behind her.

"Good morning, Ms. Grant."

Beth nearly jumped out of her skin and turned to see Todd Allman sitting at a desk in the back row. "Todd! You startled me. What are you doing in here?"

"You gave me the room code, remember?" He grinned at her from under his Dolphins' hat.

"Oh, right." She dropped her bag on the podium. "But why were you sitting in the dark?"

"I got here early and figured I should lay low." He was still grinning.

"Ah well, I guess that makes sense." Beth's heart was having a hard time getting back to a normal speed. The shock he gave her coupled with Jenna's voice in her head—*He was totally hitting on you*—sent a flush across her pale, Irish skin and she fumbled around in her bag waiting for it to pass.

"Also," he said, standing and walking toward her. "I wanted to talk to you before class starts."

"Okay. What about?" She pulled a stack of papers out of her school bag and set them on the podium before finally facing him. He towered over her, forcing her to look up. *Damn, he's tall.*

"I wanted to apologize for how I spoke to you at the football game. You were right, I was out of line." Todd said. "I had had a few drinks on the plane and the jet lag and…" He trailed off and when it was clear that he was finished, Beth stood a little straighter and looked him in the eye.

"I accept your apology and I'm sure we won't have to worry about that again."

"No, I guess we won't," he agreed, but the look of contrition had somehow taken a mischievous slant and not for the first time, Beth found that she couldn't read him. Before she could say anything else, some other students walked in and Todd returned to his seat.

At the top of the hour, Beth flipped on the projector. The picture on the slide was of an old-fashioned suitcase opened to reveal some photos, a comb, an alarm clock, and a box of shoe cream.

"Good morning, class. Today, we're going to do something a little different. Has anyone ever heard of the Willard Suitcases?"

They looked at her blankly. So Beth explained about the over 400 suitcases recovered from the attic of a mental institution in New York. They were from the people who had been admitted to the hospital years before—some in the early 1900s, many of whom lived out the rest of their lives there. The suitcases and the stories behind them had fascinated Beth. "This is just one of the suitcases. There's something very haunting about it, don't you think?" Several students nodded. "And it made me wonder, if I were going away for an indefinite amount of time and could only take one suitcase, what would I bring? What would you bring? That's what I want you to answer today. Don't overthink it, that's why this is an in-class assignment. You can take the rest of the period to answer. If you find the idea of being committed to an institution unsettling, you can imagine different circumstances. But it should be one small suitcase of things that are important to you. Let's say, no more than 4 or 5 things. And be sure to make clear the significance of each item."

The class shuffled about getting out papers and pens. "While you're doing that, I'll be handing back your assignments on magic. For the most part, they were really good but keep in mind, writing is never really done. There's just a point when we let it go. So even if you've done well on the assignment, your paper may still be covered in ink. Don't be scared, I'm always going to mark up your work with feedback and suggestions. It's my job."

She walked around the room avoiding backpacks, careful not to distract the students from their writing. The last paper she handed back was Todd's. Though she had read it first, she had graded it last. It was obvious that he wanted a reaction from her, which made her reluctant to give him one. But she felt like failing to comment on his work would be condoning it. In the end, after surprisingly few grammar corrections compared to the rest of the class, she had settled for: *Good writing but work on making your characters more believable.*

When she slid the paper onto his desk, he didn't look up. He was lost in what he was writing and Beth felt a pang as she remembered how that felt. *I used to write like that.* She thought again about the manuscript sitting on her hard drive and she resolved once again to go back to it. *Today,* she thought. *I'll open it today.*

On her couch that night, she stared at the stack of papers in front of her and knew she wouldn't be doing any writing. Beth had always hated the nasty old adage "Those who can, do. Those who can't, teach." But looking at the pile of grading, she wondered if the saying should have instead been "Those who can, do. Those who teach, can't." Sighing, she picked up the papers and flipped through them, telling herself that she was just trying to get a sense of what the students had written about. But when she came to Todd's, she stopped.

His handwriting was distinct, small and slanted, but neater than that of most of her students. She read with curiosity the description of what his suitcase contained: a picture of his family, an iPod of his favorite music, and his mother's favorite book of poetry. *Poetry?*

9

Beth was only half listening as Martha and Allie discussed the misogyny of language after Tiana called Janet a "pussy" for folding. Those were the kind of conversations had at a Ladies' Poker night filled with academics. Janet and Tiana were in the English department with Beth and had invited her to join the group when she started at the college the year before. Martha and Allie taught in the Women and Gender Studies program and had started the group. They met every few weeks for food, drink, conversation, and sometimes a little poker.

"No seriously," Martha said. "Just think about it. What do we call people who are weak? We call them pussies or little bitches. Or sissies. We tell them to 'man up' or ask them if they need a tampon. It's disgusting, really, demonizing all things woman."

Tiana rolled her eyes. "Fine," she said. "You aren't being a pussy, Janet. You're being a little, flaccid penis if you don't call my bet."

Janet shook her head. "Nope, I fold. Beth, it's to you."

"Actually," Beth said. "Instead of calling someone a pussy, we should call them a 'sack.' What is more weak and spineless than a ball sack? They're all shriveled and helpless."

"Yessss!" Martha hissed. "Sack! Ball sack if you're nasty."

She sang in her best Janet Jackson. The other women laughed.

Beth looked at her cards. The turn made her pair of jacks three-of-a-kind. "And I will not be a sack. I don't just call your bet, Tiana. I'll raise you five." She threw her chips in with a flourish. Tiana called, the next card was dealt, and Beth cleaned up.

"Okay, ladies, speaking of genitalia," Beth began, as she dealt the next hand.

"Oooh, are you finally going to tell us about having Todd Allman in your class?" Allie asked, giggling.

"What? How do you know about Todd Allman?"

"In general? I mean, I've seen He-Man. And Beth, everyone knows he's in your class. The whole school is talking about it. So what's he like? Is he that hot in real life?"

Beth rolled her eyes, then noticed that all the women were waiting to hear what she had to say about the movie star. "He's a pain in my ass is what he is. There are always groupies waiting for him in the hall. And I had like 50 requests for overrides. It's ridiculous."

"He could be a pain in my ass anytime," Janet snickered and everyone but Beth laughed.

"Beth, she didn't ask about overrides," Martha said. "She asked if he was really that hot."

"No, he's not hot in real life. He's always wearing a dingy baseball cap. And he's always late to class," Beth added. Though he hadn't actually been late again since the first week. "It's more annoying than anything else. There is a gaggle that waits outside my door for him. And I have to have these special little meetings with Hy-Gene to talk about what kind of 'special treatment' I can give him." She put extra emphasis on 'annoying' and air quotes around 'special treatment.' She was playing up the downside of having him in her class but she wasn't sure why.

"I'd give him special treatment," Allie said, fanning herself like a southern lady overtaken by the vapors.

"Meh," Beth said frowning, but the image of Todd leaning over the woman at the laundromat, the one Jenna had shown her, came to her. She could understand why the ladies would be interested in knowing more about *that* Todd. Then she thought about the Todd from the football game, so arrogant, *or was it just mischievous?* They seemed like completely different people and though she tried, she couldn't reconcile the two.

"Wait, what were you going to say about genitalia?" Martha was walking around the table refilling wine glasses.

"Oh yeah." Her thoughts turned away from the twin Todds and back to George. "I was going to ask you about this guy I was seeing."

"Wait, you're seeing someone?" Tiana said, a corn chip halfway to her gaping mouth.

"It's about time! Ladies," Martha said, tapping her wine glass with her fork and staring pointedly at Allie and Janet who were still snickering about Todd Allman. "Beth just said she is seeing someone."

"Whoa! Who?" Allie asked.

Beth told them about meeting George and dinner at Flavor and the football game. "And well..."

"Did you sleep with him?" Janet asked. "What happened after the football game?"

Beth bit her lip, beginning to feel a little self-conscious. The ladies waited, all eyes on her. "So, have any of you ever slept with someone for the first time and it was pretty bad but you kept seeing them and it got better?" She finally blurted out.

Tiana looked at her like she was stupid. "Um, yeah of course. It is almost always bad the first time."

Martha turned to Tiana. "That's not true at all. I would never sleep with a guy a second time if it was bad the first time."

"Wait," Janet said. "What do you mean by bad? Because sometimes I don't have an orgasm the first time because I'm just not comfortable enough with the person. But that doesn't mean it's bad."

"You don't always have an orgasm?" Martha was appalled.

"Um no, not always. Do you?" Janet said.

"Absolutely! Even if he finishes first, *we're* not finished until I've finished." She laughed.

"Good for you, Martha," Allie said tersely. "But for some women, it doesn't work that way."

"No judgment," Martha said, softening her tone. "None at all. I was just surprised."

"Beth, what exactly was bad about it?" Janet asked.

Beth told them about how things with George started out really nice but then progressed so quickly. About how he seemed to think her needs were inherently met just by being inside her.

"Hmmm," Tiana said. "I don't know if you can change a base-stealer."

Beth laughed. "That's what Jenna called him!"

"What's a base-stealer?" Allie asked. "Oh, wait… I get it."

"What?" Martha and Janet said in unison, looking confused.

"A guy that heads for home without stopping at each base," Allie said. Soon the conversation digressed into an argument about what each base represented, that was finally settled by Tiana pulling out her phone to check Urban Dictionary. Which led to a conversation about women being more assertive in bed to get exactly what they want.

Beth still didn't have an answer as to whether a base-stealer could be taught. But the conversation about being more assertive was inspiring and all the talk about sex made her want to try again. So when George texted her, she finished her wine, played her final hand, and got up to leave.

"You're going over there, aren't you?" Tiana asked, loading the poker chips into the case.

Even though these women knew nearly everything about her, Beth began to blush. "Maybe."

"All right," Martha said. "Be sure to report back and let us know if your base thief can be rehabilitated."

10

In the parking lot of George's condominium, she sent Jenna a text.

BETH: George take 2

JENNA: 2nd time is always better

JENNA: but don't blame me if it's not!

George opened the door in jeans and a T-shirt that hugged his muscular chest. She thought about pushing him into the wall and starting things immediately but some of the bravado she had worked up at poker had worn off on the drive over.

"Can I get you a glass of wine?" She nodded and started to sit down on the couch, but changed her mind. Determined to make this time better, she followed him into the kitchen. Like the rest of his place, George's kitchen was dark and sleek. Walnut cabinets were accented with black granite counter tops. The only bright spot of the room was the green glass backsplash.

He pulled a bottle from the wine fridge built into the cabinet under the counter and started to show it to her but she waved him away. "But how are you going to learn about wine then?" He held the label in her line of sight. *Why do I need to learn about wine?*

"Maybe," she said, pushing the hand holding the bottle

away and stepping in closer to him. "I'm not here to learn about wine. Maybe, I'm here," she ran a hand down his chest, "for a very different reason." *Let's get this party started before I talk myself out of it.*

George laughed. "Well, you can still appreciate that this is a 2007 Domaine Dominique Mugneret."

"Of course I could, if I knew what any of those words meant." She smiled at him flirtatiously. "But I appreciate even more the way you're wearing that shirt."

"Easy there, girl." He handed her a glass of red wine which she immediately put to her lips to avoid saying, *"I'm not a girl. I'm a fucking woman!"*

"Hey," he said. "You didn't even let it breathe."

"Ah, silly me," Beth said and held the glass to her nose, inhaling loudly and, if possible, sarcastically.

"That's better," he said. "Do you smell the hints of clove and raspberry?"

She swished the wine around in her glass, smelled again, and took another sip, then nodded. "Oh yeah, definitely clove." *And also, just a note of manure from a male bovine.*

But George missed the sarcasm in her voice and her sniff. "I'm so glad you came over. I've been waiting to drink this and I really wanted to share it with you."

That made Beth feel a little guilty. *But why do you want to share something with me that I'm so clearly not interested in?* George appeared to have that in common with Peter. They both seemed to think that she needed to be educated about wine—and by them—despite her total lack of interest in the topic. *Maybe I need to date a younger man,* she thought and was horrified when laundromat Todd Allman flashed into her mind. She took another, larger sip of wine, to dissolve the image, mentally blaming Jenna for showing her all those pictures.

She listened but not well, as George described how the region the wine came from affected the tannins. *What time is it?* she wondered as she took another sip of wine to stifle a yawn.

"Maybe we should go sit down?"

"Sure, but let me top you off," he said and picked up the bottle of wine.

She put a hand on her glass. "Oh, no more for me, thanks. I have to drive home."

"You could just stay the night." He smiled at her hopefully.

"I can't. The dog."

"Oh, yeah. So how was poker?" he asked, leading her by the hand to the couch.

"Fine," she grinned. "We had a few interesting conversations."

"Really? What did you talk about?"

"About how women should take more charge in bed, to get what they want."

"I'd like to hear more about that." He grinned.

"Would you?" She set her wine glass on the table and took his out of his hand, sloshing a little onto her tank top. "Oops!" The shirt was black so she just swiped at it with her finger but as soon as George saw the spill, he leapt up, pushing her away.

"Shit!" He stalked off to the kitchen and came back with a disproportionately large bunch of paper towels for the two drops she had spilled on herself. "Did you get any on the couch? On the floor?"

"Um, I don't think so." He wiped vigorously at both the floor and the couch.

"I'm sorry," she said but she wasn't sure why. After all, she had only spilled the wine on her own shirt.

"I think it's okay," he said absently, searching the couch and floor a final time before going into the kitchen to dispose of the still clean paper towels.

She sat on the edge of the couch feeling equal parts ashamed of her klutziness and indignant at his overreaction. When he sat down next to her she said, "Maybe I should just go. It's getting late."

"No, no, stay." He touched her leg. "I'm sorry if I overreacted a little. The couch is new." She hesitated, looking toward the door, when he added under his breath, "We didn't have much when I was a kid, so I like to really take care of my things."

His honesty softened her, plus she still wanted to test the 'second time is better' theory. "So this couch is new, huh?" George nodded and she decided to go for it. She climbed nimbly onto his lap, straddling him. "Does that mean you haven't broken it in yet?" she whispered into his ear. He nodded again.

Beth leaned forward and kissed him, running her hands down his chest. When she got to his jeans, she hooked a finger in the waistband and tugged. He ran his hands up her thighs under her long, cotton skirt and cupped her ass. Impulsively, she pulled off her shirt. Grabbing his hands, she placed them on her breasts so he could feel through the lace of her bra that her nipples were hard.

He yanked down the lace and started to pull roughly on each of her nipples. "Ah… gently," she whispered. But he was already squeezing her too hard again, so she grabbed his hands and moved them to her hips. Then she unhooked her bra and leaned forward, pressing her breasts into his face, so that he could take each one into his mouth. He flicked and sucked aggressively and she whispered, "softer, softer," until he complied. *Maybe he can be taught,* she thought as she unbuttoned his jeans and slipped her hand in to stroke him gently.

Abruptly, he pushed her off of him and stood up. "Let's go

to the bedroom," he said.

"But I thought…"

"I don't want to mess up the couch." He grabbed her hand and led her down the hallway.

In the bedroom, he stopped at his dresser to light a candle. Beth wrapped her arms around his waist and slid a hand into his pants while planting kisses along his back. He turned to face her, tugging at her skirt until it fell to the floor.

"No thong this time?" he asked and she couldn't tell if he was actually disappointed or just teasing her.

Before she overthought it, she unbuttoned his jeans and slid them down, then did the same with his briefs. When he was naked, she pushed him back onto the bed and straddled him. She could feel his erection through the thin fabric of her panties. Beth closed her eyes and began to rock, pressing into him and then pulling away. After a moment, George pushed her away and she opened her eyes. He was ripping open a condom. Her face fell but he was so focused that he didn't even notice.

"Wait," she said. "Let's take it slowly."

"But you're obviously ready," he grinned at her. "And now so am I."

He flipped her onto her back and pulled off her panties, then positioned himself atop her. *Here we go again,* she thought, but then remembered the conversation at poker.

"No, George, wait," she said, pushing him to the side. "I want you to touch me." She grabbed his hand and moved it up her thigh.

"Oh." He looked confused. "Okay." He slid his finger inside her and began moving it in and out rapidly. "You like that, baby?"

"Slower," she whispered. His hand moved a little slower but he was still nowhere near her clit. "Like this," she whispered, moving his hand out of her and up to where she was most sensitive.

"Oh, you want it there." She nodded and he started to rub her clit a little like he was scrubbing a pot.

"Softer," she whispered again. And for about ten seconds, he was close. She moaned in pleasure, which George took as his cue and before she knew what was happening, he was on top of her, pushing into her.

"Yeah, you're ready now, aren't you," he grunted into her ear, thrusting vigorously. *Well, I guess I have to be, don't I?* But she wasn't ready to give up yet.

"Let me be on top," she said.

He stopped moving and looked down at her, surprised. "You sure?" She nodded. "Um, okay. It's just that my ex always said I was too big to take that way."

Beth bit her lip. George was definitely not too big, but she couldn't say that. "Let's just try it," she said. So he flipped over, pulling her on top of him. As soon as she positioned herself, he grabbed her around the waist and began jackhammering into her, thrusting his hips upward. She felt like she was riding a bronco and now understood why his girlfriend had lied.

"Wait a minute," she said again. She tried to lean forward to slow him down. But George was in his own world.

"Come for me again, baby," he said slapping her ass aggressively, sweat breaking out on his forehead. *Again?!* And to her horror began picking up speed.

"Stop, I need a minute," she started to say, when George froze and then started cooing.

"Ooohooohooo oooohooohooo," he chirped, his body shuddering.

What. The. Fuck.

When he stopped making bird noises, he looked up at her. "That was amazing," he said with a smile.

"Was it? Was it really?" The words flew out before she could bite them back. But George, lost in his haze of avian orgasm, missed the sarcasm. He rolled her over onto her back, pulled out, then disappeared into the bathroom. Once again she was left on his bed, unsatisfied. *Well, lesson learned. You can't teach this base-stealer.*

Beth didn't wait for George to return. There would be no napping together tonight. *Or ever.* She bent down to pick up her panties when she felt him behind her. He ran his hand over her ass, then pinched it gently.

"You know," he said, his hand still resting on her butt. "We could tone this up in just a couple of months. You should come to my gym with me."

We?! She stood up, her eyes narrowed severely. "Oh, yeah? You think so?"

He was still looking at her ass. "Sure," he continued. "You have a really good body, you just need a little…" He had finally looked up at her face. "No, um, I mean, um, only if you wanted to." He took his hand off of her and stepped away, literally and figuratively backpedaling. "Not like you need to or anything, that's not what I meant."

She waited to see if he would apologize and when he didn't she stooped to pick up her skirt, facing away from him as she did so.

"Hey," he said, grabbing her hand. "I didn't mean it like that. Really." He kissed the back of her hand gently. *Oh, now you're gentle! With my fucking hand?* "I think you're hot." She smiled tightly at him, pulled her hand away and then slipped into her skirt.

"Well, I'm going to get some coconut water. Do you want anything? Another glass of wine?" *What? And fatten up this ass some more? You sure you want to do that?*

"No thanks, I really should get going." She dressed quickly, grabbed her purse, and was at the front door where he met her holding a glass of hazy liquid.

"Are you sure you don't want some? It replenishes electrolytes. It's really good for your system." *My system is just fine as long as you aren't in it.*

"No thanks." She opened his front door. He slipped on his shoes and followed her out. "You don't have to walk me out. I'm right out front."

"I want to," he said. "It's late and even though this is a gated neighborhood, you never know."

At her truck, he finally seemed to realize she was less than thrilled. "Hey," he said, taking her hand. "Are you upset about what I said about working out? I really didn't mean it."

And yet, you still haven't actually apologized. "No, I'm fine." And she was. Because she had realized that she didn't care at all what George thought about her. She let him kiss her cheek and got in her truck.

As she started to back out of the parking space, George stopped her. "I meant to tell you, I'm going to be really busy in London and with the different time zone, you probably won't hear from me."

Oh shucks.

* * *

When she got home, she took a shower and climbed into bed, but she was too keyed up to sleep. She thought about George. Not only was there no spark between them, there was absolutely no chemistry of any kind. Even with Peter there had been some pretty amazing physical chemistry. She remembered the time he had taken her from behind on the balcony of a mountain cabin. They were both naked, the crisp autumn air biting their skin as they looked out over a sea of changing leaves. And then there was the time he had made love to her on his boat in the middle of the ocean, her breasts bare to the sky, the salty sea on both their lips. She reached over and opened the drawer of her nightstand. Fumbling around in the dark, she finally put her hands on TOM. TOM was "The Other Man," a battery operated gift from Jenna. She had given it to Beth for her 30th birthday saying, "Welcome to the club. You're going to need this." It turned out she was right. She had never really been into sex toys but it seemed like she enjoyed TOM's company more and more each year.

She pulled off her underwear and hit the power button. He shuddered briefly then went still.

"Damn!" For a moment she considered just trying to go to sleep. *Dammit, I deserve an orgasm! Even if I have to give it to myself.* She shuffled out to the kitchen in nothing but a tank top and her bare ass and rooted around in the junk drawer next to the refrigerator.

"Where are they?" She slammed the drawer in frustration and went into her spare bedroom to search the drawers of her desk. Still no batteries. Beth was about to give up and go back to bed when her eyes landed on the television remote, a beam of hope beckoning to her from the living room. *Hallelujah!*

She threw herself on the bed and fired up TOM. At the whirring noise, Homer looked up from his bed in the corner. He got up and walked out the bedroom door, but not before looking back at Beth with his ears flopped down.

"Don't you judge me, Homer," she shouted at the retreating dog. "You lick yourself!"

Leave it to Jenna to spend a small fortune on a sex toy, but Beth was glad she did. TOM had multiple speeds and directions and a vibrating hummingbird that protruded from the shaft. She arched her back as the hummingbird settled onto her most tender spot, imagining it was Peter's mouth instead.

Closing her eyes, she saw his dark hair, flecked with gray, between her legs, the rocking of the ocean giving rhythm to his exploration of her. It didn't take long before Beth increased the speed on the buzzing little bird. She arched her hips up against the toy, moving closer and closer to orgasm. Peter was sucking her and licking her. She reached down and cupped her own breast, imagining that it was his large, strong hand gently pulling at her nipple. His lips, his hands, the vibrations between her legs. It all came together in a loud moan that shook her from head to toe.

11

Jenna stood in front of the mirror at Vintageous Fashions holding up a pair of green and yellow bell bottoms.

"I thought you said the theme was rock stars," Beth said. "Who are you going to be in those pants?" They were shopping for costumes for Asha's Halloween party.

"I don't know," Jenna said, putting the pants back on a rack. "Maybe Janis Joplin or something?"

Beth's phone chirped and she stopped flipping through a rack of dresses from the 1980s to dig it out of her purse. When she saw the screen, she grimaced.

"Who is it?"

"Ugh. It's George."

GEORGE: can u do dinner tonight?

"Is it okay to dump someone over text? I don't think I've dumped anyone since college."

"Is it really necessary to dump someone you only fucked twice?" And then Jenna giggled. "Excuse me, I mean who only fucked you twice."

Beth laughed. "I can't for the life of me understand why he thinks I would want to see him again."

"Oh honey, you have a hole and a heartbeat and that's all most guys need."

"Ew," Beth wrinkled her nose. "That's gross."

BETH: I already have plans.

GEORGE: can you change your plans? I'm pretty busy this week

BETH: No, sorry

GEORGE: well tonight is the only time I can see you :(

"I don't know what to say to this," Beth said, holding up her phone for Jenna to read the conversation.

"You want to ditch me and go hang out with Georgie Porgie?"

Beth rolled her eyes. "Do I need to call him and tell him I not interested? What is the right thing to do here?"

"Well, first of all, you don't owe him anything. Especially not a date with 4 hours notice. I'd text him back and tell him to fuck off."

"I'm going to go call him. I'll be right back." She walked out of the store onto the sidewalk and her phone buzzed again.

GEORGE: don't understand y u can't make time 4 me

She stared at her phone. *What?*

GEORGE: guess u dont have time 4 this relationship

This is ridiculous.

Beth rolled her eyes. "What relationship!?" she said out loud and dialed. The phone rang. And it rang. And rang. Then George's voicemail picked up. "Seriously? You're going to text me but you won't answer the phone to actually speak to me?" She pulled up his text and began to type.

BETH: I just tried to call you.

GEORGE: Can't talk. At the gym.

Then why are you texting me? She wondered as she walked back into the shop.

BETH: I wanted to tell you that it was nice getting to know you but I'm not ready for a relationship.

GEORGE: Are you kidding me???

She was about to write back when she saw that he was texting something else.

GEORGE: I could have hooked up with soooo many girls last week but didn't because of u

What?

BETH: I didn't realize you thought we were exclusive

GEORGE: whatever

GEORGE: I deserve better than this

"What the hell? He just told me that he deserves better," Beth said to Jenna, holding up her phone.

"I thought you were going to call him."

"I tried. He didn't answer."

"But he's still texting you?"

"Yup. He said he can't talk, he's at the gym."

"Bless his heart. Maybe he has roid rage- all the gym testosterone or something. Maybe it's the roids that make him coo like a turtle dove. Ooooohoooohooohoo…" Jenna began to make bird noises but the mocking turned into sounds of actual excitement. "Oh, wow!" She held up a white, lacy dress and turned to Beth. "I know who we're going as!"

Beth raised one eyebrow as her phone chirped again.

GEORGE: I deserve a girl who will make time for me and make sacrifices

"Ugh, then go find a girl because you obviously don't know what to do with a woman!" Beth realized she was shouting at her phone. She started to type, *Maybe you can meet someone with a 'firm' ass at the gym.* Then she sighed and erased it.

BETH: If that's how you feel, I understand.

GEORGE: fine whatever

GEORGE: have a nice life

"Ooooh," Jenna said, reading over her shoulder. "You got the 'have a nice life' line. Hahaha… That's basically a 'fuck you.'"

"So I guess I'm done with him, then?"

"Yep, congratulations. You just dumped someone over text. Or actually, I think he dumped you."

* * *

"Two margaritas, stat!" Jenna said to no one in particular as they slid into a booth.

"God, how long has it been since we've been to Pancho's?" Beth loved the place with its tiny white lights hanging from the ceiling and the black-and-white photos of old Mexican women hand-rolling tortillas.

"I don't know, but I need some serious chips and salsa. And guacamole!"

"I might need queso, too," Beth added, with a face of mock sadness. "You know, to help me get over the big break-up." She was surprised by how relieved she was to be done with George. She felt practically giddy.

Jenna nodded seriously. "Definitely cheese for your broken heart."

They were knee deep in burritos and on their second round of margaritas when Beth heard a familiar voice.

"Hey Miss Grant." Beth thought she heard Jenna's jaw hit the table. Or maybe it was her own. *What the hell is he doing here?*

"Hi, Todd," Beth looked up at him from the booth, her heart beating unexpectedly faster.

Jenna's eyes moved from Todd to Beth, then back to Todd, then she finally spoke. "You're Todd Allman!" Before he could respond, Jenna added. "I thought you'd be way bigger."

"Jenna!"

"What?" she protested. "You should have seen him in *He-Man*. He was huge!"

"Please excuse my friend," Beth said.

Todd laughed. "It's okay, I get that all the time. But to look like He-Man, I'd have to live at the gym."

"I mean, don't get me wrong," Jenna added. "You still look good."

Beth shot her a look, then turned to Todd. "What are you doing here?"

"Grabbing dinner with my manager. Hey Danny," he called to a dark-haired man who had just walked over from the direction of the bathrooms. "This is my professor, Miss Grant."

"Nice to meet you Miss Grant," he said with a warm grin of impeccably white teeth.

"Beth," she corrected as she shook his hand. "Call me Beth."

"Ah," Danny said. "I know you! You're the Ludacris fan. Something about a bitch in your way? Am I right?"

Beth found herself blushing and before she could speak, Jenna said, "Yup, that sounds like her. And I'm Jenna." She held out her hand to him.

Danny grinned, taking her hand and holding her gaze. "Well Todd, if I had known the teachers at your school were so beautiful, I'd have signed up for classes, too."

"Oh, I don't teach at the college," Jenna said, grinning right back. "I own a yoga studio."

"Is that so? I've been meaning to try yoga but the classes are usually when I'm working. Do you ever give private lessons?"

"Sure," Jenna said with a laugh. "For the right price. If you boys want to join us, we can get another round and I'll tell you all about it."

"Ah, I wish I could but I've got to go," Danny said. "Maybe you could give me your number and we could do that another time?"

"Of course." She was too busy typing her out her number into Danny's phone to catch the pointed look Beth was trying to shoot her.

"I'll join you," Todd said. "I don't have to be anywhere."

What is he up to? Before she could protest, he had slid into the booth next to Jenna who was handing her number to Danny. As if on cue, Miguel showed up with another round of margaritas. When he left, Jenna handed the drink to Todd.

"I've got to drive. I can't drink this. You take it."

Todd shook his head. "I'm driving too, give it to her."

"Seriously, y'all?" Beth said, looking at the two and half margaritas that now sat in front of her.

Jenna shrugged. "A cure for your breakup?"

Beth glared at her but Jenna just grinned back mischievously.

"Your breakup? Is she talking about the guy from Thrasher?"

Beth cleared her throat dramatically, still glaring at Jenna, then turned to Todd, "So, how is your weekend going?"

"Well, it'd be a lot better if I didn't have homework for my creative writing class."

"Oh you poor thing," Jenna said. "You must have a mean teacher, giving you homework over the weekend. What made you decide to take a creative writing class anyway?"

Gene's words come back to Beth *"his people requested it."* "Yeah, why did you take my class?"

Todd grinned. "Do you really want to to know?" He leaned forward and took his wallet out of his back pocket. He opened it and pulled out a business card. For Beth, time slowed down as he slid the card into the middle of the table. "This made me decide to take your class."

Jenna looked at it, then at Todd. "Where did you get Beth's business card?" It took a moment, but Beth finally got there. *Fuck, fuck, fuck! That's why he looks so familiar!* Red heat blazed across her chest and up her neck.

"That was you?" She said slowly, trying to remain calm.

Todd nodded, grinning like he had just won a very big hand of poker.

"What was him?" Jenna was confused.

"But that guy had a beard," Beth protested weakly. *How did I not realize it before?* She thought about the guy with the broad shoulders who had held the door for her at the convenience store and then followed her back to the drink cooler where they exchanged smiles. When he had ended up behind her again at the register they laughed and he had told her *I promise I'm not stalking you.* Her wallet was open and her business card was right there and she had turned to him…

"You said you didn't think you would mind if I stalked you."

"Wait a minute!" Jenna said. "He's the guy from the gas station?" Todd nodded and Beth cringed, rubbing the bridge of her nose, wishing she was somewhere else. Jenna dissolved into a fit of laughter. "Oh my god, Beth. This is good even for you!" Beth kicked her under the table but that made her laugh harder.

"Only you would hit on a movie star and have no idea who you were even talking to!" Jenna was practically wheezing now.

"Well, I wouldn't have if I had known who he was," she protested and began giggling hopelessly into her hand, abandoning what was left of her dignity. When she finally stopped laughing at herself and she could speak clearly, Beth said to him. "I'm so sorry. I had no idea you were going to take my class. I don't hit on my students."

Jenna was still laughing. "It's true. She doesn't usually hit on *anyone.*"

"So wait," Beth said. "You're taking my class because I hit on you at a gas station?"

"No, not really. I'm in a movie about a college student and I was thinking about taking a class to prepare for the role. Then I met you at the gas station and well…" He smiled at her and Beth was surprised to feel her heart flutter. "I guess you could say I don't believe in coincidences."

Jenna was watching her closely for her reaction but Beth just picked up one of the margaritas and finished it.

When Miguel returned to the table, Todd said something to him in Spanish.

"No no no," Beth said, grabbing her purse.

"What?" Jenna asked.

"He said he wants to pay for us. Todd, I can't let you do that."

Todd looked surprised. "You speak Spanish?"

"Yeah, I spent a few summers in Costa Rica. How do *you* know Spanish?"

"My mom was from Cuba. I grew up speaking Spanish."

"Really?" Jenna said. "You don't look Hispanic." She put her hand on his arm and studied him intently. "Oooh, except maybe your dark eyes."

Beth felt a flash of irritation with Jenna but dismissed it.

"Todd, I can't let you pay! It would be…" She struggled to think of the word, her brain foggy from the margaritas, finally landing on, "Inappropriate."

"I insist."

"Really, you can't pay. You're my student. It's not right. I could get in trouble."

"If you're worried about that, I guess you'll just have be faster next time," Todd said as he handed the check Beth never even saw back to Miguel with a black credit card.

In the parking lot, Jenna stood on tiptoe and gave Todd a hug. "Thanks for dinner," she said. "And make sure your friend calls me."

"Yeah, um, thanks," Beth said, awkwardly patting him on his arm.

Beth waited until they were in the car to blurt out. "What the fuck is going on? First he shows up in my class, then the damn football game, and now Pancho's?"

"Wrong. First you hit on him at a gas station," she said and starting laughing again. "But it sure seems like the universe keeps putting you two together. I wonder what it could mean?" She made a lewd gesture. Beth rolled her eyes trying not to imagine herself and Todd in the starring roles of said gesture.

"Click. Click. Click," said the car as Jenna tried to start it.

"Shit."

They were standing next to the car while Jenna talked to the tow truck driver when an old, black Chevy truck pulled up. The darkly tinted window rolled down and there was Todd.

"Everything okay?"

"Jenna's car won't start," Beth said and was startled to realize she was slurring her words a bit.

"Do you need a jump?" he asked.

"Nah, I think it's the starter."

Jenna hung up the phone. "Ugh, he said it's going to be two hours."

"Do you all want a ride?"

Beth opened her mouth to tell him no, that they would take an Uber but before she could, Jenna said. "Do you mind? I'll just leave the keys in the car."

And just like that, Beth found herself on a bench seat between her celebrity student and her best friend. Up close, the truck wasn't black but a deep, midnight blue. Even though it was in near-mint condition, it was definitely not the truck of a movie star. The black rims and darkly tinted windows were the flashiest things about it.

After they dropped Jenna off, Todd turned up the music.

"You listen to Tom Petty?" Beth said. This kid, this movie star kept surprising her.

He grinned at her. "You like him? I wouldn't have figured you for a Tom Petty fan."

"Me?" she said. "What about you? I'm surprised you've even heard of him. You're so young!"

He looked at her then, his face serious. "I'm not that young, Beth." The sound of her name in his mouth was startling. Not for its novelty but for how familiar it seemed. The whole night had been like that.

"Well, I still wouldn't have figured *you* for a Tom Petty fan." She glanced at him, not sure what else to say. He was watching the road ahead of them, his face still serious.

When he stopped at a red light, he turned to her. His brown eyes were almost black in the dark cab of the truck. They stared at each other. Her breath caught in her chest and she couldn't hold his gaze. *I can't believe he's the guy I hit on at the gas station.* Butterflies bobbed in her stomach and she had the overwhelming feeling that she was in big, delicious trouble. When the light turned green and the truck moved forward, she snuck a look at him, admiring his full lips and the way his big hands managed the steering wheel.

"Right, Beth?"

"What?"

"It's on the right, correct?"

"Oh, sorry. I was just... Um, yes, just up around this next corner. The blue one. See, there it is." She pointed.

Todd pulled up to the house, put the truck in park and turned to her. "So can I see you again?"

"Listen, this was fun and I appreciate the ride but you need to know that I don't hang out with my students." She paused.

"Or let them drive me home." Then added. "And I definitely never hit on them at gas stations. If I had had any idea…"

"I figured." He grinned at her, the shadowy light making him look older. "But you know how you told us in class that we need to find our magic?"

She nodded. "Mmmhmm."

"I think *you* are my magic." He was looking at her, his handsome face so earnest.

She blinked for a moment and then, unable to help herself, she burst out laughing. "Oh my god, does that kind of stuff really work on girls your age?" His look of shock cut her laughter short and she clamped a hand over her mouth. Her mother always said Beth had to be careful with her sharp tongue and the tequila had removed what little filter she had. "Of course," she said more softly. "You've probably never had to hit on anyone in your life."

He turned away from her, looking out the window, clearly stung by her response. Feeling guilty, she put her hand on his arm, conscious of his firm bicep under the soft T-shirt. *Wow, so that's what Jenna was talking about.* "Hey," she said. "I'm sorry." Todd finally looked back at her, his face unreadable. She started to apologize again but before Beth knew what was happening, he was kissing her. His full, warm lips pressed into hers so naturally that for just a moment she kissed him back. As their tongues met, Beth felt an exquisite longing deep inside her that was at once arousing and also sobering.

"Stop," she said pushing him away. "I can't. You're my student. Oh my God. This is so wrong." The words tumbled from her mouth as she shook her head and opened the door of the truck. She grabbed her purse off the floorboard and fled up her walkway, searching frantically for her keys. It was only once she was inside, the door shut firmly behind her, that she noticed her bare feet. Her flip-flops had been abandoned on the floorboard of Todd's truck.

Shit! What have I done? she wondered. Homer danced excitedly around her.

As she brushed her teeth, Beth examined her face in the mirror. It was flushed from the excitement of the evening and probably the tequila, making her look younger. But no one would mistake her for his age. *He's too young for me even if he wasn't my student,* she thought.

12

The next morning, Beth replayed the events of the night before in her head. Her stomach flip-flopped anxiously. She hadn't believed it when Jenna said Todd was hitting on her at the Dolphins' game. But after that kiss, it was clear he wanted to be more than her student. *He shouldn't have kissed me like that!* She told herself, pretending she hadn't kissed him back, re-writing what had happened in her memory. He was obviously confused by the time she hit on him at the gas station. Hanging out with him at Pancho's and letting him drive her home must have made him even more confused. *I'm just going to have to have a talk with him about what behavior is acceptable and what is not.* She would have to meet with him after class and set things straight. She felt calmer now that she had a plan. *It's fine. It was only a misunderstanding.*

On the drive to school, she psyched herself up for the conversation she needed to have with Todd. By the time she walked into the classroom, she felt strong and capable, ready to put the situation to bed. But when she scanned the room, he wasn't there.

After class, she went to her office to check her email for a note from Todd but there was nothing. *Did he go out of town again?* She was both disappointed and relieved at not having dealt with him. Beth tapped her pen absentmindedly, leaning back in her chair and watching the dust motes dance in the sunbeam coming through her window. It was a perfect, unusually clear day and she was itching to get out on her board. *Should I leave early?* She looked at the clock. *Students never come to office hours anyway.*

Screw it! Beth grabbed her beach bag from under her desk. She locked her office door and stepped into the corner that couldn't be seen from either window. Quickly, she shimmied out of her work clothes and threw them into her bag, then slipped on her swimsuit, shorts, and a tank top. When she dug to the bottom of the bag looking for her flip-flops, she came up empty handed. That's when she remembered where they were. *Damn!* She dropped the bag on her green chair and leaned back against the desk, wondering if anyone would notice if she walked through the parking lot in her beach clothes and work heels. It was a ridiculous image. *I should probably just change back into my…*

The knock made her jump. *Shit! Gene?!?* She unlocked the door and opened it just a crack. But instead of peering out into the hallway, she found herself looking directly into a broad, T-shirt covered chest.

"I come bearing gifts." He held her flip flops up to the crack in the door and waved them like a flag of surrender. She sighed and opened the door. In her bare feet he seemed taller than ever. She scooted behind her desk and sat down, attempting to look as professorial as possible with the strings of her green bikini poking out of the top of her shirt.

Todd closed the door behind him and studied her. "Can I sit down?" he finally asked.

"Of course," she said, sitting up straighter and gesturing to the chair across from her, only to realize that her bag was still there, disheveled work clothes spilling out of it. On top, like a cherry on a sundae, was her bra.

She stood up quickly, banging her knee hard on the desk. It really hurt but she wouldn't feel it until later. The only thing she could feel was her heart pounding and the flush of heat that was creeping up her face. "Let me just get that," she said, scurrying over to the chair and shoving the clothes down inside. She dropped the bag on the floor and tried to kick it under her desk but she somehow managed to send the bra flying out onto the floor.

Beth grimaced and looked at Todd who's mouth twitched at the corner. The absurdity of the situation overruled her embarrassment and she began to laugh.

"Oh well," she shrugged, slowly picking up the bra and putting it back into her bag. "It's not like you've never seen one of those before."

"Did I interrupt something?" Todd asked, no longer suppressing his smile.

"Uh, no," she said and went back behind her desk to sit down. Then more definitively, "No." She wasn't expecting him to show up at her office and now that he was there, she was thrown off guard. The speech she had composed in her head — *Todd, I need to see you in my office. We need to talk about your behavior the other night* — didn't seem to fit.

"Are you sure?" His smile had turned cocky. "Did I miss field day or something?" He gestured at her bare feet under the desk and she was tempted to pull them away, out of his line of sight. But his attitude was so relaxed and it wasn't like she was going to make it back to respectable professor after flinging her bra around.

She sighed and slumped back in her chair. "You caught me," she admitted. "I was going to sneak out of office hours early to hit the beach."

He grinned and slid her flip-flops onto her desk. "I guess

you'll be needing these then."

"Thanks," she said, then hesitated. "And about the other night."

"What about it?" He grinned, leaning forward, his elbows on his knees.

She straightened up in her seat again. "That was incredibly inappropriate." The grin disappeared and his face fell into an expression she couldn't read. "I understand why you might've felt like that was okay." She intentionally left out the words *kissing me*. "But you need to know that I don't date my students. Or hook up with them. Or whatever." She was beginning to get flustered again. This conversation was not supposed to be taking place like this. "I mean, even if I wanted to," she looked down at her hands and then back at him, his expression was unchanged. "I mean, I'm not saying that I want to. What I'm saying is, regardless, I could get fired for having a relationship, or… or… whatever with my student."

Todd pressed his index fingers together resting his chin on them and said nothing.

Beth continued. "Listen, I know I hit on you at that gas station, so I can see why you would be confused, but that was before you were my student."

He remained silent and Beth stared at him for a moment, not sure what else to say. She finally asked, "Do you understand?"

He nodded. "I think so."

"Good." She sighed. "So, we're good?"

"Sure," he said, still wearing the expression that she couldn't read. "But Ms. Grant?"

"Yes?" His return to formality was reassuring but she was worried what he might say next.

"Has anyone ever told you that this chair is really uncomfortable?"

She snickered, then covered her mouth with her hand,

looking at him with bright, mischievous eyes. He cocked his head to one side and studied her. "You knew that already, didn't you?" She didn't say anything, but her shoulders shook with silent laughter. He nodded. "Okay then." He grinned and stood up, looking down at her. "I guess I'll just see you next class then?"

At the door, he turned and looked back at her. "Oh and Ms. Grant," he said. "Your secret is safe with me."

Beth laughed again, thinking he was talking about her uncomfortable chair. But after he left, she started to wonder if that had been what he was talking about after all.

13

Just like in college, Beth was ready and Jenna was not. So she grabbed Jenna's laptop off her nightstand, sat down on the bed, and googled Todd Allman. She wouldn't admit it to herself, and definitely not to Jenna, but ever since the kiss she had found that she couldn't stop thinking of him. She clicked on *image search* and scrolled through dozens of photographs. There were only a few of him with a woman, and always the same woman, who was tall and thin and blond and *nothing remotely like me*. When she realized what she was doing, she chastised herself and closed the website.

Jenna was still blow drying her hair so Beth opened a new page and typed in the web address for the college. It took her a while to find what she was looking for, but after some searching she found the Faculty and Staff Handbook. She scrolled through rules and regulations until she found the section titled *Consensual Relations*. Her eyes scanned the screen:

> No faculty or staff member shall have an amorous relationship (consensual or otherwise) with a student who is enrolled in a course being taught by the faculty member or whose work is being supervised, evaluated, or otherwise similarly impacted by the

faculty or staff member. Such unethical behavior may constitute a violation of the University's Harassment Policy.

She was about to click on a link to the harassment policy, too engrossed in what she was doing to realize the hairdryer was no longer running. Jenna's voice came from behind her.

"What are you looking at?"

Beth jumped. "Nothing, just work stuff." Then slowly and deliberately, so as not to attract suspicion, she moved the cursor to the corner of the screen.

Before she could click on it, Jenna said, "Sexual harassment? Why are you reading about that? Did Hy-Gene make a pass at you? I'll kill him!"

She forced a laugh then closed the browser and shut the laptop. "No, we just have to do some mandatory HR training so…" Beth turned to look at her friend, the walking epitome of the 1980s. "Ah!" she squealed. "You look fantastic!"

Jenna did a little twirl. She was head-to-toe in white: a white bustier, a white tutu, and long, white lace gloves. Her blond hair was teased out and tied partially back with a white scarf. Strands of pearls and gold chains hung around her neck.

"Are we ready for the finishing touch?" Beth nodded and followed Jenna to the bathroom mirror, where she handed her a brown eye pencil. She stared at her reflection in the mirror. Her dark hair, parted in the center, fell in curls past her shoulders. Her lips were stained a shade of burgundy just lighter than her dress.

"Here, right?" Beth motioned to her face and deftly placed a beauty mark just above and to the right of her top lip. She handed the pencil to Jenna and watched her do the same.

They stood grinning at themselves in the mirror. "We look like hookers," Beth laughed.

"No, we look perfect. Hey, we should do a shot before we leave!"

Beth eyed her friend suspiciously. "I don't know if that's a good idea."

"Of course it is, we're not driving!" She followed Jenna downstairs to the kitchen.

"Okay, but only one. You know how they go right to my head." Jenna poured the tequila and handed it to Beth. The tequila was smooth going down and a pleasant warmth spread from Beth's throat up the back of her neck to the base of her skull. She grinned dopily.

"You're such a lightweight. You feel it already, don't you?" Jenna laughed and hiked up her bustier. "Are you ready to go, Madonna?"

Beth smiled and mock bowed, "After you, Madonna."

* * *

The car pulled through the gate and onto a circular driveway lined with blazing torches, the flames dancing from skull-shaped pots. The house was rectangles of concrete and glass, sleek and modern. But tonight cobwebs and orange lights festooned the entrance. Pumpkins professionally carved with the faces of Elvis, Michael Jackson, and Tina Turner lined the steps leading up to the front of the house.

As soon as the car door opened, they could hear music from the house spilling out across the lawn. The man at the door was a caricature of a bouncer, complete with a tight black shirt, bulging biceps, and a somber expression. "The Madonnas have arrived and are ready to make an entrance, Hercules!" Jenna announced.

"Invitation," the man said flatly without looking at them.

Beth's heart started to race. She hated these events where

you had to prove that you belonged. She smiled up at the man weakly. His expression remained tattooed on his face.

"Oh yeah," Jenna said and dug through her oversized purse, until she found her phone. After a few taps, she handed him her phone. He scanned the code with what appeared to Beth to be another phone. One of the devices made a ghoulish cackling noise and the man opened the door. Beth let out a breath she didn't know she'd been holding.

Just inside the door was a long table draped in black. Behind it were light-tight ceiling to floor black velvet curtains. Two women sat at the table, both in tiny black dresses, both with long, sleek hair—one purple and one pink. A man, nearly identical to Hercules, stood in front of the curtains.

"Happy Halloween," the pink-haired woman said over the music. "We'll take your bags and any cell phones or cameras you have."

"No problem." Jenna smiled at the girl then whispered to Beth, "They don't want any unauthorized photos. Do you want to put anything in my bag?" Beth looked at the small clutch in her hand, shrugged and dropped it into Jenna's purse. Jenna handed her purse to the woman who placed a plastic tag on it, then scanned the tag and held the device out to Jenna.

"Just put your first two fingers on the screen. Great, now you can come back here if you need anything from your bag or want to check your phone." Jenna nodded and the bouncer held the curtain open for them. When it closed behind them, they were in total darkness.

"Is this party supposed to be scary?" Beth whispered. "I thought the theme was rock stars."

"I don't know," Jenna said. "I think it's just a maze or something. Take my hand."

With their free hands, they felt along the wall which was

covered in the same velvet fabric of the curtains.

"Is this going anywhere?" Beth asked as they crept slowly forward.

"I'm not sure. I'm just walking toward the music." Their eyes were finally beginning to adjust to the lack of light as the wall rounded in front of them.

"I hate Halloween," Beth muttered and held Jenna's hand tighter.

"Calm down. I think we've got to be almost there. Their house isn't *that* big."

Suddenly there was a whoosh and Beth felt the air move in front of them. A figure had jumped down from somewhere above and was blocking their path. A light flashed showing Freddy Krueger right in front of them. Jenna shrieked and backed into Beth who was already yanking her friend away. Freddy let out a grisly laugh.

The bright flash plunged them further into darkness. Beth's heart pounded in her chest and she willed her eyes to adjust. *I fucking hate Halloween.* Jenna was still shrieking when Beth sensed movement behind them. She froze, her senses heightened. And that was when she felt breathing, so close to her that it moved strands of her hair. Instinctively, she dropped Jenna's hand, whirled around, and swung low and hard, her fist connecting to soft flesh. Just then, the light flashed again showing a man in a Jason mask double over.

"Jesus, lady," he groaned.

"Man down," a voice shouted from in front of them and the darkness was lifted by a dim glow. Beth found herself standing over a curled up Jason Voorhees, her hand still in a tight fist, her heart pounding furiously. Freddy pulled his mask off and pushed past them to his partner.

"Are you all right, man?"

"Ooof," Jason moaned as he let Freddy help him to his feet.

Beth looked at Jenna whose mouth was agape.

"Uh… I'm sorry?" Beth said feebly. "You guys really scared me."

"That's the point." Freddy glared at her. "It's Halloween."

"Are you okay?" she said but thought *you sort of deserved it.*

Jason lifted his mask and sighed. "Lady, you got one hell of a rip. Good thing I'm not any taller, you would have socked me right in the nuts."

After several more apologies, Jenna grabbed Beth's hand and pulled her out of the maze before someone could turn the lights back off. When they were finally in the main part of the house and out of earshot of the two horror movie villains, Jenna collapsed in laughter.

"What. Just. Happened?"

"I don't know." Beth still felt confused. She shook out her hand which was starting to get sore. "But I think I hit him pretty hard."

"I can't believe you just punched Jason!" Jenna was laughing even harder.

"I mean, I feel bad but…" Beth started to giggle. "You know I hate stuff like that."

"What's a rip, anyway?"

"No clue but I need a drink. Let's find the bar."

As they walked into the kitchen, the crowd milling around the bar started clapping. Beth was confused until she noticed a giant flatscreen television mounted on the wall behind the bar. An Axl Rose look-alike, was holding up a remote and the images on the screen were moving backwards. When he turned, Beth saw that it was Levi in a long, red wig, tied back with a blue bandana. "The ass-kickers are here!" he hooted. With shock and horror, she realized that the video was of her and Jenna and the movie villains. "Man, you really gave it to him," Levi cackled. "Watch the instant replay!"

"Levi! Are you filming people getting the shit scared out of them?" Jenna shouted at him.

"Of course. It's Halloween!" He came out from around the bar and made to give her a hug, then pulled back.

"Wait, I don't want to get punched," he said, looking at Beth. "Hey Rocky, is it okay if I hug her?"

Levi's arrogance was exceeded only by his charm. Beth rolled her eyes but laughed despite herself and accepted a kiss on the cheek from him.

"You ladies made quite the entrance. How is your hand?" He grabbed Beth's hand and scrutinized it. "Didn't even break a nail," he shouted over his shoulder to the group, who cheered in appreciation.

"Who didn't break a nail?" Asha walked into the kitchen carrying a martini glass filled with orange liquid. Her dark hair was curled into a mass of corkscrews. "Jenna! Beth! Did you just get here?" She looked back and forth between the two.

"Madonna and… Madonna?"

"Exactly," Jenna grinned. "Like a virgin," she gestured to herself, then turned to Beth. "And like a prayer."

"I love it!" Asha squealed. "You'll have to do a song together."

"Do a song?" Beth asked, her throat going dry.

"Yeah, everyone's doing a song in character. Come on, the deejay is in the back room. Levi, are you ready, sweet child o' mine?"

They got drinks and followed Asha and Levi to the back of house where a deejay dressed as Elvis was set up on a small stage. A disco ball hung from the ceiling. People were milling about, some sat on couches along the edge of the room, some danced. Beth saw a David Bowie, a Gwen Stefani, and a woman with dark hair and spinning lollipops for boobs.

Levi and Asha got up on stage. "Happy Halloween, rock

stars!" he shouted and the crowd cheered. Some people catcalled and others chanted "G N R!"

"Thanks for coming out. I'm your host Axl Rosenbloom." The crowd laughed and Levi continued, "And this is the lovely Slash-a!"

The opening notes of *Sweet Child of Mine* brought a cheer from the crowd. The energy in the room was so contagious, it felt like an actual concert. She and Jenna grinned at each other and began to sing along. Beth, still a little shaken from her altercation with Jason, downed her drink a little too quickly. So when Levi and Asha transitioned into *Patience*, Beth shouted at Jenna, "I'm going to get another drink. Do you want one?"

In the kitchen, a dozen people were watching two more unsuspecting guests on the television. An older man in a long blond wig turned to her, "Hey, it's Madonna! She's the one that punched the guy." The others turned to look at her. "These people need help. You gonna come to their rescue?"

Beth smiled awkwardly. "No, sorry. I'm taking the rest of the night off."

The bartender raised his hands in mock surrender. "Anything you want, it's yours." She blushed and ordered a vodka soda. Then a very tall Gene Simmons walked up.

"Lightweight," he said.

"What?" His voice was slightly muffled behind his mask and she wasn't sure she had heard him right.

"That drink is for lightweights. I thought you were tough. They said you punched Freddy Krueger."

"Actually, I punched Jason. But just out of curiosity, what would a tough drink be?" She held up her hands in air quotes around the word tough. It was a strange conversation but it was also a strange party.

"Shots," Gene said. "If you're brave enough." She had never

liked Kiss and this guy's attitude was starting to irritate her. *Who stands around the bar at a party trying to get women to do shots?* She stared defiantly up at the mask.

"What the hell," she shrugged and turned to the bartender. "A shot of tequila, please. And one for Gene here, since he's such a tough guy."

The bartender poured the shots and placed them on the bar. Gene held his up to hers but Beth ignored him. She took the shot, the cool tequila sliding easily down her throat, the familiar warm buzz slipping back up her neck. She turned the empty glass over on the bar and picked up her drink. Gene chuckled behind his mask and started to clap slowly. She didn't wait for him to do his shot before turning and walking out of the kitchen.

Levi was still singing *Patience* and working up a pretty good Axl Rose slither. Beth squeezed through the crowd, back to Jenna. Jenna put her arm through Beth's as they both swayed with the music. "See, I told you this would be fun."

When the song was over, Jenna leaned over to Beth. "I've got to pee. Hold my drink. I'll be right back."

"Wait, I'll go with you," she called after her, but Jenna had already disappeared into the crowd.

"My friend here wants to dedicate this next song to a very special lady," Levi announced and Beth turned back around to see the Gene Simmons from kitchen climbing onto the stage. She rolled her eyes and began to weave her way through the crowd. Soft piano notes floated down on her like snowflakes, causing her to shiver. When he started to sing, she froze.

Before she even knew what was happening, a familiar spasm of grief shot through her. Her face crumpled as a painful lump welled in her throat. The drinks, the crowd, the music—*that goddamn music*—were overwhelming, suffocating. *I've got to get some air.* She spun around and pushed her way through the crowd, dropping the drinks on a table before she shot through the back door, past the people milling around the fire pit and the outside bar, across the sloping lawn. She didn't stop until she could no longer hear that Kiss song that shared her name. When she finally settled on a chaise by the pool, she gulped in the fresh air, tears already rolling down her cheeks. *Oh Jeremy.* The liquor had made her so emotional. It always did. And that damn song had pushed her over the edge.

"Beth!" Gene Simmons was jogging toward her. *Shit! Just leave me alone!* Before she could protest, he sat down on the chair next to hers and pulled off his mask.

Gene Simmons was now wearing a Todd Allman mask. Her head swam and she blinked at him stupidly, trying to make sense of what had just happened.

"What are you doing here?" she stammered, swiping the tears from her cheeks.

"I came out here to find you. You looked so upset."

Beth stared at him, still confused. "Not here," she pointed to the ground in front of her. "Here!" She gestured at the house. "At this party."

"Oh. Right. I'm friends with Levi," Todd said, running his hand through his hair, missing a large chunk in the back that stood rumpled from the mask.

She lifted her hand to reach up and smooth his hair, but hesitated. Remembering what happened the last time she touched him, in his car, she put her hand back in her lap. "You know Levi?" Beth was still struggling to understand how Gene Simmons had just become Todd Allman.

"Yeah, we met when his band did the *He-Man* soundtrack. And he's my partner in The Meat Shed."

"Really? The Meat Shed?" She realized she was just repeating what he said but she couldn't help it. Between the scare in the maze and the drinks and the song and Todd

Allman sitting in front of her, Beth felt completely off balance.

"Hey, are you okay?" Todd was studying her. *Again with that stare.*

She waved her hand dismissively. "I'm fine," she said. Then without thinking added, "It's just that Jeremy used to sing that song to me. And," her voice broke a little so she stopped to take a breath. "It just totally caught me off guard tonight."

Todd took her hand in both of his, still staring at her intently. "No, *I'm* sorry. I had no idea that song was so important to you."

Beth was puzzled by his dramatic reaction and laughed half-heartedly, forcing herself to ignore the warm, tingling sensation from his touch. She could see the muscles move in his tanned forearm when he squeezed her hand. "It's not what you think. I actually really hate Kiss."

"You do?" He frowned. "So much that it made you cry?"

She laughed again, this time with more conviction. The whole situation was ridiculous, Todd in her class and at this party and the kiss from the other night. "It's kind of stupid, really." She took her hand from Todd's to hold her stomach. "He would sing it to torment me." Beth tried but couldn't seem to stop laughing. Her words came out in a gasp now. "It drove me fucking crazy!"

When she finally got a hold of herself, she sighed deeply and swiped under each eye with her index fingers. "Whooo, I'm sorry," she said and let out a last little giggle. "You must think I'm nuts."

"Not at all." Todd continued to watch her, unfazed by her outburst. "But who is Jeremy?"

She bit her lip and searched his face. It had been so long since she told someone about Jeremy. She took a deep breath. "He was my... person."

The first time that someone called Beth a widow, she began

to refer to Jeremy as her fiancé instead. She hated the term widow. Beyond the sad, spinster connotation, the word implied a life lived together. She had been cheated out of that life and that was a very different kind of loss, the loss of what might have been rather than what had been. In some ways, she wondered if it was actually a *more* painful loss. Telling people that Jeremy had been her fiancé instead of her husband elicited a different kind of pity, though. Some people, even in the grief support group, seemed to think her pain was less because they hadn't had much time together. It didn't take long for her to realize that neither pity was something she wanted, so she had stopped telling people altogether.

Todd didn't respond. She looked down at her hands, trying to decide whether to share more. He continued to wait until she finally said, mostly to her lap, "He died." Beth braced herself for his pity and met his eyes through two fresh tears. "Sometimes it still gets to me," she said in stronger voice.

"I'm so sorry," he murmured and reached for her face. With thumbs on either cheek, he wiped away the tears. His touch made her heart beat faster. Beth searched his dark eyes. There was concern but no pity. And there was also something deeper… *longing.* She leaned in unconsciously and held her breath. Todd pulled her face closer and she let him until their lips brushed softly together. Her mind told her to pull away but his kiss was magnetic and she felt herself melting into him.

"Beth?" Jenna called from the patio area. "Are you out here?"

Beth snapped her head back and Todd dropped his hands.

"Over here," Beth shouted back.

They looked out across the lawn and saw Jenna trying to negotiate the grass in her heels.

"There you are. Are you okay? I heard some asshole was singing *Beth.*"

"Yeah, I'm okay," she said pulling further away from him as Jenna made it to the pool deck, noticing Todd for the first time.

"Todd Allman," she said and bent to hug him. "I didn't think you were coming." She looked at the mask on the chair next to him, then to Beth, and back to Todd. "Ohhhhhh," she said. "You're Gene Simmons."

"Yep, I'm the asshole."

"Yikes, sorry." Jenna winced, then looked back to Beth. "Am I interrupting something?"

"No!" Beth said too quickly.

"Oh-kay." Suspicion dripped from each syllable. "Well, if you're all right, I'm going to head back to the party. Bye, Todd." She kicked off her heels, picked them up, and walked back up the lawn toward the house, but not before shooting a pointed look at Beth.

She stood up and smoothed out her dress. Jenna's interruption was like being doused by a cold bucket of water. *What were you thinking, Beth? You just kissed him again! He's your fucking student!* "Well, um, it was nice to see you. Have a good night." She turned to follow Jenna back up the hill when Todd grabbed her hand.

"Don't leave," he said.

She looked down at him, the tenderness on her face replaced with frustration. "Why not?" She snapped, angry at herself for letting this happen again. Startled, he let her hand go with a wounded look. "I'm sorry," Beth sighed. "But really, what do you think you're doing? Why are you singing a song to me? Why are you kissing me? You're 24 years old and..." She gestured to him dramatically. "You are my *student*."

"Yeah, you mentioned that," he snapped back.

"Listen, I shouldn't have let you kiss me just now. But what exactly did you think was going to happen here tonight?"

"I like you." He said as he stood and moved closer to her. She couldn't meet his eyes so she stared at his chest instead. A blush crept up her neck to her cheeks. "And I think you like me. Plus, you know I'm not a real student." He bent his head down, so she had to face him. Instead of meeting his eyes, she concentrated on the scar that ran through his eyebrow beautifully flawing his perfect face. His face so close to hers now that their noses nearly touched. "I think you just use that as an excuse." Her heart thudded in her chest, her lips still slick from where they had met his.

"An excuse for what?" she asked, feebly attempting scorn.

He leaned in even closer, so close their bodies were touching. She stifled a gasp but didn't step back. "An excuse to not give me a chance," he whispered, his lips brushing her ear, sending an explosion of heat through her. Her body was pressing against his when her brain shouted *No!* The school's sexual harassment policy flashed in her mind. With all the restraint she could muster, she put both hands on his chest, pushing him away.

"Well, thank you for that analysis. I didn't realize you were taking a psychology class, too."

"Are you kidding me? What is wrong with you?" He looked at her indignantly.

"What's wrong with me?" Beth glared at him, flushed with anger. "What's wrong with you? What are you trying to do to me? Is it some kind of teacher fantasy? Or are you just trying to get me fired?" She thought of all the students in the hallway at school, always waiting around for him. *Easy prey.* "It's not like there's a shortage of young women throwing themselves at you! Why don't you go find someone your own age?"

"Whatever," Todd said grabbing the Gene Simmons mask off the chair. "I guess if you're into that douchebag from Thrasher, I'm not your type anyway." And in two long strides, he was across the pool area and walking up the lawn.

Fucking Todd Allman! She watched him go, pretending to herself it was the cool night air and not the interaction with him that was making her shiver. When she walked back into the house, Jenna pounced on her.

"What is going on? What just happened out there? Did I see you guys kissing?"

Beth sighed, "Nothing happened."

"Bullshit. Do you think I'm stupid? I know something is going on with you two."

"No," Beth said. "It's not. He's my student. And that's all."

Jenna grabbed her by the hand, pulled her into the bathroom and gestured toward the mirror. Beth looked at herself. The beauty mark was smudged along with her lipstick.

Jenna's reflection glared back at her from over her shoulder. "Now you want to tell me what's going on?"

Beth sighed and grabbed some toilet paper.

"Here let me," Jenna said, more softly, wiping away the beauty mark and the smudges around her mouth.

"Let's get another drink and I'll tell you everything."

"You better."

In the kitchen, Beth was dismayed to see Todd in the corner with a group of young women, each one slimmer, younger, and glossier than the next. Her reaction to the scene only served to irritate her further. Without his mask on, he had become the center of attention. The young woman with lollipop boobs was reaching up to smooth the rumpled section of Todd's hair. She swished her dark hair over her shoulder and laughed playfully, leaning into him. Beth seethed. *What the hell?* Trying to ignore the swirl of jealousy and confusion that was turning to rage, she marched up to the bar, Jenna right behind her.

"Two shots of tequila, please," Beth announced.

"Tequila? I don't want to do shots," Jenna protested.

"Fine, I'll do them both," Beth snapped as the bartender filled two shot glasses in front of her. *Well, that's not a good idea,* her sensible side said. To which she replied, *Shut up!* She had never done two shots in a row in her life. Even though she felt like a child throwing a temper tantrum, she knocked back the first shot and then the second.

Jenna leaned over to the bartender. "Um, you better give me a water, too, please." She was no stranger to the volatile energy coming off Beth but it had been years since she had seen her in such a state. "Let's go back outside." She led Beth by her elbow to an empty corner of the patio, near the fire pit and sat down.

"What happened?"

"Gah!" Beth said in frustration and put her hand to her forehead. The shots were starting to make her feel dizzy. "Okay," she started. "You know how I said nothing happened after we left Pancho's?" And she told her friend everything. "Then we go in there and he's hanging all over that girl with the lollipop boobs!"

"That's Katy Perry," Jenna said. "But yes, I can see your dilemma." She was nodding sagely.

"You can?" She hadn't expected Jenna to understand.

"Actually," Jenna said, cocking her head to the side. "No, I can't." And she began to laugh. "You have mutha-fuckin Todd Allman in your class, up your ass, trying to get with you and all you can say is 'wahh, he's my student.'"

Beth was indignant. "So you think I should potentially get fired to hook up with some stupid actor?"

"First, he's not some stupid actor. An actor is the guy that makes your coffee at Starbucks. Todd Allman is a *movie star.* Second, he's right, he's not a real student. And third," Jenna stopped. She had worked up quite the speech but Beth could tell she wasn't pausing for effect.

"You don't have a third!" She poked her friend and began to laugh.

"Of course I do!" Jenna protested. Then after a moment, she poked Beth back. "Third, he's mutha-fuckin Todd Allman and he's hot and young and you need to hit that!"

Beth laughed and stood up, a little unsteadily. The shots had definitely gone to her head. She thrust her hips back and forth obscenely and in a meathead voice said, "Yeah, I'm gonna hit that! Uh uh uh!"

Jenna cackled with laughter and it was a moment before Beth's dulled senses realized she was not laughing at her, but at something behind her.

"Haven't you hit enough tonight?" a male voice asked. "I'm going to have to give Jason hazard pay." Beth whipped around so fast, she lost her balance. Levi grabbed her waist and righted her. "Whoa. And why is my boy Todd singing to you?"

Beth felt woozy, but something was tickling the back of her mind. "Hey," she pointed her finger up at Levi. "You own The Meat Shed." It came out as a slurred accusation.

Levi laughed. "I do. Todd and I opened it a few months ago."

Beth turned back to Jenna, her eyes narrowed dramatically. "Did you know that? Did you know he was going be here tonight?"

"No, of course not. It's news to me," she said. But Beth was sure she saw a look pass between Jenna and Levi.

Levi slung an arm around her neck and looked at Jenna, who was still feigning wide-eyed innocence. "Todd's a good kid, Rocky. You could do worse."

Before she could respond, Asha walked up. "Hey! We've been looking for you. You two have to do a song together."

"I don't know, Beth might be too busy hittin' it," Levi said, thrusting his pelvis.

"What?!?" Asha looked from Levi to Beth, who was laughing too hard to speak. The only thing coming out of her mouth was a silent wheeze.

Asha began to laugh, too. "Jenna, how much has she had to drink?"

Jenna shook her head. "More than she can handle, clearly. But not too much to sing!" She handed Beth the glass of water. "Drink this, Madonna," she commanded. "Then let's hit the stage."

14

Jenna helped the unsteady Beth to the stage and Elvis waved them over. "Okay, ladies. What will it be? You want *Like a Virgin* or *Like a Prayer?*"

"I'm crazy for you!" Beth blurted out.

"Thanks sweetie, but I'm married," he said with a wink.

"No!" Beth protested. "I want to do *Crazy For You.*" She enunciated each word slowly, her tongue feeling too big in her mouth.

"Oooh that's a good one," Jenna agreed. The deejay nodded and pressed some buttons. "You got this," Jenna said in Beth's ear as the music began.

Beth nodded solemnly. "I got this," she said, but into the microphone. Some people in the crowd whistled and clapped.

She began to sing. "Wait, literally," she interrupted herself. "The room *is* swaying and the music *is* starting." A few people in the crowd laughed and Beth grinned. Jenna raised an eyebrow at her, so she looked back down at the words on the screen. They were swimming so she closed her eyes and tried to remember the words. When she opened them again she found Todd, a head above most of the other guests. Her eyes locked onto his. The women surrounding him chattered and preened trying to get his attention, but he was watching Beth.

She was starting to get into the song now and she reached out her arm in what she thought was a dramatic gesture but the imbalance caused her to sway. Jenna moved beside her to steady her and joined in the chorus. With his eyes on Beth, Todd put his arm around Katy Perry. She looked up at him adoringly and Beth cringed but continued to sing. Jenna followed Beth's gaze across the crowd to where Todd was standing. In horror she watched as, after a pointed look at Beth, he leaned over and put his tongue into the woman's mouth.

"*I'm crazy …*" Beth stopped mid-lyric. She turned to Jenna whose mouth hung open.

"I'm done," she said, holding her arm out and dropping the mic. It thumped to the floor emitting a screech of feedback. Jenna looked at Elvis and mouthed "sorry," then followed Beth off stage, but not before glaring at Todd.

"Beth, wait!" Jenna ran to catch up with her friend.

"Jenna, I can't. I'm sorry. I've had too much to drink. I'm just done." Her eyes were glassy.

"It's fine. But I have to say goodbye to Asha before we leave. Come with me."

"No, I need some air. I'm just going to head outside. I'll wait for you there."

"Okay, but don't leave without me. I'll be there in just a sec."

Jenna found Asha in the kitchen, said goodbye and headed back down the hall, almost bumping into Todd.

"Hey! Um hey!" he stammered.

"It's Jenna," she said coldly. "My name is Jenna."

"I know," he said.

"Really, because it sounded like you didn't when you were calling me 'Hey um.'"

"Give me a break," he said and rolled his eyes.

Jenna put her hands on her hips and looked him up and down. "Yeah, I think I was wrong and Beth was right."

"Wait, what do you mean?"

"I told Beth to give you a chance. But clearly, I was wrong. She'll be thrilled to know that she's right about something else. Excuse me."

She tried to walk past him but he put his hand up to stop her. "Hey, that's not fair. She's the one that blew me off. What am I supposed to do?"

"Well Sherlock," Jenna said, each word painted in sarcasm and disgust. "If I really liked someone and they objected to me being their student, I don't know… call me crazy but maybe I would just stop being their student!" She brushed past him.

"Yeah, I've thought about that," he said.

"Really?" she called over her shoulder. "Because you didn't look like you were thinking about anything but being a dick when you had your tongue down that girl's throat."

* * *

Her first thought was that she had eaten cotton candy. Her mouth was so dry. *No, not cotton candy. A gym sock is what I must have eaten. A dirty gym sock.* The thought made her stomach roll which triggered a pounding in her head. She wanted to pick her head up, to see where she was, to check the time, to see if her drunk self had left her hungover self the present of a glass of water. Something moved next to her.

Am I in my bed? Who is next to me? She thought back to the party and the tequila and the singing and Todd's tongue in another woman's mouth. *After his lips had just been on mine.* Her stomach rolled again, this time constricting her chest. She tried to open her eyes but her contact lenses were dried out making her eyelids too sticky to move.

"How are you feeling Madonna?" Jenna's voice cut through the fog in her head.

Beth moaned.

"That's what I figured. You had quite a few tequila shots last night."

Beth moaned again, then whispered. "Where are we?"

"At your house."

"You stayed?"

"Yeah, I wasn't sure I should leave you alone."

Beth pulled her eyes slowly apart frowning at her best friend. "We had a sleep over and I missed it?"

"Yes, you did."

"Tequila," Beth groaned and closed her eyes.

15

Beth wasn't surprised when Todd didn't show up to the next class. She had another speech about inappropriate behaviors prepared just in case. Only this time it was edited to concede her own inappropriate behavior. *But it's not like I was hanging out at a student bar getting drunk. It was a private party that I was invited to by my friends.* Either way, the best way to deal with this would be to admit her own fault, something she was loathe to do. So when he didn't turn up, she was relieved.

She half expected him to show up during her office hours, the way he had after she left her shoes in his truck. But no one came. She graded papers until it was time to go and just as she was about to shut down her computer her email pinged with a new message. Beth's hand hovered over the mouse, trying to decide if she should check the email or just go home. Curiosity won out and she pulled up her mailbox to see a message from Gene. The subject line was written in all caps and her heart dropped into her stomach, forming a nasty pit there.

To: Grant, Beth
From: Walker, Gene
CC: Hatton, Marcia
Re: TODD ALLMAN

Beth,

Mr. Allman's assistant contacted the college today to withdraw from your class. Needless to say, the dean and I are extremely disappointed by this development. I thought I made it very clear to you that Mr. Allman's success here was a top priority. I was under the impression that you understood his unique situation and that you were willing to work with him. You were instructed to contact me with any issues yet I heard nothing from you about this student. Dean Hatton and I would like to meet with you to discuss your role in this situation on Friday. I hope that you have ample proof that you tried to accommodate his needs.

Best,

Gene Walker, Ph.D.

Fucking Todd Allman! Beth's heart pounded and her face burned with anger. *Oh, he wanted accommodations all right.* But what could she tell the administration? That he left because she wouldn't hook up with him? Then she would have to explain why there had ever been a reason for him to think he could hook up with her in the first place. The pounding in her chest crept up her neck to her head. *What am I going to do?* She reread the email and dropped her head into her hands, wishing she had just gone home. Several times, she started a response only to erase it.

She was digging through her bag for an aspirin when her cell phone rang. "Hey Jenna," she muttered.

"What's wrong with you? You sound like you're still hungover from the weekend," she laughed, and Beth winced.

"No, I wish it were just that." Beth sighed. "Todd just dropped my class."

"Good!" Jenna said cheerily.

"What? No. Not good, Jenna. I just got a nasty email from Hy-Gene. I have to meet with him and the dean on Friday to explain why he left my class and prove that I tried to accommodate him."

"Oh." Jenna said, then went quiet.

"Oh what?" Beth's fingers tightened around the phone, her pulse quickening.

"Um..."

"Jenna," she said through clenched teeth. "What did you do?"

"Um... I may have told him that he should drop your class."

"What?! Why would you do that?!" Beth's fingers were beginning to cramp from squeezing the phone.

"Well he said he wanted to be with you but you wouldn't because he was your student so..."

"Seriously, Jenna?! What am I going to do now?" She was shouting into the phone. "Should I tell the dean that my best friend thinks I should fuck him so she told him to drop my class?"

"I'm sorry," Jenna said meekly. "I was just trying to help."

"No, you weren't," Beth was about to add *you were just trying to use my life for your own personal fantasy*, when there was a knock at her door. "Shit. I gotta go," she said and hung up the phone.

"Come in," she said, her voice strained in frustration, her head aching, badly wishing she had just gone home.

He slipped wordlessly into her office and closed the door behind him. She glared at him, livid that he had brought so much trouble into her neatly organized life. Todd stood his ground and silently returned her stare. Neither of them spoke. Finally, Beth couldn't restrain herself any longer. "What do you want, Todd?"

"I'm not your student anymore." He walked over to her

until he was close enough that she could smell him, that she could feel the warmth of his energy mixing with hers.

She looked up at him. "I heard."

"So," he said again, leaning into her. "I'm not your student anymore." She watched his eyes close and his full lips part just slightly.

Before he could move any closer she said, "What are you doing? Are you serious? Why are you even here? The last time I saw you, you had your tongue in some girl's mouth. Then you drop my class and get me in trouble with my bosses. And now you're standing in *my* office trying to kiss me with the same filthy mouth that has been god knows where," she hissed at him in a furious whisper.

"What trouble?"

"They're mad that you dropped my class. They think I wasn't a good teacher or that I didn't help you enough. I'm being called before the dean to explain myself."

"Wait. What?" Todd was finally jarred out of his own cockiness.

"And it's not like I can tell them the real reason you're dropping my class," Beth continued, her voice trembling with anger. "*That* could get me fired. So, you need to go now." Suddenly feeling weary down to her bones, she picked up her bag and her keys and herded him to the door with a wave of her hands.

"Wait, I can fix this," he stammered.

"No, I don't think you can." She locked her office door. "Good luck with your movie, Todd," she said and walked down the hall away from him.

* * *

The next day, she sat in her office trying to hash out exactly what she was going to say to the dean. She contemplated coming clean, just explaining the whole thing and facing the consequences. But then she thought of Gene Walker's pompous face and anger bubbled up inside her. She wished like hell that he wasn't going to be at the meeting, but there was really no way around it. The notepad in front of her was covered with more doodles than anything useful. She was putting the finishing touches on a devil-horned likeness of Gene's bobbly head when the phone on her desk rang.

"Beth, Marcia Hatton."

"Oh, hello Dr. Hatton."

"I'm calling to let you know that we received the nicest letter about you from Todd Allman. Apparently, despite what Gene initially thought, he is dropping the class due to schedule conflicts. He's also made a generous donation to the English department for what he calls…" Beth could hear paper being shuffled in the background. "Hold on Beth, let me put my glasses on. Ah, here we go. He says 'I found Ms. Grant to be an exceptional teacher and her willingness to go above and beyond to work with me was invaluable. I know she won't take personal credit for the help so I'd like to make a donation in her name to your department's scholarship fund so other students can benefit from her teaching.' So, there you go. No need to worry with meeting."

"Okay," Beth said slowly, not quite able to believe that she was off the hook.

"I'll be giving Gene a copy of this for your personnel file. But let him know if you want your own copy. Oh, and Beth, I've talked to Gene about jumping to conclusions. You know he can be a little," she paused and Beth's mind filled in the blank with several adjectives before Dean Hatton added, "high strung."

"Okay. Thank you, Dr. Hatton."

"Call me Marcia," she said. "And have a great weekend."

Before Beth could thank her again, the dean had hung up. She stared at the receiver for a minute. When she finally hung it up, she leaned back in her chair and let out a sigh of relief. An image of Todd standing dumbfounded in the hallway came to her. *I guess he did fix it,* she thought. It occurred to her then, that after their last conversation—the way she had talked to him, she would likely never see him again.

16

When she got home, Beth took a long, hot shower, letting the events of the week wash over her and disappear down the drain. There would be no school work tonight. Tonight, she was going veg out. She had just flopped onto the couch when her cell phone rang. It was Jenna. Beth considered not answering it. She was still angry with her for meddling. But she really wanted to tell someone about her conversation with the dean and no one else knew about Todd.

"Hi Meddlesome," she said.

"Have you forgiven me yet? Please say yes! When do you have to meet with the dean?"

Beth told her about being off the hook, about Todd's letter.

"Wow," Jenna said. "That's really good, right? How much was the donation for?"

"I don't know. She didn't say." Homer ran to the front door and began barking.

"What is Homer barking at?"

Beth got up and looked out the window. "Jenna," she said over the noise of the dog. "Someone is here, let me call you back."

Beth looked down at her tank top and pajama bottoms. *Shit!* There was a knock and she opened the door to Todd Allman standing on her front step in dark jeans and a white T-shirt, his wet hair disheveled, his grungy baseball cap absent. He smelled clean and he was holding a bottle of green liquid. Homer bolted before she could grab his collar, circling the visitor excitedly, his tail thwacking Todd's legs.

"Hey, buddy." Todd squatted down to pet him. "What's your name?"

"Homer." Beth folded her arms across her chest, trying to hide the fact that she wasn't wearing a bra.

"Homer?" Todd said, finding the spot on the dog's belly that sent his leg twitching. "Like Simpson?"

"No, like the *Odyssey*," she said, smirking.

He looked up at her. "Oh… really?"

She laughed. "Nah, I'm just messing with you. He's named after Homer Simpson. The dog likes donuts more than I do."

"I think he likes me, too." He grinned up at her, as happy as the dog. She didn't have the heart to tell him that Homer, terrible watch-dog that he was, liked anyone who scratched his belly. Beth opened her mouth to ask him why he was there when he stood up to face her.

"I wanted to call you but I don't have your number. So I came by to tell you that I sent the dean a letter. They shouldn't blame you for me dropping the class."

"I know," she said, smiling despite herself. "She called me this afternoon."

"Oh, good," he said, but looked disappointed.

It occurred to Beth then that her neighbors might see him so impulsively, she invited him in and closed the door behind him. When her cell phone chirped, she was surprised to find it still in her hand. Jenna had texted her.

JENNA: you haven't been murdered have you?

Todd stood, filling her foyer, watching her. She texted back.

BETH: No I'm fine. Call you tomorrow.

When she looked up, she noticed the bottle in his hand.

"Is that," she leaned forward to look more closely, "mouthwash?"

He grinned, the cockiness back, and held up a bottle of Scope. "You were worried about where my mouth has been, so I wanted you to know that it was clean."

She laughed. "And why would I care about the state of your mouth?" He handed her the bottle and before she could protest, he took her face into his hands and kissed her hard. His full lips pressed against hers, his mouth opening, his tongue tentatively exploring. Beth felt herself melting into him. She knew she should protest, should stop him, but she was so tired of pushing him away. Her resolve was a chain of dominos and he had knocked over the first tile. *He's turned me into a romance novel cliché,* she thought as he slid his hands down her body.

Todd pulled back to face her. "Are you okay?" Beth knew couldn't turn him away. She couldn't even speak. So she just kissed him and pressed her body into his. She felt him harden through his jeans. They kissed their way down the hall to her bedroom. At the foot of her bed, she stood on tip-toes and ran her hands through his wet hair. His hands moved up her shirt, caressing her bare breasts. She sighed softly as he untied her pants and slid them down her legs. Then he pushed her back onto the bed and kneeled in front of her.

I shouldn't be doing this, she thought, leaning up on her elbows to look at him. He grinned, grabbed the edge of her panties with his teeth, and slowly pulled them down. Starting at her left knee, Todd's tongue made gentle contact with her skin as he slowly kissed his way up each of her thighs. Every place his lips met her body tingled until her whole body was humming. A little moan escaped her throat as he pushed her legs apart. She looked down at him again and his eyes, nearly black, met hers as he tentatively touched her clit with the tip of his tongue. *Oh my god, I could come right now.* She closed her eyes.

Todd began lazily moving his tongue in circles around her clit. Beth gasped and she could feel him smiling between her legs. When he plunged his tongue inside her, she arched her back against the sensation. His tongue moved slowly back to her clit and she felt him slide a finger into her. He moved it in and out, stroking her deeply while his tongue kept circling her clit. As he slid a second finger inside her, she squeezed her body around him and this time it was Todd who gasped. Her hips moved in rhythm with his fingers and she reached down, grabbing a fistful of his hair. His fingers moved faster, his mouth sucked at her hungrily. The sensation was exquisite and Beth lost herself, one hand in his hair, her other thrown across her face.

"Oh fuck!" she cried out as her body shook with waves of orgasm, her breath ragged. She had never come so fast and so hard and when she finally opened her eyes, she saw Todd watching her. Gone was the boyish smile. The face that was staring back at her was all man. *All man? Allman.* Beth giggled.

"What?" he asked.

"Is your name really Todd Allman?" she asked.

He looked surprised. "Yeah, why?"

"I didn't know if it was a stage name or something."

"You've found me out." He grinned up at her from between her legs. Then with an exaggerated southern twang he said, "My real name is Jedediah Huckleberry."

She laughed and fanned herself. "Oh Mr. Huckleberry, I do believe you've given me the vapors." Then she leaned forward and grabbed his hair with both her fists, drawing him to her. "Can I call you Jed?"

"You can call me anything you want," he said and kissed

her. She pushed him onto his back, then climbed nimbly on top of him. She ran her hands down his soft shirt, her fingertips tracing every firm muscle through the thin fabric. Then she leaned back and pulled her shirt over her head. Before the shirt hit the floor, his hands were touching her, stroking her breasts softly, his erection straining his pants.

Beth grabbed his hands and pinned them over his head then leaned over him, rubbing her breasts across his face. Todd opened his mouth, circling each of her nipples with his warm tongue. They ached deliciously as she bent toward his pinned left hand and ran her lips over the tip of his index finger. When she took it into her mouth and sucked it gently, he closed his eyes and sighed. Her lips left his finger and moved to his ear, kissing it and softly biting his ear lobe.

"I want you inside me," she whispered and moved her hand to his crotch. His eyes flew open and she grinned down at him.

Todd smiled slowly and sat up, shifting her onto his lap. He pulled his shirt over his head and threw it to the floor. A surge of electricity shot through her when the warm skin of his bare chest pressed against her naked breasts. He tilted his face down and moved his lips softly across hers, almost a whisper. Her body ached for him.

Beth reached between them and undid his pants, then pushed him back onto the bed. He raised his hips so she could slide his pants off. When he lay naked beneath her she ran her hands slowly down his broad chest, letting the tips of her fingers be tickled by the trace blond hair, following the trail down, down to what rose between them. She wrapped her hand around him, pleasantly surprised when her fingers didn't touch. Then she stroked him gently until, smiling, he pulled her toward him.

They were nose to nose when she whispered, "Do you have a condom?" His face froze in panic and Beth had to bite her lip not to laugh. He took his hand from her ass and rubbed his temple in frustration, his face a mask of anguish. "Really? You brought mouthwash but no condoms?" She could no longer hold back the laugh. He started to protest but she kissed him quiet, then leaned over to her nightstand and found the box of condoms she had bought when she moved out to LA.

She felt relief radiating from him as he grinned up at her. Without a word, she ripped open the condom and rolled it onto his erection. Then she slowly lowered herself onto him. She could feel her body pulsing as it accepted each exquisite inch. For a moment neither of them moved, savoring the sensation. He stared up at her in awe and she smiled down at him. Then slowly she began to rock her hips back and forth, contracting her muscles each time she pulled away, releasing them as she sank back on to him. Todd's breath quickened and she closed her eyes, her hands pressing into his chest. Before she could really lose herself to the rhythm of their movement, he grabbed her hips hard. She looked down in time to see him gasp and shudder, squeezing his eyes shut. When he covered his face with one hand, she knew.

Gently, she moved his hand from his face and before he could say anything, she kissed him, her tongue pushing into his mouth. With a little guidance, his hands found her breasts again and he palmed each of them gently. She moved to his neck kissing him and biting him gently. By the time she kissed her way down his chest, reaching down to remove the soiled condom, she found that he was already getting hard again.

Beth leaned over to the nightstand again and grabbed another condom. Then slowly and methodically she began to move atop him again.

"You're so sexy," Todd whispered, his dark eyes drinking in her face. He pulled her toward him until they were kissing. Then he deftly flipped her onto her back without breaking their connection. She wrapped her legs around his waist as he moved inside her.

Beth kissed his chest and his shoulder, gently biting him anywhere she could. She ran her hands down the back of his neck, across his sculpted back and to his firm ass, pulling him further into her. Each stroke seemed to fill her more and push her closer and closer to ecstasy.

"Oh," she gasped into his ear and ground her hips into him. Every nerve in her body was singing. As her body began to tremble, she dug her nails into his back and cried out. Before she even came back to herself, Todd had dropped his face to her hair and moaned, Beth's body still quivering around him.

* * *

Beth awoke to the sound of Homer whining outside her bedroom door. She had shut him out during the previous night's festivities and forgotten to let him back in.

Poor baby! she thought. Carefully, so as not to wake him, she untangled her legs from between Todd's. She grabbed his shirt off the floor and threw it over her head. At the bedroom door, Beth paused and looked back at the man dwarfing her queen-sized bed. They had found each other again in the middle of the night, coming together more slowly this time, like a dream. Then he had wrapped his arms around her, her back to his chest. Like a Lego piece, she fit perfectly. She had fallen back to sleep happily with his breath on her neck. Now, she couldn't quite believe what had happened. Nor could she believe that he had stayed the night. A giddy smile spread across her face. *Definitely not my student anymore.*

Beth fed Homer, then checked the clock over her stove. If she left in the next 15 minutes, she could make the morning yoga class. If she waited, she'd have to hit one of the afternoon classes, both of which were taught by Jenna. And Jenna would know immediately that something had happened. Beth could never hide anything from her. As much as she loved Jenna, and as much as she wanted to shout about her night from rooftops, guilt was creeping in with the sunlight. She needed to keep this to herself for at least a few more hours.

Plus, she reasoned, *Todd will probably want to sneak out anyway. I'm sure he does this kind of thing all the time. If I stay and we have to talk it will probably be awkward, right?* Beth had no clue. She had never had a one night stand before.

She plucked yoga pants, a sports bra, and a tank top from her dryer so she didn't even have to go back into the bedroom. Now she could slip out without disturbing him and give him an easy getaway. If that's what he wanted. *Do I want him to do that?* Beth felt a pang at the thought of him leaving but panic at the thought of him staying. Yoga was definitely the answer.

After brushing her teeth and running a brush through her hair, she unlocked Homer's doggie door and a patted his head. *I guess I should tell him why I'm not here. That's only polite, right? What IS the protocol for these things?* She scribbled a quick note stopping at the T in Todd before giggling to herself and changing it to a J.

Jed-

Decided to hit an early yoga class. Help yourself to whatever. Just lock the door when you leave, please.

-B

She bit down on the cap of the pen, then added:

PS- last night was fun

Climbing into her truck Beth mulled over the note, hoping it came across as casual without being insulting. If it had been any other man in her bed, she would have texted Jenna and asked her what to do. But Todd Allman was definitely not any other man.

* * *

Despite the scenes from the night before that flashed through her mind during savasana, Beth felt completely relaxed after class. Of course all of the contorting of her body had contributed to that, but surely the orgasms deserved some credit. That, and the fact that she had managed to dodge questioning by Jenna, made her downright cheery. The weather was beautiful, her windows were down, and she was singing along with Tom Petty when she made the sharp turn onto her quiet little street and almost ran into her neighbor's mailbox. Todd's truck was still in front of her house.

How late do 24 year olds sleep, anyway? She sat in her driveway for a few minutes trying to decide what to do. Pulling the rearview mirror down, she examined her reflection. Despite the ringlets that frizzed out from her temples, she didn't look too bad. She grabbed lip gloss from her purse, swiped it on and headed inside.

Both Homer and the smell of bacon greeted her when she opened the front door. He whined and danced around her, wagging his tail happily.

"Hello?" she called tentatively.

"In the kitchen!"

Her stomach rumbled as she walked into the kitchen, the banana she'd grabbed on her way out the door was long gone. Todd was standing at the stove in his jeans and her "Cupcake Princess" apron that hardly covered his bare chest.

"I hope you're hungry. I thought you might be after yoga." He grinned at her. "And last night."

She laughed. "Nice apron. And yes, I'm starving."

"Yeah, I couldn't find my shirt and the bacon grease kept splattering me." He looked down at his chest. "Why is this apron so small anyway?"

Beth took a piece of bacon off the plate. "My mom ordered it for me online. She didn't realize it was a kid's apron."

"The 'Cupcake Princess' didn't give it away?"

Beth shrugged. "She knows I like cupcakes."

"And you're a princess?"

"More like a queen." She grinned and popped the bacon into her mouth. Todd smiled, leaned over, and kissed her on the forehead. If she hadn't been chewing, her mouth would have hung open in surprise at the ease of the whole exchange. It seemed so natural that he was there in her kitchen, making breakfast.

"You're making pancakes, too? But I didn't have any pancake mix. Did you go to the store?"

He laughed at her and expertly flipped the last pancake. "You don't need a mix to make pancakes. It's just flour and a few other things. You had all the ingredients."

"I did?"

They sat across from each other at her little, yellow kitchen table.

"Thanks for making breakfast," Beth said, feeling suddenly shy.

He smiled at her. "Thanks for letting me eat all your food. I was actually afraid you were a vegetarian with the whole yoga thing."

"Yeah, I think it about it all the time." She sighed. "But, bacon." He laughed as she bit into another crispy piece and grinned at him over the table. "So where did you learn to cook?"

"From my dad. He did most of the cooking."

When they were done, Todd went into the living room to return a call from Danny. Beth got up and cleared the plates. But before putting them in the sink, she absentmindedly wiped her index finger through the maple syrup on her plate and put it in her mouth, a habit of hers from childhood.

"That looks good," Todd said from behind her and she jumped. Then smiling flirtatiously, she put her finger back in the syrup and brought it to his lips. He sucked it off slowly and something deep inside her clenched in pleasure. She dipped her finger into the syrup again, this time swiping it across his lips. Before he could protest, she pulled him to her and put her lips on his, savoring the sweetness of the syrup and the fullness of his lips. When they parted, Todd ran his own finger through the syrup and held it up. She licked his finger slowly, sucking the last of it from the tip. He groaned.

Grabbing her by the waist, he hoisted her onto the kitchen counter, covering her lips with his. She wrapped her legs around him, pulling him closer while he ran his hand up her back, up her neck and into her hair grabbing her ponytail and pulling it tightly. She gasped. With his other hand, he pulled up her tank top and palmed her breasts over her sports bra.

"Take this off," he whispered and in one swift motion, she pulled off her tank top and her sports bra. This time he ran two fingers through the syrup and traced it over her nipples, which were already firm. Todd bent down and ran his tongue over each of her breasts, lapping up the syrup. He grabbed at the waistband of her yoga pants.

"Wait," she said panting, pushing him back. "Let's take a shower first."

He grinned down at her and shook his head slowly. "No time," he said and pressed his mouth to hers as he continued to tug at her pants.

Beth pulled away and whispered into his ear. He stopped, spun around and ran to her bedroom. She hopped off the counter to shimmy out of her pants. Before the pants hit the floor, he was back.

"Hold on a second," he said, smiling slowly. Then he spun

her around so her bare ass faced him. *Whoa!* She thought he was going to take her from behind but he just ran a hand over her left butt cheek. "An angel?" She looked over her shoulder at him. He was smiling, examining her tattoo. "Finally."

She laughed. "Yeah. Jenna and I got them on spring break our freshman year. I thought it was funny to have an angel watching over my ass. Corny, I know."

Todd shook his head. "No, I like it." Then he playfully nipped her flesh with his teeth. She started to protest but he spun her back around and lifted her onto the counter. With one hand, Beth pulled him to her by the waistband of his jeans. The other hand worked the button and zipper. When she got the pants to his hips, she hooked her toes into his belt loops and pushed them the rest of the way down with her feet.

She took the condom from him. "Let me." And as soon as their maple syrup-covered lips found each other again, he was inside her.

17

She was in the bathroom of a little bagel shop when Todd texted her the next day. Unfortunately, her phone was on the table with Jenna. Beth knew as soon as she saw Jenna's face that she was busted.

"Well," Jenna said, dramatically indignant. "Todd wants to know if you want to come over to watch the Dolphins' game."

Beth tried to look nonchalant but she could not hold back the grin that spread from ear to ear. Jenna squealed. "Tell me!"

So she started with mouthwash and ended with the syrup.

"Oh my god, I knew it!" Jenna was practically dancing in her seat from excitement. "You have to go over there."

Beth sipped her coffee. "I don't know Jenna. I mean, I sort of thought it was a one-time thing."

"Why the hell would you want *that* to only happen once?"

She giggled, thinking about running her hands down Todd's sculpted chest. She stopped giggling when she thought about Todd's dark eyes looking up at her from between her legs. "I mean, I don't. But this is crazy, right? He's way too young for me and he used to be my student and, and…" She looked around then lowered her voice to a whisper. "And he's fucking Todd Allman."

Jenna squealed. "And you're *fucking* Todd Allman. All the

more reason you have to go. It's not like you have to marry him, Beth. But why not ride it out?" She raised her eyebrow and rocked suggestively in her chair.

Beth's hand flew to her mouth to stifle her laughter. "All right. Maybe I'll go. Just for a little bit."

* * *

Now that Beth was winding up the hill toward Todd's house, she was having second thoughts. Her heart fluttered anxiously in her chest and she almost missed the entrance that was hidden from the road by lush green foliage. She drove slowly up the winding driveway until she got to a large wooden gate. A keypad stuck out of the plants. She leaned out of her truck and pressed the intercom button.

"Come on in," someone shouted out of the little box. *Was that Todd?* It didn't sound like his voice but it was hard to tell. Plants were nearly overtaking the property, making it impossible to see from the road and giving it a remote yet cozy feel. The house was not at all what she expected, not sleek and modern like Levi and Asha's. It had the gray wood of a Cape Cod bungalow but with wide sweeping windows. Several cars were backed in against a low brick wall, with steps leading up to the front door. She wondered if all the cars were Todd's.

When she got out of the truck, Beth heard shouts and laughter coming from the back of the house. Briefly, she considered turning around and going home. *What am I doing here?* Then she remembered the camera at the gate. Someone knew she was there which would make it really awkward to leave. She hesitated at the foot of the steps. *Oh, what the hell? I can do a party.*

Marching decisively up the brick walk, she knocked on the big wooden door. Nothing happened. She peered through the glass panels on either side of the doors, but all she could see was a hallway. *Someone knows I'm here. Why aren't they answering the door?* She wondered if she was supposed to go around to the back of the house but had no idea how to get there. After another minute of waiting, she tried the door and it opened, so she let herself in.

The hallway opened up to a large living room that was empty. At the far end, two sets of French doors stood wide open overlooking a deck. She crossed the room and walked toward the sounds. There she found a bunch people, none of whom were Todd. No one noticed her. Not sure what to do next, Beth turned around and nearly bumped into a tray full of hamburgers and hot dogs.

"Oh! I'm so sorry!" she said, helping his steady the tray of meat. It was Todd's manager. Her mother would have described him as tall, dark, and handsome. He was in his late 30s, thin, yet muscular, with tousled waves of dark brown hair.

"You're Beth, right?"

"Uh, yes, right. We met at Pancho's, right? I'm sorry I have totally forgotten your name."

"Danny," he said with an easy smile then gestured over his shoulder. "Todd's playing Madden in the den." Beth nodded like she knew what he was talking about and walked in the direction he indicated.

She poked her head through the doorway of the den and saw Todd and another guy sitting on a huge, brown leather sofa. They were both staring intently at an equally large television. And though there was plenty of room to sit on the couch, a slender blond woman perched on the armrest nearest Todd. She had the exaggerated features of a fashion model, big doe eyes and even bigger lips that looked amazing in magazines but somewhat alien in person. Her purple bikini was completely visible under a white crocheted dress that fell just below her crotch. Her long tanned legs ended in impractically high espadrille sandals. She was the first one to spot Beth and when she did, she casually draped a hand on Todd's shoulder. He ignored her but also didn't notice Beth.

She stood uncomfortably in the doorway with her arms crossed pretending to be interested in the video game. Animated football players moved around the screen as Todd and the other guy intensely punched buttons. When the play was over, the guy started laughing triumphantly and Todd groaned. Beth was wondering if she should say something before the next play started when he glanced over at her.

"Hey Beth," he said, with a grin that she hadn't seen before. *Shyness?* She wondered if she should give him a hug. But he didn't get up and she wasn't sure the blond would let her by.

"The game's on out by the pool. There are drinks in here," he pointed to a small fridge next to the doorway, "and in the kitchen. Help yourself to anything."

Beth nodded. "Okay, thanks," she said.

"Second half," the guy shouted and with that, Todd's entire focus was back on the video game.

Back in the living room, she again contemplated going home. When he had texted her, she had visions of the two of them snuggled up together on a couch, watching the game and then maybe… *What am I doing here? Why did he even invite me and who the hell is that?* Her phone buzzed in her back pocket.

JENNA: How's it going? What's his house like? Don't text me back if you're making out! Squeeeeeeee

BETH: Not making out. Would probably disturb glamazon sitting in his lap. It's an f-ing party.

JENNA: What??

BETH: Whatever. I figured he dated other people. Just didn't think he would expect me to hang out with them. Leaving now

JENNA: Sorry :(

BETH: Don't be. It's fine. I'll call you later.

Beth tucked her phone back into her pocket and headed toward the front door, planning to slip out unnoticed.

"Hey Beth!" Danny called from the patio. She flinched, then turned around. He had a spatula in his hand and was waving her over. She rearranged her face into a smile and walked outside to where he was standing over the grill. The burgers smelled amazing and her stomach growled. *Hmmm, might as well eat before I go.*

Sitting on lounge chairs by the pool were two clones of the young woman inside, except that one had brown hair. A shirtless guy was splashing around the pool with yet another blond, while three other guys were setting up a game of beer pong.

"Everyone!" Danny said over reggae music pumping out of invisible speakers. "This is Beth."

"Hi Beth!" two of the beer pong guys said in unison. The people in the pool waved and the women on the lawn chairs remained so still that Beth wondered if they were real or just some type of weird Hollywood lawn ornament. She waved feebly at the people who had acknowledged her and when she turned back to Danny, he was shoving a plate with a burger on it into her hands.

"Thanks," she mumbled.

"Drinks are in the fridge," he said pointing with the spatula. So she helped herself to a beer and parked at a table in front of the Dolphin's game. They were losing, of course.

"What am I doing here?" Beth thought.

"You're eating a burger," a voice said from behind her. Before she could turn around, Danny sat down next to her with a plate of his own.

"Did I just say that out loud?" She cringed. "Sorry. I hate it when I do that."

Danny laughed. "No worries. I often think the same thing when I'm at Todd's house." He lifted his burger to his mouth then looked at her. "Um, you have a little..." He gestured to her cheek and she raised a hand to her face, her fingers coming back with mustard.

"Thanks," she said, wiping her face with a napkin. "By the way, this is delicious. Is that one of your jobs as manager, to make awesome burgers?"

"Thanks but I can't take the credit. Todd made them, I just threw them on the grill."

Beth was taking a sip of beer when she felt hands on her shoulders. Her heart skipped. *Todd!* But when she looked up, it was one of the beer pong guys.

"Hey, we need a fourth for beer pong. Either of you want to play?" She looked over to where they had set up a floating table in the pool.

"Not me." Danny shook his head. "I have work to do this afternoon."

"I don't have a bathing suit," Beth said. She was glad he hadn't told her to bring a suit. Even though she was rarely self-conscious anymore, she couldn't help but feel shy around these statuesque women 10 years her junior. *What am I doing here?* she thought again.

"I'm sure Todd has some extras lying around you could wear. Chicks are always leaving them here," Danny said, shoving more burger into his mouth. *Bathing suits lying around? People always leaving them? Like the groupies that he has sex with every night? Ugh, I can't believe I was one of those!* Then she remembered his mouth on her and she could completely believe it. Her face grew hot.

"So, you're in?" The beer pong guy was still waiting for an answer.

"Sorry, no." He left disappointed and Beth turned to Danny "Hey," she said quietly, leaning in to him. He looked away from the television, giving her his full attention. "Um, I just want you to know, that I um, don't usually do this," she whispered.

He looked confused. "You don't usually eat burgers?"

She shook her head. "I don't usually, you know… hang out with my students."

"Oh, Todd? Well, he's not really your student is he."

"No, I guess not. And he did drop my class, so…"

"He dropped your class?" Danny looked surprised.

Beth nodded. "Yeah, why?"

"Nothing, he just didn't tell me that." He let out a frustrated sigh.

"Is that a bad thing?"

"I guess we'll see," Danny said cryptically.

She started to ask him what he was talking about but he took another big bite of his burger and stared out toward the pool, deliberately avoiding eye contact. So she decided against it and returned her focus to the game.

"Well, this game isn't getting any better. I'm going to head out."

Danny looked surprised. "Already?"

"Yeah, I have a lot of school work to do. It was nice to see you again."

"You too. And tell that cute little yoga friend of yours that I'm gonna be calling her for a lesson."

"Will do." She gave him a quick hug and briefly thought about popping her head into the den to say goodbye to Todd, but decided against it.

Later that night she was sitting in bed reading when her phone buzzed.

TODD: Where'd you go

Beth glared at the screen.

BETH: Home

TODD: Why

"Seriously?" she said to no one. "Um, because you totally ignored me." *And because of purple bikini...* She was irritated, not only because he was just now concerned with her whereabouts, but also because hearing from him had made her heart start to flutter. She began typing "Because you clearly didn't want me there..." and then erased it and started again. "Because a video game is more interesting than I am..." And then erased that, too.

BETH: Thanks for the burger. Have a nice night.

She had almost texted "life" instead of "night."

TODD: Come back over

TODD: And get in my bed

Beth rolled her eyes. *He must be drunk.*

TODD: You know you want me

She considered texting him back and telling him to go to bed. But instead, she just put her phone on silent. The next morning she had two more messages from him.

TODD: I'm a naughty student, come punish me

TODD: I wish you were here

What's wrong Todd? Did purple bikini abandon you?

After class, there was another text.

TODD: Sorry about last night. That was bad form.

Which part? Inviting me over and ignoring me or drunk texting me after I left? She was tempted to text him that very thought, but decided against it. Instead, she deleted his messages and mentally deleted him. It had been fun and she didn't regret it. But she certainly wasn't going to compete for his attention. *I'm too old to play games and you're obviously too young to know better.*

18

She almost ignored his call the next day, but she was curious about what he would say.

"Hi," she said and waited.

"I, um," he paused, and she thought she could actually hear him swallow. "I just wanted to um, apologize."

When she didn't say anything, he added, "For yesterday?"

Beth's heart was beating hard now. *Ugh, I thought I was done with him, with feeling like this.* "Are you sure? You sound confused."

He sighed and she shivered at a flashback of his breath on her neck. *Be strong, Beth!*

"I'm sure. I'm really sorry about the party and the dumb texts I sent."

"Well, thanks, but you don't owe me anything," she said coolly.

"Yes I do. All I wanted to do was to spend time with you but when you got there, I don't know. I just didn't know how to act, so I acted like an idiot."

"You acted like a child, Todd. Because you practically are a child," she blurted out before she could stop herself.

"Maybe I did act like a child, but I'm trying to be a man and apologize." She was surprised by how frustrated he sounded.

"Listen, I wanted you to be there yesterday. It was just supposed to be a couple of us but then Tara showed up with her friends and I should have told them to go but... Well, I didn't. And that wasn't fair to you. But I really want to make it up to you."

Tara... is that purple bikini? Who is she? "Listen, I appreciate the call but really, it's fine."

"Okay," he hesitated. "So will you let me make it up to you?"

"That's not necessary. It is what is. I think we're just in two different places."

Todd was silent for a long moment and Beth thought the call had been dropped. "Hello?" she said.

"Do you really not want to see me again?" he blurted. The disappointment in his voice melted her heart.

"I don't know. I mean, the other night was great but..." she trailed off, not knowing how to finish. She did want to see him again but she couldn't see any future in it.

"So will you please let me make it up to you? Come back over. I'll make you dinner."

"I don't know. I don't think that's a good idea." Beth was shaking her head, even as her stomach rumbled at the memory of the burger.

"Please give me another chance. This time no singing, no football, no other people. I'm not your student, you're not my teacher. Just you and me and some good food. Like a normal date. What do you say?"

Nothing about this is normal. Nothing about you is normal. Her heart was skipping all over the place. The idea of an entire night alone with Todd was so very appealing. *I wish I could talk to Jenna. Why? You know Jenna would tell you to go for it.*

"I'll even make dessert. And if you don't want to see me again after that, I promise, I won't bother you anymore."

She bit her lip. "Something chocolate?"

* * *

Beth took her time getting dressed. More time than she had taken to dress for anything in a very long time. She tried not to think about what that meant. "What do you think, Homer?" she asked, staring at herself in the mirror. She fed him, unlatched the doggie door, and then stared at the dog, trying to work out what she was forgetting. He put his chin on his paws and looked sad until she gave him a treat.

It wasn't until she was half way to Todd's that she remembered what she had forgotten to put in her purse. Beth checked the time on her phone and pulled into the parking lot of a drugstore. She headed to the back and looked at the display of condoms.

A three-pack? No, definitely a twelve pack. Wait, the 24 pack is only $2 more than the smaller box. Holy crap, the 36 pack is only $4 more than the 12 pack!

She thought about the first night they were together. She thought about Todd with his shirt off. She grabbed the big box and threw it in the basket. *Thank God I remembered these. Do I need anything else?* She stood thinking at the end of the aisle. *A toothbrush! Just in case.* She grabbed the first toothbrush she could find, then headed up to the register.

"Beth!" A nasally voice came from behind her. She turned to see Gene Walker's wife coming down the aisle from the pharmacy toward her. *Shit!* She glanced into her basket where a 36-pack of condoms in its neon-packaged glory dwarfed a SpongeBob SquarePants toothbrush. Frantically, she grabbed the first thing she could off the end cap, dumping five boxes of Band-Aids on top of her other purchases.

"Hey there," Jean drawled, dripping with what she no

doubt considered southern charm.

Beth forced a smile over her gritted teeth. "Hello, Jean. How are you?"

It wasn't the southern part of Jean Walker that annoyed her so much. It was her inherently antiquated and sexist viewpoint. The first time she had met Jean, they were at the English department's annual back-to-school picnic. Mistaking Beth for someone's wife, Jean had leaned over to her and said, "Gosh, don't you just wish we could be smart like all these brilliant professors."

Beth had had to bite her lip so hard to not say something condescending, coming out instead with, "Actually, I'm a professor here, too."

But Jean must not have been listening because when her husband walked up, she had said to him, "This little lady and I were just saying how we wish we could be as smart as you all." Gene had beamed at his wife and puffed out his chest.

Beth suppressed the urge to shout, "I said no such thing!" But being new to the department, she felt like she had to keep up polite conversation with the department head's wife. So for the rest of the afternoon, she was treated to stories about the couple's pet ferrets and commentary on the calorie count of each food item. Since that day, she avoided Jean as much as possible, going so far as to map escape routes at each college function. Unfortunately, there didn't seem to be any escaping her here in the drugstore.

"Well, bless your heart Beth, I haven't seen you in so long!" She leaned over and hugged Beth awkwardly, leaving behind a cloud of pungent, grand-motherly perfume. "How are your classes going?"

"Fine, fine. Thanks for asking."

Jean leaned in and whispered conspiratorially, "Big Gene tells me that you have a movie star in your class!"

"Um, oh. I did, but he dropped."

"He did?" Her thin, drawn-on eyebrows raised in surprise. "Did he not… you know… were you not… Maybe they should have put him in Gene's class. Some people just learn better from a stronger teacher, someone who's more of an authority figure."

Beth felt her eye begin to twitch as she fought all of her instincts and bit back every retort that came to mind. "Actually, he really loved my class. He just had a lot of scheduling conflicts with his new movie." *And I'm about to go give him some private tutoring right now!*

"Oh," Jean said, confused.

"Well, it was really nice to see you, Jean. But I've got to go." Inadvertently, Beth glanced down at her basket, realizing that a quarter of the condom box was still showing under the boxes of Band-Aids. Jean followed her gaze into the basket.

"Oooh, are Band-Aids on sale?"

"Um," Beth glanced at the end cap. "I don't know. I, um, just cut myself a lot."

Jean laughed. "Oh honey, we've got to get you a husband to do the chopping up. Big Gene is so good with a knife. You know, we ladies just don't have the hand eye coordination they do."

Beth's eye twitch was about to turn into a full on spasm. "Well Jean, I really have to get going. I'm meeting a friend and I'm already running late." She turned away from the woman and took a step toward the register.

"Okay, dear. Well, if Gene or I meet some nice single boys, we'll give you a call. His nephew will be in town next month, maybe the four of us could go out."

Beth knew that it was no longer possible to respond politely so she just waved and walked away, hoping that Jean had more shopping to do and wouldn't end up behind her in line.

In the car, she shoved the shopping bag in her purse. One glance at her phone told her that she was going to be late, but she stopped for wine anyway and briefly considered opening the bottle in the car just to calm her nerves.

19

This time when she pressed the intercom, it was definitely Todd who responded. And when she walked up the path to his house, he opened the door before she could even knock.

"I'm sorry I'm late. I, um, ran into someone at the store." She handed him the bottle of wine and he kissed her on the cheek. The encounter was a little too scripted and Beth felt a pang of disappointment, missing the ease of their pancake breakfast.

"No problem. Dinner's just about ready. Come on in." He led her back to the kitchen, a large room under an exposed beam ceiling. Copper and stainless steel pots and pans hung expertly over a long wooden island in the center of the room. She loved it immediately.

"Sit here while I finish up." He gestured to two worn leather chairs in the corner on either side of a lit fireplace. "Can I get you some wine? I was going to make margaritas but I didn't realize those assholes finished my tequila the other day."

"Uh, that's all right. I think I'm, um, off tequila for a little while."

"Me, too." He winked at her and handed her a glass of wine. Beth tried not to blush.

Eager to change the subject she said, "What are you making? It smells amazing."

"It's palomilla, my grandmother's recipe. But I know you like Mexican food so I figured we could just eat it in tacos."

"That sounds good. Can I do anything to help?"

"Nope, I just need to cut up the steak and throw the tortillas on the grill to warm."

She sipped her wine and drank in the cozy room. Her eyes settled on Todd and the way he moved around the kitchen. The Viking range in the corner was clearly not just for show.

"If you want to head to the dining room, I'll bring the food."

"Why don't we just eat in here?" she gestured to two stools at the end of the wooden island. As she watched him lay out the food, Beth's stomach rumbled.

"Wow, Todd, this is really, really good," she said after her first mouthful.

"You sound surprised." He raised one eyebrow, the one with the scar, and grinned at her.

"Hey, where did you get that scar?"

He pointed to his eyebrow and she nodded. "Oh, that was courtesy of my sister. She was chasing me around the pool when I was little and I fell onto the corner of the diving board. Well, she says I tripped but I think she pushed me."

"Ouch."

"Actually, I don't remember the accident at all but I remember my parents having a big fight after we got home from the hospital. Apparently, my mom had been bugging my dad to take out the diving board for years. And she thought I was going to be scared of the pool because of the accident."

"Were you?"

"Nope. I actually didn't want them to take it out so while they were still arguing I went out there to stand guard. And I guess I got tired because they found me asleep on the diving board."

"So no problem with pools, then?"

He shook his head. "None at all. I spent most of my childhood in one."

"Me too. I think that's why I can never stay out of the water. I wish I had a pool."

"Do you want to go for a swim?"

"Right now?"

"Sure."

"It's a little cool, don't you think?" Though she wasn't feeling cool at all. With the fire and the wine, she was actually feeling quite warm.

"Nah, the pool's heated."

Beth wasn't sure why but she suddenly felt shy. "I don't have a suit." Then she winced and looked down into her wine glass, waiting for him to echo what Danny had said about 'chicks' leaving bathing suits there *'all the time.'* Or worse, to lecherously say that she didn't need one. So she quickly added, "Maybe some other time."

"Are you sure? You can wear my rash guard, if you want."

* * *

The pool was an oval with a rock waterfall at the edge of the deep end. The vegetation growing up around the far side made it seem more hidden and tropical than any place she had ever been in the city. Todd put on music as she eased into the pool. The warm water was like silk against her skin but the cool night air was giving her goosebumps. His rash guard was big and it covered her, but it was thinner than a bathing suit and clung to every curve, accenting each of her firm nipples. *Well, it's not like he hasn't seen them before.*

Beth watched him walk across the deck. His torso was tanned and muscular and his black board shorts hung low on his hips. She snuck a look at his feet and sighed in relief. *He even has nice feet.*

Their rapport was comfortable, but the nearness of him, bare chest and soft smile, was causing her heart to beat erratically. She felt so timid, as if the party on Sunday had erased the happy ease of their first time together. He seemed to sense it too, sitting back on one of the steps with his wine instead of moving toward her.

Beth put her glass down on the edge of the pool. Then she slipped under and swam to the deep end, enjoying the weightless feeling of her body in the water. When she popped back up, he was still sitting on the steps.

"It's really nice and peaceful back here."

"Yeah, that's why I bought this place. I couldn't believe it could be this quiet so close to the city. But I guess I'm an old soul. That's what my family always says, anyway."

"Oh yeah? Why do they say that?"

"Ah, I don't know. I guess because I was kind of a shy kid. And I always loved my dad's old records."

"Records? Really?"

"Yeah, he had a huge record collection when I was little. But then..." He laughed to himself. "Then we got Duke."

"Who's Duke?" She was slowly treading water, watching him from across the pool.

"Our dog. When he was a puppy he got into my dad's records and pulled them all out of the sleeves. We came home and found Duke pouncing on the records and sliding across the floor on them. He had the entire Beatles collection and a bunch of other old stuff and it was just ruined. All scratched up."

"Oh no! That's terrible! Your dad must have been so upset."

"He was! I thought he was going to cry. Especially since my mom was the one who had gotten him most of them."

"Yeah, is she a big music fan?"

"Was," he said, not meeting her eyes. "She died right after He-Man came out."

Beth's heart ached at the pain in his voice. She swam back over to him. "How did she die?"

"Breast cancer. She fought it off the first time, when I was eight. But it came back."

"That fucking sucks," Beth said, studying his face as he looked past her across the pool.

Todd laughed. "Yeah. You're right. It really fucking sucks."

"Would you like to tell me about her?"

He finally met her eyes. "Yes. But not right now." He stood up as Otis Redding began to play.

"Oh I love this song," Beth said.

"Me too." He was watching her as he walked down the steps into the pool. A shiver spread all over her body. She glanced down into the water and saw the rash guard had ridden up and her thong was showing. But when she back up at him, he wasn't looking at her underwear, but at her face. Otis was singing about how it was too late to stop now. Her heart was beating so loudly as he came closer that she thought he must be able to hear it. He sank down into the water in front of her so they were the same height. Beth took his face into her hands and looked into his eyes.

"I'm sorry about your mom," she whispered.

"I'm sorry about your person," Todd said.

And then they were kissing. His arms wrapped around her and she could feel the muscles of his chest through the tantalizingly thin fabric of the shirt. He tugged the shirt off of her and took each of her breasts in his mouth, his tongue circling her tender nipples. She ran her hands through his hair and pulled his head back so her mouth could again find his. Before Otis finished his song, they were lost in each other.

They kissed for a long time, until she was dizzy with desire.

When she found herself desperate for more, she grabbed his hand and led it to the front of her panties. Needing no more encouragement, he pulled them aside and slipped a finger inside her. She gasped and he kissed her neck while sliding his finger gently in and out, his thumb finding the bundle of nerves that sent shockwaves through her. Then he took his hand away and hoisted her up onto the deck of the pool. The cool night air was a shock and her bare nipples ached with a delicious tightness.

Todd grabbed either side of her thong and pulled it off, then wrapped her legs over his shoulders. When his mouth touched her, she leaned back and looked at the night sky. He swirled and flicked and plunged his tongue into her and she trembled and shivered and moaned softly.

"Are you okay?" he whispered.

"Yeah," She looked down at him.

"Are you sure? You're shaking."

Beth sat up and looked at her body, covered in goosebumps. Her teeth chattered involuntarily. "I guess it is a little chilly."

He pulled her back into the warm water, wrapping his arms snuggly around her. "Let's go inside," he whispered into her ear. "Wait here, I'll get towels."

Her eyes followed him out of the pool, admiring the way the muscles of his broad back came together in deep grooves that sank into his board shorts. When she caught a glimpse of his erection straining his shorts, she stifled a giggle.

"It's freezing out here! I'm sorry," Todd said, jogging back to the pool. She stepped quickly out of the pool and he wrapped her in the towel. Before she could protest, he scooped her up and carried her across the patio.

Inside his bedroom, they fell onto the bed giggling and shivering and kissing. He pressed his wet shorts against her and her bare body responded immediately. But despite the warmth of his mouth and his body on hers, her teeth were still chattering. He looked down at her. "Do you want to get in the shower?"

Beth followed him into an expansive bathroom covered in gray tile and dark wood. He stepped through a big glass door into the steam shower and turned the water on. She huddled in her towel, shifting from foot to foot, while he pressed some buttons on a panel. The bathroom lights dimmed and the music that had been playing outside streamed softly through the room. In the shower, tiny white lights set between the gray tiles sparkled like stars.

"Wow," she said, forgetting her chill for a moment to take in the constellations peppering the shower walls.

"Pretty cool, huh?"

"Yeah, I've never seen anything like it."

"Don't tell anyone, but that's the real reason I bought this house."

She giggled at the thought of He-Man being captivated by little, twinkling lights. Todd held out his hand to her and she dropped the towel and joined him under the water. He slid his arms around her bare body and she rested her head on his chest until she felt warmed through.

"This is really nice," she murmured, not sure if she was talking about the warmth, the twinkling shower lights, or being in his arms. He kissed the top of her head and she pulled away to look up at him.

"Hey, why do you still have these on?" She tugged on the ties of his board shorts, then unfastened the Velcro and let them fall to the floor. He took her face into his hands and kissed her while she let her hands explore his lower back, his firm ass. When she began to gently stroke his erection, he sighed deeply and leaned back against the shower wall. She stood on her toes and kissed his neck, then his chest, making her way down to his stomach. Crouched down and about to take him into her mouth, he grabbed her shoulder.

"Wait," he said. "I'm not finished with *you* yet. Come here." He helped her up onto a wide ledge built into the back of the shower. Standing naked before him, his face was level with her navel. He bent slightly, slid his hands under her ass, and buried his face in her. She leaned against the side of the shower wall and threw one leg over his shoulder. Without anywhere else to hold on, she weaved a hand into his hair.

"Oh my god," she breathed, creeping toward orgasm. He pulled back. "Don't stop!" she cried. Todd grinned mischievously. He touched her gently with his tongue then pulled back, watching her for a reaction. Beth held her breath. He moved back toward her and began stroking her with his tongue. She sighed deeply and he pulled back again. She glared down at him and he laughed, then slid one finger into her and put his tongue back on her clit. She moaned, but he stopped again. Frustration got the better of her and she tried to put her leg down, but he was too fast for her. He grabbed it and wrapped it around his waist, then pulled her forward until she wrapped the other leg around him. He turned and pressed her into the shower wall, his mouth finding hers. She felt his erection near her own swollen crotch and shifted so they were touching. Deliberately, she rocked her hips back and forth, savoring the feel of him, so smooth and hard, so nearly inside her. Beth didn't think she had ever wanted anything more than she wanted him at that moment. They were wet and warm and slippery and with the slightest tilt of her hips, the tip of his penis entered her. She moaned again and he looked at her, his eyes wide, searching her face. Before he could say a word, she arched her back against the wall, thrusting her hips down and forcing the length of him inside of her.

Condom, a voice inside her head whispered, but it was

drowned out by the roaring waves of her ecstasy.

"Oh god," he moaned into her ear, pushing her into the wall, moving deeper and deeper inside her. She ran her hands over the firm muscles in his shoulders and back, taut with the strain of holding her.

"Put me down," she whispered. He pulled out and kissed her madly before putting her down. She turned, bent over the ledge, and guided him into her. With each thrust, a doubt she had was squashed. *Thrust,* she no longer cared that he was too young for her. *Thrust,* she no longer cared that he was a movie star. *Thrust,* she no longer cared that he had been her student. From behind, he reached a spot deep inside that sent an electric current crackling and snapping through her whole body.

He bent forward and whispered in her ear, "I want you to come." His fingers found her clit just as she neared climax. A primal sound came from her throat as an orgasm made her legs tremble so badly beneath her that she thought they might give out. But he held her firmly to him, still moving slowly in and out of her. A few moments later, he pulled out and she felt him shudder against her. She stood up and he wrapped his arms around her from behind, his hands on her breasts and kissed the top of her head. "That was amazing," he murmured into her hair. Then he turned her to face him and took her chin in his hands, guiding her face to his, kissing her sweetly on the lips.

When they were wrapped in dry towels he led her to his bed and pulled her on top of him. Beth sighed deeply and propped her chin up to look at him. He was impossibly handsome, his wet, blond hair framing his chiseled face, his brown eyes so full of depth beyond his years. He gently stroked her shoulders and back with his fingertips and she shivered. "Are you cold?" he asked. "I'll be right back." Before she could respond, he was up and walking out of the bedroom. He came back a moment later with a pink terry cloth robe. She looked at it and, suddenly, Danny's words were in her head *"Chicks are always leaving them here."* And then she saw an image of the young woman in the purple bikini, her hand draped possessively on Todd's shoulder.

Now her brain wouldn't stop flashing images: the woman at the laundromat in the magazine spread, the girls waiting in the hall outside her classroom, the young woman with her tongue in his mouth at the Halloween party. *Why didn't I use a condom?* Beth rubbed her forehead, trying to remove the images of every eager young woman she had ever seen him with.

"Are you okay?" Todd was still holding the robe out to her.

"I, um, should probably go," she croaked, getting up from the bed and stumbling a little. Before he could respond, she was heading out of the room.

"Beth, wait!" he called after her. She was halfway across his living room before he caught up with her.

"What's the matter?" She didn't see the stunned look on his face because she wouldn't meet his eyes.

"Nothing," she said, trying to keep her voice calm. "I, um, just have a lot of work to do, and um, the dog and you know..." She went to grab her purse and knocked it over, sending the bag from the drugstore onto the floor. The yellow box of condoms landed face up with the boxes of Band-Aids scattered around it. *Shit!* But before she could stuff them back into her bag, he had bent to pick them up.

"I guess we didn't need these," he said, laughing.

She winced and took the box from him. "Yeah, I really shouldn't have done this."

"Done what?"

She sighed and shook the box. "Sex without these."

"Hey, I tried to pull away but you were the one who..."

"I know. I know. I know exactly what I did." Her jaw clenched painfully.

"But I pulled out, you know. We should be fine."

Her eyes flashed in frustration, and she saw him visibly shrink back from her. "Seriously? Do they not have health class in Miami?"

"Well, can't you get the morning after pill or something?" he offered feebly.

"I'm not worried about getting pregnant!" she snapped. Even though she was really furious with herself, she couldn't help but yell at him. How dare he make her want him so badly that she was that careless?

He was confused. "Do you think I'm going to give you something?"

"Um, no. I'm sure a guy like you is perfectly clean." Her anxiety had turned into biting sarcasm.

"Hey," he held up his hands defensively. "I don't have anything. I swear." Todd leaned against the arm of the couch relieved and started to laugh.

His nonchalance was irritating and she could no longer hold back her temper. "That's what everyone says! Do you really expect me to believe that? Coming from you? You *always* have women hanging on you. I had to beat them out of my class with a stick. And the one in the purple bikini and her friends apparently have a standing invitation here. For chrissake, you had your tongue down some girl's throat in the middle of the Halloween party, right after you kissed me!" The accusations spilled forth and she hated the bitter taste they left in her mouth.

"Whoa, you were the one that turned me down at the Halloween party!" The look she gave him made him quickly switch gears. "Anyway, I don't have sex with any of them." She rolled her eyes. "Honest," he said. "Really. I get tested every year. I can show you the results. And I haven't had unprotected sex with anyone since I got tested last."

She wanted to believe him but... "Bullshit."

"No, seriously," he said. And his face was serious.

"You expect me to believe that you don't hook up with *any* of the women that throw themselves at you."

He folded his arms over his chest. "I said, I don't have *sex* with any of them."

"What's that supposed mean?"

He sighed and looked down at the floor. "Gahh... I don't know how to put this without sounding like a dick."

She waited, an eyebrow raised.

"Well, apparently you think I'm a dick anyway so..." he paused. "I sometimes hook up with girls. Or let them hook up with me, I guess." He put air quotes over hook up. "But I only sleep with people I'm in a relationship with."

"What the hell does that mean?"

He sighed again, in exasperation. "It means if I'm not really interested in a girl, I only... I just... they just..." He started to gesture vaguely to his lap but then stopped and crossed his arms back over his chest.

Understanding was beginning to dawn on Beth. "Wait a minute. You mean to tell me that you let those women go down on you but you don't have sex with them?"

Todd winced but nodded, suddenly very interested in the hair on his forearm. She was speechless. She didn't know whether she felt disgusted or relieved. "I don't want to get anything either," he mumbled.

"Well, how do you know that I don't have anything?" she stammered, still dumbfounded by his answer.

He smiled at her tentatively. "I trust you." She rolled her eyes so hard it made her head hurt. "Listen, I know how it all sounds—like I'm a jerk."

"Um, yeah…" She glared up at him and he met her gaze defiantly.

"But you have to understand, in my position people try to take advantage. Some women try to get pregnant on purpose. It's happened to a lot of guys I know. I have to protect myself."

"Well, how do you know that I won't get pregnant?" She blurted out before she could stop herself.

His eyes lit up and he flashed her his movie star grin, then stood and walked toward her. "I'll take my chances with you." He wrapped his arms around her waist and leaned his forehead down to hers. "No one has ever looked at me the way that you looked at me in the shower. That was so. Fucking. Hot. And I think you'd make really cute babies."

Todd's nose was nearly touching hers and her heartbeat quickened. "That's a really stupid answer," she said softly, still feeling a little confused and a little disgusted but also safe.

"Maybe," he grinned. "But it's true. Don't leave. We haven't even had dessert yet."

His touch and the ache in her sweet tooth were too convincing. Todd held the robe out to her.

"Whose is this?" she asked, still suspicious.

"Relax. I have it here for my sister. She visits sometimes." Beth did relax. A little. Enough to notice that he appeared to be going commando under his navy sweatpants.

"So tell me about your sister," she said, plopping down in one of the oversized leather chairs in the corner of the kitchen, by the fire.

"Elena? She lives in Las Vegas," he said, his back was turned as wrestled with something in the refrigerator. "She used to come out here a lot but then she met Nico."

"Nico?"

"Her husband. He's a developer," he said, walking toward her with a large blue pastry box, big enough for a sheet cake.

"What's that?"

"You said you wanted chocolate, but I didn't know exactly what that meant. So I went to the bakery and got a few things."

Her eyes grew wide, a grin spreading across her heart-shaped face. "Really?"

He nodded and bowed to her, laying the box on her lap. "Open it."

Feeling like a kid on Christmas Day, she undid the brown ribbon on the box, slid her finger under the sticker with the bumblebee on it, and lifted the lid. There were brownies, chocolate cookies, a large slice of chocolate cake covered in chocolate frosting, and two chocolate covered mounds with drizzles of white icing on them.

"Oh my god," she laughed, clapping her hands in delight. "I can't believe you got all of this stuff!"

"I wasn't sure what you would like. Oh, and I have chocolate gelato, too. It's in the freezer." He was smiling, pleased with himself.

"What are these?" She pointed to the chocolate covered mounds.

"Those are homemade ring-dings. That's their specialty."

"Ooh, that sounds good. Can I have one of those?"

"You can have it all. I got it for you."

She picked up one of the ring-dings. It was the size of a tennis ball and she tried to figure out a lady-like way to eat it, eventually giving up and taking a big bite that smeared chocolate on her lips and the tip of her nose. Todd laughed and handed her a napkin then polished off his own cupcake in two huge bites. She wiped off her face while he set the box on the counter and came back with two new glasses of wine. Beth shifted to face him, swinging her legs over the arm of the chair, her feet dangling in the space between them. He grabbed one and held it up against his hand. Her foot was the same size as his hand. "Your feet are so small. How do you stand on these?"

She shrugged. "Sometimes not very well."

"I like them," he said and kissed her big toe.

The small gesture was surprisingly intimate. She flushed and changed the subject. "So, you mean to tell me that a hot, young, movie star doesn't sleep around at all?"

He grinned. "You think I'm hot?"

She rolled her eyes at him and he laughed. "Answer the question."

Todd shifted in his seat uncomfortably. "Honestly?"

"Of course. Do I seem like the kind of woman who wants you to lie to her?" Something passed across his face for a moment, so fast Beth wasn't sure she had seen it at all.

"Well, when He-Man first came out, I ended up with more than my share of girls chasing me. And, I mean, I'm a guy. Of course I was into it. I wasn't some kind of stud in high school or anything so I… um, took advantage of the situation. But when Danny realized what I was doing, he sat me down and told me about all of the guys in my position that ended up with surprise babies, paternity lawsuits, and all that. That kind of put a damper on things."

"I guess it would."

"Don't get me wrong, for a while I just tried to be really good about protection. But sleeping around isn't all it's cracked up to be. Those kinds of girls, they don't really want to sleep with me. They just want to sleep with He-Man. You know what I mean?"

"Actually, I don't. I've never had a one night stand."

"Never?" He looked surprised.

"Nope. I thought you were going to be my first."

He studied her then said, "Well, you aren't missing much."

"I'm sorry if I overreacted." She paused before the rest came out in a rush. "I just felt so stupid. We had this conversation at poker the other night about diseases and how nearly everyone has one or another. And I even picked up that huge box of condoms on the way here, I just didn't want to..." Finally, she stopped herself and began to blush.

"I get the condoms." He grinned. "But what about the Band-Aids? Do you have some injury that I missed?"

She laughed. "No, I was trying to hide the condoms because I totally got busted at the drugstore by my boss's wife."

"That makes sense, it is a pretty big box." He grinned at her. "Were you planning on using those all tonight?"

She blushed again. "Well not the Band-Aids..."

He looked serious for a moment. "Hey, do you want me to get my test results to show you? I really don't mind." He made to get up but she waved him back to his seat.

"I think," she said, getting up from her chair. "That I want you to stay." She slid onto his lap, straddling him, her bathrobe bunching open so that her breasts were mostly exposed. "Right. Where. You. Are." He wrapped his arms around her and sighed with pleasure or relief or both. Through his thin sweatpants she could tell that he already had an erection. *Well, that's one advantage to dating a younger man.*

20

Beth called Martha's raise and stared at her cards realizing she had nothing. *What am I doing? I should have folded.* When the next card was flipped Beth bluffed, throwing in half of her chips. It worked but that was the last hand she would win that night. She couldn't concentrate on the game, her thoughts floating off into daydreams about Todd. He had asked to see her but she refused, on principle, to bail on poker night. When she went all-in on an obvious straight draw with only a pair of twos, Martha called her out.

"Earth to Beth! What is going on with you? You haven't really been here with us."

"You got something on your mind?" Janet asked.

"Or someone?" Tiana added, winking at Beth.

Shit! Has she heard something? Are there rumors going around school?

"I heard that hunky He-man dropped your class. What was that all about?" Tiana said.

"What? Who?" Beth's faced flushed as she heard the false tone of her own voice.

"Don't play dumb, Beth. Give us the scoop. Were you too hard on him or something?" Allie asked. *Not exactly.*

Janet chimed in, "I'd give him some extra credit." And then

in a sultry voice, "Come to my office kid and we'll work *something* out."

"No, no," Beth said, wondering if she was protesting too much. "He dropped the class because of work. Not his grades."

"Then what are you all dreamy about?" Martha asked. "Did you rehabilitate the base-stealer after all?"

"What? Oh, George? God no. I didn't tell you about him last time?" The women shook their heads. "Well, that's because there was nothing good to tell. He was just awful. The slower I tried to get him to go, the faster he went. And did I tell you about the noise he made?"

The women howled with laughter as Beth explained what happened. Which led to more conversations about sex.

"I can always tell when I'm ovulating if I see a guy walking a dog and I look at the guy, not the dog."

"I know, right?" Janet said. "It seems like the moment I turned 35 all kinds of lights went on and I started looking at every guy I come across."

"It's just primal, ladies. We're hard-wired to give mating a last ditch effort in our late thirties. That's why so many women cheat and with guys that they wouldn't have looked twice at in their twenties."

"So you're saying that we're all wearing the evolutionary equivalent of beer goggles?" Beth asked.

"Sort of," Martha said. "But I don't want to make it sound like it's a bad thing. I've learned more about my own sexuality in the past five years than I did in the fifteen before. Hell, I hadn't experienced the trifecta until a couple of years ago."

"What's the trifecta?" Beth and Tiana asked in unison. Martha proceeded to explain that the trifecta was when a man is behind a woman and he is able to be inside her while stimulating her clitoris with one hand and her breasts with the other.

"I think it only works with tall guys," Allie said.

"You can actually do it on all fours just fine," Martha said. "As long as they can reach all three spots."

"I've only done it when I'm on his lap, leaning into his chest."

"His chest?" Tiana was confused.

"Yeah, facing away from him. On his lap, with his arms wrapped around me. But I've only dated one guy that was tall enough to do it that way. And it was the best orgasm I've ever had."

I know a guy who's pretty tall. Beth shifted uncomfortably in her seat as the blood rushed to a trifecta of places. "I've never done it. Too bad I don't have anyone to try that with," she said with an awkward noise that was supposed to be a laugh. Had it been any earlier in the night or the wine, the ladies surely would have noticed it. She stood up. "Does anyone else want some water?" But the women were already engrossed in a discussion about the merits of doggie style versus reverse cowgirl.

In the kitchen, Beth pulled her phone out of her pocket. There was a text from Todd.

TODD: how's poker?

A giddy smile spread across her face.

BETH: I'm up $1,000

That couldn't have been further from the truth. She had lost all her chips a half hour before and now was splitting her time between grazing the snacks and daydreaming about Todd.

TODD: Really???

BETH: Ha! Nope. The buy-in is $5 and I'm already out

TODD: In that case, you should come over

Beth bit her lip. She had been planning to cool things off with him a little, concerned that anything too serious would be trouble. But her trifecta was still tingling from the talk at the table.

BETH: Hmmm… I should probably go home for the dog. Do you deliver?

TODD: I do

BETH: In that case, I'd like to order one large Cuban

TODD: you want pickles on that?

BETH: wouldn't be a real Cuban without a great pickle, right?

TODD: HA! Okay, I'm on my way

Now her panties were getting damp.

BETH: see you soon

TODD: You are talking about my pickle, right? Or do you want me to bring you a sandwich too?

* * *

Todd's truck was parked in front of her house when she got home. He slid out of the driver side, his baseball hat pulled low and followed her inside. Homer danced and whined and spun around Todd.

"Can I get you something to drink?" Beth asked over the whirligig dog.

"Just water." He crouched down. "Hey buddy, hey buddy. Who's a good boy? You missed me didn't you?" Beth went into the kitchen to get the water when she felt strong arms snake around her waist. Todd kissed her gently just below her ear and she leaned back into his chest, remembering what Allie had said about the trifecta. He breathed in her hair and sighed. "How was poker?"

She turned to face him, handing him a glass of water. "I didn't win, but we had some interesting conversations."

"Oh yeah? What about?"

"Maybe I'll show you later," she said coyly. "So what did

you do tonight?"

He laughed. "Nothing. I played some video games, tried to read, but then gave up and texted you. I couldn't concentrate on anything else."

Beth's heart began to race and she felt tingly all over. "I had a hard time concentrating at poker, too," she said softly.

"I knew you missed me," he said. "It's like I could feel it."

She could feel it, too. Even more so now that he was in her kitchen dwarfing her appliances and radiating masculinity. She leaned against the counter—the very same spot where they had had maple syrup-induced sex. The tingle shifted to a gentle pulse.

"So," she said. They both knew why he was there.

"So." He seemed to feel a little awkward, too. His cocky grin replaced with something more unassuming.

She grabbed his hand and she led him into her living room. Gently, she pushed him down onto her arm chair. He took his hat off and ran his hand through his hair. Before he could get comfortable, she grabbed the hem of his shirt and pulled it over his head. Beth ran her fingertips down his chest and just like that all the nervous energy between them turned into sexual tension. She climbed atop him and kissed him feverishly until he slipped a hand under her shirt. The conversation at poker had been more than enough foreplay so she leaned back and pulled off her shirt, unclasped her bra and threw it all on the floor. He palmed her breasts, then gently traced his finger around her taut nipples. The gentle pulse shifted to an aching throb.

Beth slid off his lap. "Stand up," she said. Todd stood before her and she rubbed her palm across the front of his jeans, squeezing him gently. He sighed and bent his forehead to hers, smiling.

"You smell good." He inhaled. "Like coconuts."

He smelled good, too, an intoxicating mix of deodorant and clean male skin. She unbuttoned his pants and slipped a hand in, caressing the tip of his penis. Todd put his hands on her shoulders and stepped on the heel of each of his shoes, kicking them off. Then he unbuttoned her pants, pushed them to the floor, and sank to his knees in front of her. He peeled off her panties and wrapped his big hands around her waist, steadying her as she stepped out of the clothes. Beth stood naked before him. He cupped her ass in his hands and smiled up at her. Then, he pulled her to his mouth. The breath caught in her throat as his tongue met her flesh and traced slow, exquisite circles.

"Oh my god," she sighed, her head tilting back in raw pleasure. His tongue moved faster, flicking her lightly. Beth shivered. She was so turned on, she was already nearing orgasm. "Wait," she whispered.

Taking his hand in hers, she helped him stand and unzipped his pants. He kissed her as his pants fell to the floor and she blindly tugged at his boxer briefs, pushing them toward his crumpled pants. Now they were both naked. Again, she pushed him back onto the chair and straddled him, rubbing her damp skin against his hard flesh. He kissed her cheek, and then her ear, and then her neck. When his mouth made its way to the place where her neck met her shoulder, she shuddered. He pulled away from her and smiled, then went back to the spot, sucking it gently. Beth moaned. Todd's hands found her breasts and he bit her gently on her lower neck until she cried out.

She was so close but she didn't want to come without him inside her, so she climbed off of him and stood up.

"Wha…" Todd sat up in surprise.

Beth turned around and lowered herself onto his lap, guiding him into her, leaning back against his bare chest. He relaxed and they began to move together. He brushed her hair to the side and continued to kiss her neck. She reached behind her for his hands and brought one to her breast. As he began to tease her nipple, she guided his other hand to the spot between her legs, just above where they were connected.

Everything fit and they moved together, her tiptoes touching the ground, giving her just enough leverage so she could rock up and down on him. Her entire body was singing as he stimulated each of her most sensitive parts at once. She was gasping, overwhelmed by so much sensation in so many places. Beth's body started to tremble, but Todd held her tight. Between her legs, his fingers moved faster. Her nipple buzzed as he squeezed it softly. He touched his teeth to the sensitive and exquisite place on her neck as she bucked against him. It felt like he was growing even harder, expanding to fill her. The instant she began to cry out he bit her neck gently but firmly, sending her spiraling into ecstasy. She trembled wildly, pleasure singeing every nerve of her body.

Several moments later she came back to herself. Todd's arms were wrapped tightly around her waist, his head on her shoulder, his body shuddering beneath her. It took her a second to realize that she was still moaning softly. When his body was still, he leaned back in the chair, shifting her against him so he could cradle her in his arms.

"Hey," he said when he saw her face, a streak of worry creasing his brow. "Are you okay?" He put his hand to her face and brushed away a tear.

"Oh," Beth said, bringing her hands up to her face. "Wow." Her cheeks were damp.

Todd was frowning at her, fear in his eyes. "Did I hurt you?" he asked, his voice unusually hoarse.

"No, not at all." She wiped her eyes and smiled at him. She felt completely stoned but in the best way possible.

"Are you sure you're okay?" He didn't look convinced.

"Totally sure. I'm fine." Then she laughed softly and added, "I'm better than fine." She was actually getting giddy. Giddy with him, with them. "I've never felt *anything* like that before."

"Really?" he said, beaming.

"Definitely not." She couldn't wipe the grin off her own face. "But don't let it go to your head now, Jedidiah."

"Too late."

21

"What are you doing tomorrow?" he had asked her before he left. She had told him that if the weather was good she would be out on her paddleboard. He had said that sounded fun, she had offered to take him sometime and now he was standing in her driveway.

She gestured to the back of his truck. "I thought you didn't have a board."

"I just bought it."

"Seriously? We could have just rented you one."

"I didn't want to bother with all that."

"No, of course not," she laughed, shaking her head. His new board was slimmer, which would move faster in the water. *But might not be the best choice for a beginner.* "This is nice."

"Do you want me to drive?" he asked.

"Does your truck have 4-wheel drive?"

"Uh, no."

"Then you'd better let me drive. It's a little off the beaten path but it's great because only a few people know about it."

Beth climbed onto her bumper while he got his board, then helped him secure it to the roof. They threw the paddles in the back and she looked up at him. "Where's the rest of your stuff?"

"What stuff?"

"Did you bring your wetsuit? Or a towel or anything?"

"Ummmm…"

"Todd, the water's pretty cold."

He shrugged. "I'll be fine."

"I'll you a grab towel," she said.

"Can I say hi to Homer?"

"Sure. We can bring him if you want."

"Really?" Todd looked so excited that she couldn't help but laugh.

"Yeah, I take him all the time."

She backed out of the driveway with Homer's head resting on Todd's shoulder, Todd scratching him behind the ears. They drove out of the city toward Malibu. After a while, Beth made a few turns and soon the old truck was bouncing along a dirt road. Todd held onto the door frame.

"Sorry," she called over the noise of the engine. "This thing drives like a tractor."

When they came to a fork in the road, Beth slipped the truck into 4-wheel drive and they went right. Slowly, she made her way down the nearly overgrown road and after one more sharp turn, they came to a clearing. There was only one other vehicle there, a Jeep that used to be white but was now the grayish brown of the mud that covered it.

She opened the back of the truck and Homer hopped out, bounding down a path at the edge of the clearing. Todd helped her get the boards off the roof and they followed the dog down the path. It wound down a small hill and opened into a beautiful, quiet cove. Todd sucked in his breath.

Beth grinned up at him. "I know, right?" The day was spectacular and the calm little cove, nestled between tall, sandy cliffs, looked more peaceful and majestic than ever. She waved to the two figures that were out on the water. "That's Matty and Dev. They're always here, too."

It was an unusually warm day for November and the sheltered cove held the heat in nicely. She pulled off her sweatshirt then dug around her bag for her hat.

"Where's your wetsuit?" Todd asked, gesturing to her board shorts and tank top.

"I don't have one."

"Won't *you* be cold?"

She looked up at him and grinned. "I don't fall in." Beth waded knee deep into the water, then climbed on her board. When she whistled, Homer came bounding across the beach. She moved to the back of the board on her knees while the dog scrambled onto the front. When he settled, she stood up. "Okay," she said. "Now you try."

Todd waded in and got on the board without any trouble.

"You can always practice on your knees for a little bit to get your bearings."

"I think I've got this," Todd said, his surfing experience working in his favor. He stood up slowly, crouched in surf form, before raising himself fully. "Not too bad for a beginner," he said.

She didn't respond, waiting for him to realize that he had left his paddle on the board between his feet.

"Shit," he said and bent over to grab the paddle, but he had shifted too far forward and the board rocked under his weight. For just a moment, she thought he was going to be able to steady himself but he overcorrected and ended up falling off backwards.

"Ahh!" he shouted when he came up out of the frigid water.

"Are you okay?"

"It's fucking cold." Unable to help herself, she started to laugh.

"You knew that was going to happen, didn't you?"

She nodded. "Yeah."

"Homer," Todd called to the dog. "Come here and warm me up." Homer knew many words but his favorites, after "treat," were "come here." And he liked Todd. A lot. So without hesitation, he leapt from the end of Beth's board.

"Homer, no!" she shouted but it was too late. Everything happened in slow motion, her board tipped precariously and she was sure she was going to fall off the back. But her pride kicked into high gear and her core took over. She shifted her weight far enough forward that she fell to her hands and knees on the board. Beth looked up to see Todd holding all 60 pounds of Homer like a baby, the happy dog licking his ear.

She sat back on her heels and raised her middle finger at him. Todd laughed and covered Homer's eyes. "Is that any way to behave in front of the little one, Ms. Grant?" Homer wriggled out of his arms and swam to shore, barking and spinning in excitement. Beth looked over her shoulder to see Matty and Dev coming toward them.

"Hey Beth!" Dev said, swinging her long black braid over her tanned shoulder. Matty was as fair as she was tan. His ginger hair was almost translucent in the sun, his forearms covered in freckles.

"Matty, Dev, this is my, uh...," Beth paused for just a moment, then rushed on as if that might disguise her hesitation. "My friend Todd. Todd, this is Matty and Dev."

"Hey man, did she swear you to secrecy?" Matty said in a slow, southern drawl.

Todd was confused. "Uh, what?"

"About this place. Did you take the oath not to tell anyone about it?"

Beth laughed. "Don't worry. I blindfolded him on the way here so he can't find it without me."

"Ah, right. Your secret is safe with me. Plus," he gestured to the board in front of him. "If I don't get the hang of it, this may be my first and last time."

"Nah, you'll be fine," Dev smiled down at him. "Everyone falls the first time."

Matty scratched his thick red beard. "Are you sure you haven't been around here before, bro? You look awfully familiar."

Todd grinned. "I get that a lot."

"Matty," Dev said. "That's Todd Allman. That's why he looks familiar."

"Todd Allman? No shit," Matty said, still scratching his beard.

"He-Man?" Dev sounded exasperated but waited for him to get there. She looked at Beth and put her pinched finger and thumb up to her mouth and inhaled. Matty didn't notice.

"Ohhhh man, you are him, aren't you?" Matty paddled closer to where Todd was standing in the water and held out his hand. "Nice to meet you, man. I mean He. Man." He pronounced the name like it was two separate sentences, then chuckled to himself.

"Nice to meet you, too." Todd shook his hand.

"My little brother is going to flip out when he hears about this. He fucking loves you, man. Hey, do you think I could get a picture with you?"

"Sure." Todd followed Matty and Dev to the shore.

"Do you want me to take the picture?" Beth called after them.

"Nah, man. We're gonna do a selfie, right He. Man?" She watched as Todd posed patiently for a picture with Matty, then one with Dev, then one between both of them. And then for good measure, one with Homer who was very excited to be included.

When the couple headed back up the hill, Beth asked, "Does that happen a lot?"

"What? People recognizing me?"

"Yeah and wanting to take pictures and stuff."

"Well, not all the time but yeah, it does happen a lot." Todd grinned at her and hoisted himself back onto the board. "Beth, I think you're the only person who's spoken to me in public who didn't know me from those movies."

"Really?" She couldn't imagine being recognized wherever she went. "How do you deal with that?"

"Well, it helps that I don't have Danny text TMZ every time I go somewhere."

"People do that?"

"Some people do, if they want exposure. Also little things like wearing a hat and sunglasses help. And driving the truck. No one looks twice at the old Chevy."

Once he was steady, they paddled from one cove to the next. When they got back to the car and put the boards up, he grabbed her by the waist.

"Hey. Thanks for bringing me here. This place is really... amazing." She smiled up at him, her heart starting to race, their bodies pressed together. "And so are you," he added softly. He bent to kiss her and she wrapped her arms around his neck, pulling him closer, tasting the ocean on his full, warm lips. *Should we go further down the path and find some privacy?* Beth wanted him and from the feel of things, he wanted her, too. Then there was a low grumble from between them and they both pulled back, laughing. "Was that my stomach or yours?"

"I don't know. Maybe we should get something to eat."

They got in the truck where Homer was already curled in the back, exhausted. Before they got back to civilization, Beth pulled off the road at a little shack. She cut the ignition and looked at the other two cars in front of the place.

"Do you want to wait here while I grab some food? We can take it to my place. You know, if you don't want to be recognized."

"Nah, it's fine. Most people don't even notice me if I'm wearing a hat." He pulled his Dolphins' hat lower and opened the car door.

They sat at a picnic table, Homer at their feet and ate fresh fish tacos and drank cold beer. They talked about movies and books and when there was a lull in the conversation, Beth glanced up to find him staring at her. Instinctively, she wiped at her face with a napkin. "What? Do I have food on my face?"

"No," he laughed, shaking his head. "You're fine. But I was wondering if I could ask you a favor."

"Sure, what's up?"

"Will you teach me how to drive your car?"

That was not what she was expecting. "You mean a 4x4?"

He shook his head. "A stick shift."

"You don't know how to drive a manual transmission?" Todd actually looked bashful, staring at his hands on the table, then peeking back up at her. He shook his head again and she smiled. "Of course I'll teach you. I know just the place."

She pulled into the deserted parking lot of the college, turned the car off and handed him the keys. "You should know, though, learning on this beast is definitely the hard way. But if you can drive my truck, you can drive anything."

Beth taught him in the same firm but patient manner that her grandmother had used to teach her. It took him a while but he eventually got the hang of it. Homer swayed patiently in the back seat through all the stops and starts, shudders and stalls. By the time Todd was shifting smoothly, Beth thought the dog looked a little queasy. "So, do you want to drive us home?" He looked at her, surprised.

"Do you think I should?"

She shrugged. "What's the worst that could happen?"

"Um, well, I could stall or flood the engine, we could have to push the car out of the road and the paparazzi might drive by taking pictures that will end up on the cover of some tabloid."

"Oh," she was taken aback. "Well, in that case, maybe I should drive."

As Beth buckled her seatbelt, Todd asked, "So where did you get this truck anyway?"

On the drive home, she told him about how the Land Cruiser had been her great grandmother's truck. How she had bought it because it reminded her of the Jeeps she drove when she was in the Army. Before she got too old to drive, Beth would ride with her grandmother up and down New Smyrna Beach helping to pull stuck cars out of the sand. She told him about how when her great grandmother died, she had left the car to Beth and the house to Beth's mother.

"I drove it in high school, but when I moved away to college, my mom was worried about it making the drive to and from South Carolina so I ended up with her old Honda. The Land Cruiser sat in our garage for years until I ended up back in New Smyrna and my cousin helped me fix it up."

"Ah, so let me get this straight. Your great grandmother was in the Army and loved driving trucks so much that she bought one and towed people's cars for fun."

"Pretty much. She also drank beer, cussed like a sailor, and burped louder than any man I've ever met."

Todd laughed. "So, you come from a long line of women who don't take any shit?"

"I guess I never thought about it that way," Beth smiled. "Tell me about your grandmother."

"Well, my grandmother on my mom's side didn't speak English and hated my father. She would either clam up when he came in the room or she would yell at him in Spanish. And my dad's mom was like exactly what you would think a grandmother would be. She was sweet and had white hair and baked cookies and pies. She also had a huge crush on Don Shula. She's the one who got me watching football."

"Really?"

"Yeah, she never missed a game. I think she was disappointed that I was too small to play football in high school."

"How are *you* too small for anything?"

"Oh I wasn't this size in high school. I grew like six inches my senior year."

They got back to her house, washed off the boards and the dog. "Hey, do you mind if I rinse off, too?" Todd asked. She showed him to her shower and got him a fresh towel.

"Did you bring a change of clothes?"

"Uh, no..." He was already pulling off his shirt.

"Just give me your stuff. I'll wash it." She turned to give him privacy, but changed her mind, instead watching as he untied his board shorts and pulled apart the velcro. Beth had never thought that the sound of ripping velcro could be sexy until that moment. Todd smiled at her.

"Like what you see?"

She shrugged. "Maybe."

"You're not looking away."

"Nope."

He grinned and slid down his shorts, his erection already growing. "Do you watch all of your friends undress?"

"My friends?"

"Yeah, you said I was your friend. But friends don't usually watch each other shower."

"No," Beth said, taking off her own shirt, then tugging at the strings on her bikini top. "I suppose they don't." He stood in the shower, the water running over him and watched as she pulled down her shorts and bikini bottoms at once. She joined him under the water. Her shower was much smaller and more intimate than his and they had to maneuver carefully. Slowly and methodically, they took turns washing each other, lingering over chests and thighs, exploring each other's warm, wet bodies. He picked up the shampoo bottle and turned her away from him. She leaned into his chest as he gently lathered her hair and began to massage her scalp, his strong hands at once relaxing and arousing. She moaned involuntarily and he slipped a wet, soapy hand to her breast, teasing her nipple.

When they were clean, they moved to her bed where they very deliberately devoured each other.

After, he stood in her living room in just a towel, his clothes in the dryer. "Mind if I check the score on the game?" he asked, reaching for the television remote.

"Of course not," she called back from the kitchen where she was getting them drinks.

A moment later, Todd poked his head into the kitchen and held up her remote. "Do you have any more batteries? There aren't any in here."

"There aren't? Hmm… I wonder where…" She stopped mid-thought. "Oh! Hang on…"

Beth went down the hall to her bedroom and pulled open the drawer of her night stand. There was TOM in all his multi-functional glory, waiting patiently for her. She opened the bottom of the vibrator dropping the batteries into the palm of her hand when she heard Todd say, "Hey do you have a shirt I can… Oh wow…"

She looked up to find him standing in the doorway. Willing herself to meet his eyes, she tried to act like holding a vibrator was the most natural thing in the world. But the heat making its way across her cheeks, forced her eyes to the floor. He looked from her red cheeks to what was in her hand.

Beth glanced up and laughed uncomfortably. "I, um, found the batteries."

"I see that," he said, leaning against the door frame. He crossed his arms cockily over his chest and stared her down. "You know, I thought you were satisfied, but I can go again if you didn't get enough." That twinkle was back in his dark eyes.

She looked from Todd to TOM and back. Then she dropped the vibrator into the drawer and meeting his gaze said, "Prove it."

He didn't hesitate, crossing to her in one long stride. Before she knew what was happening, he was pulling her sundress over her head and flinging it across the room. It felt like his lips were everywhere at once, her mouth, her neck, her breast, her thigh. He pushed her back onto the bed and yanked down her panties, slipping a finger inside her. Her body was wet for him before her mind even knew she was turned on. Todd grabbed her wrists in one large hand and pinned them over her head, glancing at her face before kissing her hard on the mouth. She tugged his bottom lip between her teeth, while his hand stroked her between her thighs.

Wrapping her legs around him, she tried to grip his towel between her toes and pull it off. He drew back and with one flick of the wrist the towel disappeared.

"Is this what you want?" His voice was a husky growl in her ear.

She nodded and rocked her hips up toward him. Still holding her arms above her head, he entered her so swiftly she gasped. He moved in and out of her vigorously, deliciously. When she responded by trying to match his thrusts, he drew back, pulling out of her completely.

"Don't move," he commanded, letting go of her wrists and

kissing his way down her stomach. He pushed her legs open, parting her with his tongue. Beth moaned and started to tremble. She lowered her arms and ran her hands through his hair.

"Uh uh, I told you not to move," he said positioning himself on top of her, grabbing her wrists and pinning them again over her head. This time, he entered her with an excruciating slowness and she bucked her hips trying to take in more of him. In response, he pulled away, until just the tip of him was touching her. She wrapped her legs around him and tried to pull him closer, but he was too strong. He grinned, sliding slowly back inside her, but stopped halfway. Once again she tried to wriggle toward him, pull him deeper into her and once again he backed away.

They danced like this for what felt like hours. Todd entered her in maddeningly short, shallow thrusts until she was panting, on the verge of begging. When he slipped all the way into her, filling her fully, she sighed in pleasure. Yet for every time he gave her all of him, he teased her with a dozen shallow thrusts. Beth felt like she was going mad. When she thought she could take no more, a strangled whimper escaped her throat and he let go of her wrists and held her face in his hand.

"You feel so fucking good," he whispered, staring into her eyes as he began to enter her again slowly. But now that her hands were free, she grabbed his ass and pulled him into her, bucking up against him, riding the building wave. Her urgency was contagious and they dissolved into a sweaty fury of lips and fingers and tongues. Beth's body was coiled so tightly that she thought she might scream. Todd's body strained against hers. They pressed together deeper and harder. And in one final motion they exploded together, trembling and shuddering and clutching each other desperately. He lowered his chest to hers and as she caught her breath she ran her fingers over the goosebumps that covered his back.

When the beating of their hearts had slowed to a normal pace, he entwined his fingers in hers. "Are you good now?"

She shrugged. "I guess so. For now."

"What?!" He pulled away from her, stunned.

She grinned and kissed him lightly, then rolled out of bed. When she tried to stand, her legs felt like Jell-o and nearly collapsed underneath her. She sat back down on the bed.

"Are you okay? Is there something wrong?"

"Seriously?" She looked at him to see if he was teasing but he appeared to be genuinely concerned. "Where did you learn to fuck like that?" The concern was replaced with a sly, cocky smile. Beth rolled her eyes and threw her hands up in the air in disgust. "Ugh. Never mind, I don't want to know." She started to get back up but he grabbed her before she could.

She squirmed, struggling to get away from him. "No, no, it's not what you think." He was laughing, his arms wrapping more tightly around her waist. "I read it in a magazine." She stopped fighting and turned to look at him.

"What?"

"Danny brought one of those men's magazines with us to Japan and I got bored and read the sex articles." She narrowed her eyes, skeptical. "No, seriously, I've been wanting to do that with you ever since I saw you at the Dolphin's game."

Beth tried to keep the smile that was tugging at the corner of her lips from spreading into a full blown grin. "So," she said, "what else have you been wanting to do with me?"

Todd thought for a moment, then matching her cheeky grin, he whispered into her ear.

* * *

She hadn't known she had fallen asleep until she awoke to Todd stroking her hair. They were still in bed. The sun had gone down and the room was dark and she lay on top of him under a velvety, soft blanket with all of her most tender parts slightly sore and completely sated. Beth swiped at the corner of her mouth to make sure she hadn't been drooling, then looked up at him.

"I fell asleep," she said.

"You did." Todd kissed the top of her head and she rested it back on his chest, listening to the steady thrum of his heart. Their fingers entwined, he stroked her thumb gently with his own. It was so comfortable, being with him like this. "This is really nice," he murmured and a lump welled unexpectedly in her throat. She squeezed her eyes together, willing it away.

"Beth," he whispered.

"Hmmm?"

"I want to be more than friends."

She propped her head up on his chest, then leaned over to turn on the lamp. "What do you mean?"

"I mean I'm not seeing anyone else." He stared at her, his expression much more serious than she expected. "And I don't want to see anyone else."

"Okay," she said, slowly. *Are we really having this talk?*

"I told you, I don't have sex with anyone I'm not in a relationship with."

"What are you trying to say?"

"I'm trying to say that I need to know that you aren't sleeping with other people."

"Oh!" she said. "I thought you were trying to say that you wanted to be my boyfriend or something. But no, I'm not sleeping with anyone else."

"Not even that guy from Thrasher?"

"George? Oh god, no. We only went out a few times at the

beginning of the semester."

Todd looked relieved and she placed her head back on his chest. "Would it really be so bad if I were your boyfriend?" he said softly.

She sighed and sat up. "In theory no, of course not but…"

"But what?"

She sighed again. "Well, for one thing, you're too young for me. For another, you said yourself that you get recognized a lot and probably every single person at the college knows that you used to be my student. We could never be seen together, I could lose my job. Or at the very least my reputation. I don't sleep with my students, Todd."

He smiled up at her. "I'm not too young for you and I'm not your student. Plus you don't need that job anyway. I can take care of you."

Beth did not smile back. "What makes you think I'd be happy with that? Do I strike you as the type of person who wants to be taken care of?"

"I didn't mean it like that. I just meant that we could make it work."

"That's easy for you to say. What do you have to lose? I could lose everything!"

"Hey, calm down. I'm just saying that we could be careful. No one would have to know if that's how you want it."

She didn't say anything. Beth didn't know what she wanted. Since the first time he had kissed her, she'd known they had a connection. But she had been telling herself that it was purely physical. Now, she wasn't so sure.

"Beth," he said, running his fingertips down her spine. "I don't care what you want to call it. I don't care who knows or if we keep it a secret. I just want to be with you." She looked back at him, into his earnest face, not sure how to respond. "And I really, really don't want you to be with anyone else," he added.

She bit her lip as images of all the women that threw themselves at Todd Allman flashed through her mind. "I don't want you to be with anyone else either."

He grinned. "Woman, you don't leave me any energy to be with anyone else."

"So no more blow jobs from groupies?"

"Definitely not."

She laid her head back on his chest. "Okay," she said softly. "But it has to be on the down low. If it gets out that we're together, who knows what will happen."

"Okay, baby." Todd snickered. "We'll keep it on the *down low*."

Beth looked back up at him. "What? Do you young people not say that anymore?"

22

"What did you say?" Jenna asked.

"I told him I didn't think it was a good idea. I mean, it's not like I can be seen with him. But he really wants me to go so I said I'd think about it." Before he left, Todd had asked Beth to come to his birthday dinner.

"And?"

"He said it's in the private room at The Meat Shed and no one will see us together except people we already know. He wants me to bring you."

"Me?"

"Yeah, then we can come in together. Plus, Levi and Asha are coming. And Danny, you remember him?"

"The guy we met at Pancho's?"

"Right." Beth was biting the side of her thumb. "So what do I do? Birthdays are kind of a big deal. And this thing with him is supposed to be really casual."

"First, I will go with you if you want me to. Second, birthdays are not *that* big of a deal. It's not like meeting someone's family or spending a holiday with them or something. And third, is it really all that casual? You've been seeing him a lot."

Beth rubbed her forehead like it might give some clarity to

her thoughts then sighed in an audible puff. "I don't know, Jenna. I thought it was. But he acts like..." She thought about her time with Todd laughing on the paddle board, teaching him to drive her car, arguing about the future of the Dolphins. It certainly seemed like more than a fling. "I don't know. I think it's getting too serious and I don't want it to. But at the same time, I really like being with him. And the sex..."

"Yeah?" She could hear the grin in Jenna's voice.

"The sex is unbelievable." Beth told her about the trifecta and how he bit her neck right as she was coming. "So it was like a trifecta plus one or something. He hit *all* the spots," she whispered.

"Yeah, that's a superfecta," Jenna laughed. "Dammit that sounds hot."

"It was, but it was also really..." She tried out several adjectives in her head before landing on, "tender. You know what I mean? Like, unexpectedly so." She sighed again. "Gahh. What am I doing? This can't go anywhere."

"Why can't it?"

"Jenna, he's almost 10 years younger than I am!"

Jenna snorted. "Well, that seems like a good reason not to date someone."

"Okay, maybe not. But, I can't be seen with him. At least not any time soon. Everyone knows he was my student. I could really get in trouble. How can you date someone you can't be seen with? Especially, when everyone that sees him wants to take his freaking picture. I should probably just end it but..." She bit her lip, her heart sinking at the thought of not seeing Todd again, not being with him.

"You can tell yourself whatever, Beth, but you're already in it. Why don't you just take it one day at a time? Go to the birthday dinner and just see where it goes from there."

"Will you go with me?"

"Of course!"

"Okay," Beth said hesitantly, still not sure she was making the right decision.

"Now you just have to decide what to get him for his birthday."

* * *

This time Beth was even more nervous than the first time she had come to The Meat Shed. The hostess ushered them through a set of double doors into the kitchen, then to the freight elevator in the back. When the elevator doors opened, the hostess leaned in and pressed a button, then held the door open for them. "Enjoy your evening," she said.

As the elevator lurched upward, Beth's stomach stayed on the ground floor. Her mouth was dry and her palms were clammy. Even though this was a private party, it marked the first time she was going to be somewhere as Todd's guest. Jenna squeezed her shoulder.

"Take a deep breath. It's going to be fun."

They stepped through the threshold together into a room that was a more subdued, sophisticated version of the downstairs. On one of the white brick walls hung a large bronze steer head. A wide red velvet couch sat across from the massive oak dining table. There were ceiling-to-floor windows with a view of the twinkling city and a small bar in the corner where everyone was gathered.

"Here you are," Todd said, wrapping one arm around Beth and pulling her close for a kiss. Beth cut the kiss short and gently pushed him away, flustered. Todd laughed and held the palm of his hand to her already burning cheek.

She looked around to see if they were being watched but Jenna was already engrossed in conversation with Asha and

Levi. So she flicked open the top button of her blouse and leaned in, giving him a peek at what was underneath. She whispered into his ear, "I'm wearing part of your present." She hadn't known what to get a guy who could afford to buy anything he wanted but she could give him something he couldn't buy.

His dark eyes widened. "I have a driver out back so you can leave with me without being seen."

"Good," she grinned. "Because there's more of your present in my purse." Before he could respond she re-buttoned her shirt and walked away to say hi to Asha, a little more sway in her hips than before.

They were taking their seats at the table when the elevator dinged and Danny stepped out. "Happy Birthday! Sorry I'm late!"

"You're not late, you're just in time for the first toast," Levi said, raising his glass. Danny smiled and slid into the empty chair and held up his water glass to Levi. "To the birthday boy, wishing you as much success for your next quarter century as you've had in the first, kid! Cheers."

As they clinked glasses the elevator door dinged again and Beth got a heady feeling of déjà vu. A leggy brunette stepped out of the elevator. "Happy birthday, little brother," she said, opening her arms wide.

"Elena!" Todd jumped up and crossed the room to her, easily picking her up and swinging her around as she laughed. "I can't believe you're here. How did you..."

Elena? Beth's stomach tightened as she realized she was about to meet Todd's sister.

"Danny called to see if I wanted to come out and surprise you. It's not every day you get to crash your baby brother's birthday party."

Crash, indeed. Beth's stomach did a backflip as she watched

Elena survey the rest of the table. Elena, like Todd, was tall, her skin impeccable, her smile perfect, and her hair radiant. *Guess Todd wasn't the only winner in the gene pool lottery.*

"Todd, introductions, please?" She said, looking pointedly at Beth. She was smiling but it didn't reach her eyes.

"Elena, this is my girlfr…"

"I'm Beth," she cut him off, standing up and shaking Elena's cool, slender hand. She was so not ready to do this. "And this is my friend Jenna." Jenna waved from across the table.

Elena leaned up and mock-whispered into her brother's ear. "Todd, you didn't tell me you had a lady friend." It was hard to tell whether she was being sarcastic, or threatening, or protective. But Beth was pretty certain her tone was aggressive. Her face flushed and she took a deep breath. This was his sister after all, she was bound to be concerned about who her brother spent time with. Todd gave his sister a warning look.

"Sit down, Elena. Have something to eat."

"I'd love to!"

Before he sat down, Todd put his arm around Beth and nuzzled her ear. "I can't believe you got to meet my sister."

"I can't believe I got to meet your sister," Beth echoed. She was quiet for the rest of the meal, taking it all in. Elena was magnetic and she held court about her life in Las Vegas with her husband Nico.

It wasn't until Todd was saying goodbye to Asha and Levi that Beth felt a hand on her shoulder. She turned and saw Elena smiling at her.

"Well, Beth, now's as good a time as ever to get to know you a little better. What do you do? What's your angle?"

"My angle?" She was confused by the questions but the intent behind them seemed clear enough. "I don't have an angle."

Elena glared down at her. "Sure you do. You all do. So what's yours? You want his money? You want to use him to meet producers? What is it?"

Beth sucked in her breath, shocked more by the underlying venom than the directness of the question. Though her tone was menacing, Elena's beautiful face remained placid. From where Todd was standing across the room watching them, it looked like they could have been talking about the weather.

"I'm a teacher," Beth said, plastering on the sweetest smile she could muster.

Elena's face gave nothing away. "Well, that's good, I guess. At least you're not another actress looking for a break."

She bit her tongue to keep from saying *Actually, I'm just using him for sex.* "Break? The only break I'm interested in is winter break."

"What do you teach?"

OH SHIT. She was so not prepared for this conversation and wished very badly that she hadn't agreed to come to this dinner. Then she remembered what Jenna had said, she was already in it whether she wanted to be or not. *I guess I'd better just own this.* She lifted her chin and met Elena's eyes, nearly as dark as her brother's. "I teach at the college. That's how we met." She wasn't about to tell her about the gas station.

"Really?" Elena looked genuinely shocked by the admission and Beth felt a satisfying little thrill at throwing the ice queen off balance. "So you were his... teacher?"

"Yes, but he's not in my class anymore." She caught Jenna's eye and threw her friend a subtle but distinct "please help me" look. The one they had perfected over so many years of friendship.

"So, you're dating your student?" Elena asked, not even trying to conceal her contempt.

"Actually, we didn't start seeing each other until after he

dropped my class." Before she could say more, Jenna interrupted.

"Danny has had a little too much to drink, so I'm going to drive him home. You okay with that?"

"Sure," Beth said. She had been planning to go home with Todd anyway.

"Elena, it was a pleasure to meet you," she said, peppering the word pleasure with a trace of condescension. "Will you be in LA long?"

Elena shook her head. "I leave tomorrow."

"Ah, that's too bad," Jenna said.

"So, ladies, what have you been talking about?" Todd asked as he approached the women.

"Oh, you know, just trying to get to know Beth a little better," Elena said with a terse smile.

"Todd, happy birthday, darling." Jenna gave him a hug and then headed to the elevator with Danny.

"They seemed to have hit it off," Todd said and slung an arm over Beth's shoulder. "So should we grab a drink somewhere?"

"Actually," Beth said, squirming. "It's getting late and I have a lot of work to do."

"Yes," Elena added, raising an eyebrow at her brother. "You didn't tell me you were such a teacher's pet."

He grinned, unfazed. "I wasn't actually. She wouldn't have anything to do with me until I dropped her class."

"Ah, how moral of you." Elena wasn't even pretending to smile anymore.

"I really should get going." Beth slipped out from under his arm and grabbed her purse off the back of the chair.

"Wait," Todd said. "You can't leave." He leaned over and whispered in her ear, "What about my birthday present?" She felt the hairs on the back of her neck stand up, a familiar tingle warming her thighs. But one glance at Elena shut it down.

"If you two have plans, Todd, I can just head back to your house," Elena said.

"Nonsense," Beth said. "You came all this way."

"But I leave tomorrow for Florida." Todd said, his eyes pleading. She had forgotten that he was going home for Thanksgiving and the thought of not seeing him for a week pained her.

"Go spend time with your sister, Todd. I'll see you when you get back. It was nice to meet you, Elena." She shook the cool hand again.

"Happy birthday." She kissed Todd chastely on the cheek and didn't look back, grateful the elevator doors opened as soon as she pressed the button.

In the corner of the elevator, out of view of the room, Beth slumped against the wall. As the doors began to slide toward each other, she closed her eyes and let all her nerves out in one big sigh. She was trying not to think of the birthday sex they weren't going to have when one of the waiters grabbed the door.

When Beth saw him, she rearranged her face into a polite smile. "Hi."

"You're going down, right?"

"Um," she said, beginning to feel flustered, wondering if he could read her mind.

The waiter looked confused. "You didn't press the button."

"Oh, right! Yes, I'm going down."

Outside in the cool night air, she realized she didn't have a ride. The restaurant was opening up into the night club and the line was already down the street. She walked to the corner and pulled her phone out of her purse to get an Uber.

"Beth, what are you doing?" Jenna had pulled up right in front of her and was leaning over Danny, yelling out the window of her car. "I thought you were going home with Todd!"

She rushed over to the car and hopped in the backseat. "Can you say that louder? I don't think everyone in line heard you."

"Oops, sorry."

Danny laughed. "Elena scare you off? She's enough to scare anyone."

"Yeah, what happened?" Jenna asked.

"I don't know, Danny. You tell me. You were the one who invited her."

He laughed again. "Sorry about that. Todd didn't tell me you were coming or I wouldn't have. She can be really overbearing since their mom died."

It suddenly all made sense and the irritation Beth had built up for Elena deflated like a popped balloon. She could easily see how Elena took over the role of protecting her little brother and she couldn't blame her. Beth knew all too well how grief changed people.

Back at her house, she tried to brush off the disappointment that clung to her as she shimmied out of the expensive lingerie and into her sweatpants.

"It's just you and me tonight, Homer."

23

Beth was falling asleep when her phone rang. She pulled it off her nightstand without looking at it.

"What did you do, hussy?"

"Who are you calling hussy?" A deep voice cut through her drowsy brain.

"Todd! I thought you were Jenna." She sat up, awake now.

"Apparently. What are you doing?"

"Falling asleep. What are you doing?"

"I'm calling to apologize for my sister. She can be a little…" *Rude? Condescending?* Beth bit her tongue. "Overprotective."

"It's fine, Todd. I get it. She's your sister."

"Yeah, she always thinks that people are trying to take advantage of me."

Beth thought about all the ways she wanted to take advantage of him, or his body at least, but said. "It's fine. Really. Did you have a nice birthday?"

"Yeah. It's not over yet, though," he said, his voice growing husky. The clock on her nightstand read 11:29.

"And what are you going to do with the last 31 minutes?"

"Well, I was hoping to come over and get my birthday present."

"Hmm…" she said, thinking about how much she wanted

to see him, feel him, be with him. She thought about how she wouldn't get to see him again until after Thanksgiving and how long that was going to be. She thought about the lingerie and what she had planned for him. Then she thought about Elena. "What about your sister?"

"What about her?"

"Well, I don't want her to think badly of me."

"I gave her two glasses of wine and she's already asleep. Plus, who cares what she thinks."

Beth bit her lip, trying to decide.

"Come on, it's my birthday," he whispered into her ear. "I can be there in twenty minutes."

"Okay," she said and was climbing out of bed before they even hung up. Standing in front of the bathroom mirror, she yanked and tugged and wriggled into the black lace corset, contorting herself to get it fastened. After carefully unrolling each silky stocking and attaching them to the garters, she looked at herself in the mirror. It was a ridiculous outfit but the boning of the corset cinched her waist, accented her hips, and pushed her breasts up to astonishing heights. Beth's gaze drifted up to her face. *Shit!* She had already taken off her makeup, thrown out her contacts, and piled her hair up in a topknot.

She was digging through her bathroom drawer when there was a knock on her door. *That cannot have been twenty minutes.* But it had taken her quite a while to wrangle the lingerie back on. Homer barked loudly while she swiped on some red lipstick and wrapped herself in a bathrobe. The dog followed close behind as Beth padded out to the front door. She stood on the tiptoes of her stocking covered feet and looked at him through the peephole. He was rocking back and forth running his big hand through his blond hair. Seeing him like that, waiting for her, sent a thrill of excitement down her spine and she watched him for another minute before she finally opened the door.

Todd let out a sigh of relief when he saw her. "I was afraid you'd fallen asleep." Homer spun around him and he reached down, absentmindedly petting the dog.

She shook her head. "Nope." The nearness of him was making her giddy. He grinned down at her and she pulled him inside. "I'm not quite ready for you yet. Do you want something to drink?"

But he was already behind her, wrapping his arms around her. "What do you mean you're not ready?" She turned to face him and gestured at her glasses. "I need to put my contacts in."

"Why? I love the glasses. You look hot."

"Really?"

He nodded. "You were wearing them the first day of class. I thought I was in the wrong classroom because I didn't recognize you. Then I realized you're just a sexy Clark Kent."

She laughed. "Oh my god, you *do* have a teacher fantasy."

"Maybe I do." He grinned and reached for the belt of her robe.

She swatted his hand away. "Not yet." Pushing him toward her bedroom, she added, "It may be your birthday, but I'm in charge." They stood at the foot of her bed and he reached again for her robe. "Nope. No touching."

His eyes lit up with excitement and he dropped his hands to his side. "Yes ma'am."

Beth tried to look serious, biting back a smile as she reached up and began to undo the buttons on his black shirt. When his shirt hung open, she ran her fingertips down his warm, firm chest. He sighed and tried to pull her to him, but she pushed him away hard. "Uh-uh." She poked him in the chest with her index finger. "No touching." An idea occurred to her then as she stared up at him. "Close your eyes." He looked down at her skeptically and his disobedience lit a fire in her. "Close your eyes, Mr. Allman," she said in her most stern teacher voice.

"All right, all right." He raised his hands in surrender and closed his eyes. She opened her closet door, took off the robe, and put a blazer over the corset.

Todd still stood at the foot of her bed, eyes shut. "And keep them closed," she said over her shoulder as she left the room. When she came back a minute later, he opened one eye and looked down at her. Swiftly, she stepped behind him and smacked him on the ass with a ruler.

"Ow," he said, more in surprise than pain.

She stood on tiptoes and hissed in his ear. "I. Said. Eyes. Closed."

"Okay, okay," he laughed. "I just wanted to look at you."

"You'll get to look at me when I *let* you look at me." She ran her hand over his ass, then squeezed it hard. "I'm in charge," she said, surprised by how much she was enjoying this. "Do you understand?"

He nodded and she pulled his shirt off, dropping it on her dresser. Then she ran her nails down his back. He shivered and goosebumps prickled his skin. Still behind him, she snaked her arms around his waist and unbuttoned his pants. Her fingertips dipped under the waistband of his boxers, exploring the trail of soft hair. Then she unzipped the pants and pushed them to the floor. "Step out of your pants," she commanded and he did. Beth let her eyes wander across his broad shoulders to the muscles of his back and waist, down to his firm round... He glanced over his shoulder at her and as fast as a striking snake, she snapped the ruler across his ass, harder this time. "Did I give you permission?" Todd turned back around and shook his head. She walked around to face him and found him grinning, his eyes closed tight.

"Look at me," she said and his eyes flew open. She watched as he took in the blazer, the corset, the stockings. His dark eyes grew wide when he saw the ruler. "Are you okay with this?" She studied his face for any sign of hesitation.

"Absolutely." He grinned down at her.

"Do you need a safe word?"

He shook his head. "No ma'am."

She pressed the end of the ruler into his chest and traced it down to his underwear. "Take these off," she demanded. He bent over and slipped off his boxers, his eyes never leaving her. When he stood naked before her, she allowed her eyes to feast on every inch of him. She stepped forward and ran her fingertips over the scar in his eyebrow, down his cheek, and along his strong jaw.

"Permission to speak," he said.

She looked up at him, taken in by his handsome face, lost for a moment in the depth of his dark eyes. "Permission granted," she finally said.

He leaned down and whispered. "You look unbelievably hot right now."

She smiled and traced one finger around the tip of his cock. He closed his eyes in pleasure and she placed her hand on his chest and pushed him backward. Todd laughed as he fell onto the mattress. She opened the drawer of her nightstand and was about to pull out what she had bought for his birthday but then her eyes fell on TOM. She bit back a smile. He was on his back, arms folded behind his head, watching her with a cocky smile.

"Turn over," she said. It was a struggle but she somehow maintained a straight face.

When he saw what was in her hand, his eyes grew wide and he sat up. "Beth, I, uh… wait…" he stammered.

"What's the matter?" She smiled sweetly at him. "I thought you didn't need a safe word." The look on his face, a mixture of surprise, anxiety, terror, was too much for her and she broke into laughter.

"Oh my god," he said, visibly relaxing. "I thought you." He gestured to TOM with one hand, rubbing his temple with the other. "I mean, I guess if it's something you really want to try maybe someday…"

She laughed and dropped the vibrator back in the drawer. "Nah, I was just messing with you." Then she pulled out two long, velvet, black cords. When he saw them a look, an unspoken memory, passed between them. "Happy birthday," she said. "Now, lie back down." He did what he was told.

Gently but firmly, she wrapped a rope around each of his wrists, knotting them securely. Then she threaded the ropes through the slits on her wooden headboard and tied the two ropes together in a bow. He looked up at his wrists. "You're pretty good at this."

"I was a Girl Scout," Beth said. She had actually learned from watching YouTube videos and practicing a dozen times the day before. "And I didn't give you permission to speak."

He nodded solemnly and she stood at the foot of the bed to admire her own handiwork. Todd Allman, He-man himself, was naked on her bed tied securely to her headboard. She was tempted to get her camera but settled for a mental picture, taking in the landscape of his beautiful body. He watched her watching him, his erection between them. Beth put the ruler between her teeth and pushed his legs apart. Then she climbed onto the bed, kneeling between his legs, and took off her blazer. She let him watch her as she traced a path with the ruler, up the inside of his thigh. He twitched but continued to stare at her.

Bending down on all fours, she opened her mouth and followed the same path with her tongue. Then she did the same to his other thigh. Slowly, she made her way to the crease where the muscles of his torso met his leg, her cheek brushing the side of his cock. As she moved to the other side, her breasts pressed into his erection and he gasped. She stopped and smiled up at him, then she climbed gingerly over his erection and straddling his chest, she took his face in her hands. When she just barely brushed her lips across his, he lifted his head for more, but she pulled away. She leaned forward again, softly pressing her lips to his, letting just the tip of her tongue graze his bottom lip before pulling back. He groaned and tugged at the ropes. The third time she kissed him, she did it hard and fast, pressing her lips forcefully onto his, pushing her tongue into his mouth. He kissed her back hungrily, still pulling at the ropes, rocking his hips up so she could feel his erection beneath her. She ground into him and moved in rhythm with his rocking. When she broke away, he was panting.

As Beth bent over him again, his greedy mouth desperate for hers, she turned his head to the side and kissed his cheek instead. He groaned. She planted soft kisses along his jaw, his chin down his neck, nipping gently with her teeth. She kissed his shoulder and down his chest, circling each of his nipples with her tongue. And then she kissed her way down the center of his stomach, letting his soft blond hair tickle her tongue. When she got to his erection, she looked up at him through her dark frames, the tip of her tongue barely touching the tip of his penis.

"Beth," he whispered.

She narrowed her eyes at him. "Shhhh. I didn't give you permission to speak." He looked like he was about to say more. "If you're not good, I won't let you watch." Then, very deliberately, she ran her tongue from the base of his penis to the tip. Todd moaned softly and her body began to tingle all over. She did it again, stopping short of the tip, watching him watch her. The power she had over him was intoxicating. The third time, she didn't stop. She took him into her mouth, as much of him as would fit, and he moaned louder. His pleasure, her control, were both so exciting that she found herself getting wetter as he got harder.

Beth wrapped her hand around him, squeezing him as she circled the tip of his penis with her tongue again and again. He twitched beneath her, breathing harder. She used her other hand to gently cup him while taking him back into her mouth. He was gasping now but she kept squeezing and sucking and stroking. It was a turn on, handling him like this, and her panties were damp. Todd trembled beneath her but she kept going.

"Beth," he panted, a plea, a warning. She paused to meet his eyes and considered for just a moment letting him finish on her chest. Even though she had started this game as a present for *his* birthday, she found that she wanted him in her mouth. She couldn't get enough. So she licked every inch of him with her tongue and then opened her mouth wide and took him in, all of him.

The headboard creaked as he strained against the binds. "Oh my god," he cried out as she finished him. He shuddered beneath her for a while and when he finally looked back down, she was smiling. He sighed deeply and she made her way up his chest until she was straddling him on all fours. She kissed his chest and neck, then whispered in his ear, "You make me so wet." Her panties were completely soaked through.

"Show me," he said, his voice a husky whisper and she pressed her damp, swollen crotch into his stomach. He moaned happily.

She looked down at him. "You like that?" It was more of a statement than question but he nodded emphatically. "You want to feel that?" He nodded again so she reached her hand between her legs. Todd watched her with wide eyes and bit his bottom lip. Pulling her panties to the side, she slid a finger between her slick lips. She was so turned on that her own touch made her eyelids flutter and sent her eyes rolling up into her head.

"Give it to me," he said, his breath still short. Beth took her wet finger and traced each of his nipples with it, watching them stiffen under her touch. "More," he said. She raised an eyebrow and looked down at him. He bit his lip again, adding softly, "Please."

She reached back between her legs and stroked herself with two fingers. When she held up her hand, he smiled at her and nodded. Beth tentatively raised her fingers to his mouth. He leaned his head forward and she watched in awe as he slowly rubbed his bottom lip along her fingertips. It was the slightest movement, the faintest touch, but it felt like he was teasing every nerve in her body. When Todd dipped his chin, closed his eyes, and took her fingers into his mouth, she gasped. His warm tongue stroked her fingers gently and as he let them slip from his mouth, he opened his eyes and smiled up at her.

Beth watched how his face transformed as she slid her fingers back between her legs. He wanted to see her, he wanted to watch her. And she wanted to show him. She pulled at her panties, only then realizing she had put them on under the garters, not over them, so she opened the drawer to her nightstand and got out a pair of cuticle scissors. Todd watched as she snipped the sides of the skimpy black thong and threw the wet panties to the floor. Then she sat on the bed next to him, one stocking clad leg over his chest, the other stretched up toward his bound arm. His broad chest heaved in anticipation. She leaned back, propping herself up with her arm and rolled her hips forward, showing herself to him. He was still biting his lip, mesmerized. Slowly, she slid her hand over her breasts, down her corseted stomach and onto her thigh. His eyes followed her hand. When her fingers hovered over her pubic bone he lifted his head to get a better view, pulling at his binds. She lowered two fingers, parting her damp, swollen lips and stroked gently. The usual tingling sensation was magnified exponentially under Todd's gaze and her legs began to quiver.

"I want you," he whispered.

"Not yet." Beth rubbed his growing erection with her silky foot and continued to move her fingers between her legs. He closed his eyes and moaned.

When he opened them, she saw new determination in his face. "Come here." She raised an eyebrow and kept stroking them both. "Please," he said firmly. She didn't move. "Please," he said again, more tentatively. She still didn't move. "Beth, please." His voice was soft with supplication.

"Tell me what you want." She stared him down.

"I want you."

"Where?" She demanded without stopping her slow, rhythmic movements.

"Here," he said, lifting his chin and licking his full bottom lip.

Beth moved deftly atop him, pausing to grind into his erection, then climbing up his body to hover above his face. Todd strained against the ropes, lifting his head as she tentatively lowered herself to his mouth. She was already so turned on that when they touched, it felt like his tongue was everywhere and wave after wave of ecstasy flooded her body. She grabbed the headboard, desperately trying to hold off her impending orgasm, to make it last just a little bit longer. But he flicked and sucked hungrily, her body trembling above him until she was no longer in control. She cried out his name, bucking and shuddering as the sensations tore through her.

When she opened her eyes, she was on her knees, clutching the headboard. He smiled up at her from between her legs.

Gingerly, her breath still rapid, she collapsed on his chest. He leaned his head forward and kissed the top of her head.

"I think you can untie me now," he said and she could hear the cocky smile in his voice.

"I don't think so," Beth said to his chest, reaching down to let her fingertips rest on his erection. He shivered and she slid down his chest until the folds of her damp flesh pressed against his cock. "We're not done yet." Todd moaned as she rocked up and down him without letting him inside her. She ran her fingertips down the sides of his chest and he twitched and jerked. Slowly, more slowly than she would have thought possible, she lowered herself onto the tip of his cock but as soon as he thrust his hips up to meet her, she pulled away. Again she lowered herself and again she pulled away. He yanked at his binds in helpless frustration. She smiled down at him and lowered herself again, this time just grazing the tip before pulling away.

"Gahh!" He threw his head back onto the pillow and she began to laugh.

"Jedediah Huckleberry did you just snarl at me?" He glared at her and she wiped her thumb across his mouth then kissed him. But he was still frowning. "What's the matter?"

"I just want to touch you," he pleaded.

She kissed him again. "Soon." Then she lowered herself onto the tip of him. And back up. Then a little further. And back up again. Each time taking in a little more of him before pulling away. Finally, with agonizing slowness, Beth lowered herself all the way down. Todd let out a deep sigh and for a moment, she didn't move. She just felt him, how he filled her. She took her glasses off and put them on the nightstand. Then pressing her hands into his chest, she began rhythmically rocking back and forth. He was matching her tempo and their hips danced together, unhurriedly. She reached up and tugged at the elastic, her hair falling past her shoulders. They moved together until she finally leaned forward and pulled at the bow that held the two ropes together, freeing Todd's hands. Immediately, he took her face into his hands, kissing her feverishly. Then, while still rocking beneath her, he touched her everywhere, her ass, her waist, her back, running his hands up into her hair. It was as if he had been in a drought and she was his water. Greedily, he tugged at the bustier undoing the front clips, freeing her breasts so his big hands could explore them. She continued to move atop him, her breath getting more shallow.

"I'm so close," she whispered, a hot ecstasy sweeping over her body as he moved in and out of her. Todd pressed one hand into her lower back, wound the other into the hair at the nape of her neck and held her to him.

"Me too," he breathed. They moved faster and faster and Beth began to lose control. Everything was a blur as the familiar pulses grew and swelled until they crashed over her, sweeping her away. She and Todd cried out in unison as they both began to shake.

They collapsed together, panting, his arms still around her. She didn't know she had fallen asleep until she felt him stir, slowly untangling himself. She heard him find his jeans and put them on and she thought about getting up to walk him out and kiss him goodbye. But she couldn't move, her eyes too heavy with sleep, her body too exhausted and sated. So he didn't know that when he bent down and kissed her forehead, she wasn't quite asleep.

"I love you," he whispered. And then he was gone.

The next morning she lingered in bed, wrapped in sheets that smelled of Todd. When she finally leaned over to check her phone, there were two texts from Jenna. The first read "good thing you didn't leave with him." The second was just a link which she followed to a webpage with the headline "Todd Allman Leaves Meat Shed with Mystery Woman." Underneath were several pictures of Todd and Elena leaving the back entrance and trying to get into the car. She laughed to herself that the stupid gossip site didn't even realize it was his sister. Then the reality of what had almost happened sank in. *That could have been me.* Beth's stomach turned. *Shit! That almost was me!*

24

She checked her teeth in the rearview mirror to make sure they were free of lipstick. Though they emailed occasionally, she hadn't actually seen Peter since she moved to Los Angeles. She didn't know why she was so nervous. It was Peter, after all. Peter who had seen her at her worst, puffy-faced from crying, overweight with that terrible haircut she had gotten after Jeremy's funeral. It was as if back then she was doing everything in her power to not be seen by anyone. Peter had seen her then and she wanted him to see her now—the improved version.

She walked into the bar area of the restaurant, dark and masculine in woods and leathers. Though his back was to her, she picked him out right away. Beth knew him, the shape of his head, the set of his shoulders, the trim hairline along the back of his neck. She felt something she couldn't articulate— *excitement? relief? love?*—and she had to stop herself from running to him. He was looking at his phone and didn't notice her, so she slid into the seat next to him and motioned to the bartender.

"What can I get you?" he asked.

"I'd love an old fashioned." At the sound of her voice, Peter looked up.

"Beth?" He stood and gave her a big warm hug. "Wow, I almost didn't recognize you." Holding her hand in his, he looked her up and down. "California agrees with you, sweetheart. You look incredible."

"Thank you. You're looking pretty good yourself." And he was. His salt and pepper hair was freshly cut and maybe just a bit saltier than the last time she'd seen him. He looked relaxed and tanned and happy, if predictable in his blue blazer and khaki pants— what Beth had always thought of as the uniform of the well-to-do Charleston man. Two fingers of scotch sat in front of him on the bar.

The bartender set the drink in front of her and Peter raised one thick, dark eyebrow.

"When did you start drinking whiskey?"

"A wise man once told me that you should drink dark liquors in the winter."

He smiled at her, the corners of his blue eyes crinkling. "That's right. And clear in the summer."

She held up her glass. "To old friends?"

"And to young ones," he nodded to her with a grin and they clinked glasses.

"So, your email was pretty vague. What brings you to LA?"

He told her about the lecture he was giving at UCLA Medical School. "I was hesitant at first with the holidays next week but, to be honest, I really wanted to see you. And here you are." He swirled the scotch in his glass. "I have to say, I had my doubts about you in Los Angeles. Tell me, are you as happy as you look?"

She beamed at him. "I think so. It doesn't feel like home yet but there are parts of it that are becoming comfortable." Unbidden, an image of sitting with Todd in his kitchen in front of the fireplace made her breath catch in her throat. Feeling Peter's eyes on her, she tried to cover it with a soft cough.

"Excuse me," she said and took a sip of her drink. When she put the glass back down on the bar, he covered her hand with his own. She looked at it for a moment, the familiar way the black hair crept out from under his watch band. Then she met his eyes.

"You okay?"

"Yes," she said. "Just a bit of a tickle in my throat." She smiled at him reassuringly but he didn't move his hand. He continued to look at her.

"I've missed you," he said simply. His openness caught her off guard and she felt a stinging behind her eyes. She swallowed, forcing herself to stay composed. *Why am I so emotional?*

"I've missed you, too," she said, putting her other hand on his and then taking it back to dab under her eyes. "I guess I didn't realize how much until just now." Before they could say more, the hostess came to get them. He paid for their drinks and she let him, knowing from years of experience that he would never let her pay. She thanked him and with a firm hand at the small of her back, Peter guided her through the restaurant and pulled out her chair. When she thanked him again, he leaned over and whispered "you're welcome" in her ear, notes of his classic, familiar cologne lingering after him.

The waiter came to give them the wine list and Peter waited until he left to ask, "So, who is it?"

She raised her glass to her lips to hide her grin. Once she felt composed she said. "Who is what?"

He shook his head. "Beth, who is making you glow? You're positively radiant."

She shrugged in a way she hoped was nonchalant. "I'm just happy."

"I haven't seen you like this since Spain."

Beth sighed with nostalgia. "Ah, Spain. That was such a nice trip, wasn't it?"

"It was," Peter agreed and Beth was glad to have changed the subject. The trip to Spain had been for her birthday and she often wondered if that had been the beginning of the end for them. When she protested the extravagance of the gift, he had convinced her that it was she who would be doing him the favor because he had always wanted to go but was terrible at Spanish. Beth was happy to act as his interpreter, especially when the man at their hotel, assuming Peter was her father and not her lover, had made a pass at her. Though she was quick to play off the exchange as something else, she always suspected that Peter had understood perfectly. In the end, the trip had not been the leap forward in their relationship that she thought it would be.

When the waiter returned, Peter ordered a bottle of wine.

"But I can't," she protested. "I'm driving."

"I haven't seen you in years. Enjoy yourself. I'll get you a cab."

While they ate, they traded stories, occasionally wandering back to their shared moments. Beth was feeling so comfortable that she never even noticed the dessert menu until the waiter returned to take their order. Peter smiled and ordered the chocolate torte and two glasses of expensive Spanish brandy.

"Peter, I really shouldn't."

"But you like this brandy. It's the same one we had at that little restaurant in Majorca."

"But now I really can't drive."

"Sweetheart, I wouldn't let you drive anyway. I told you, I'll get you a cab." He paused and then watching her intently added, "Unless of course you'd like to stay with me this evening."

"Um." She bit her lip and he smiled patiently.

"I didn't think so." He folded his hands atop the table and

leaned toward her. "Now, tell me. Who is the unbelievably lucky man?"

So she told him about Todd, from the convenience store to the classroom to the birthday party. "I know it can't go anywhere so I'm trying to just have fun. I mean, there can't possibly be a future there, he's practically a child." She trailed off, staring into her brandy.

Peter laughed, a deep joyful sound and she looked up at him. His eyes were shining in delight. "Oh the irony."

"What?"

"Beth, you're the one that showed me that age has no bearing. I never thought I'd be *that* guy, an old man dating a woman nearly half his age, but we worked, for a while anyway. I wouldn't change any of that."

"You're not that old. And I would never, ever, want to change our relationship either. You meant the world to me, Peter. You still do." She put her hand on his and smiled at him. "But this guy, this *kid* really, he's only 25."

"Sweetheart, you were only a little older than that when we met. And I was much older than you are now. I'm surprised that you of all people have such a double standard about this." He gave her a knowing smile.

"Touché," she said frowning. "But what about my job? How is that ever going to work?"

Peter shrugged. "These things have a way of working themselves out. If he makes you happy, be with him."

Beth took a sip of brandy, realizing for the first time that Peter had ordered the wine and the brandy knowing that it would make her open up. She looked from the glass in her hand to his face, a silent accusation. "You knew exactly what you were doing."

His eyes twinkled merrily. "Some things never change, love."

He hailed her a cab, kissed her cheek, and promised to pick her up in his rental car the next day.

The next morning before he took her to her truck, they went to breakfast. Over omelets he told her again that she should follow her heart. She was surprised to feel so relieved about it. Beth wanted to be with Todd and for whatever reason, Peter's encouragement gave her permission to admit that to herself. After breakfast, he dropped her at her truck with a long, tight hug and a chaste kiss.

"Don't be a stranger," he murmured into her hair.

25

Todd had texted her from the airport and she barely had time to shower before there was a knock on her door. Homer was beside himself barking and whining but Todd went right for Beth. It felt as if her whole body sighed in his embrace. He kissed her deeply, breaking away only to hold her closer, inhaling the coconut scent of her shampoo and murmuring, "I've missed you, I've missed you, I've missed you."

"I've missed you, too," she said and tried to pull away but he held her tighter until Homer had just about given up on getting any attention. Finally, he let her go and stooped to scratch the grateful dog behind his ears. Beth watched him, unable to stop smiling. His hair had been trimmed and though it was still longish, it was neater, more sophisticated. He looked older than he had the week before and better than she remembered. The nearness of him made her pulse quicken and her body hum.

When he finished with the dog, she took his hand and wordlessly led him to her bedroom. By the soft candlelight, they slowly undressed each other fighting an urgency fueled by their separation. Once they were naked, on their sides, they faced each other kissing softly. Todd stared at her, his eyes mapping her face. She smiled as he traced her skin with his fingertip, brushing past her eyebrow, down her cheek, landing in her dimple. He drew her to him so they were skin to skin, nose to nose, mouth to mouth. When she could wait no longer, she wrapped her leg around his waist and pulled him onto her, into her. Beth tried to feel every place where their skin met. Overwhelmed by the sensation, she closed her eyes.

"Look at me, Beth," he whispered. When she did, he softly kissed her forehead and each eyebrow and the tip of her nose and her chin and finally her mouth. Then his dark eyes were locked onto hers as he moved slowly in and out, her body responding in tandem. His focus was too much for her and she turned her head to break the connection. With one hand, he brought her face back to him, the full force of his intensity pouring over her. She gasped as the heat built between them. Again she felt too much and tried to turn her face, but he held it steady. "I love you," he said simply. Before she could respond he covered her mouth with his and quickened his pace. They moved, clasped together until her climax shook them, her mouth pulling from his to cry out. His body followed and gently, he lowered his chest onto hers and sighed. She ran her hands over his shoulders and across his back as he shifted to rest his head on her chest. *He loves me.* A pleasant warmth spread through her at the thought. Beth was wondering if she should say it back when she heard his even breathing. He was already asleep.

Later, they sat in bed, a bowl of fresh pineapple between them, and he told her about his Thanksgiving. "It was good. We had a bunch of family come and my dad and I cooked." He sighed and his face became serious. "It's just still so weird without my mom."

"How could it not be? That must be really hard." Beth said, putting a hand on his arm.

"I keep thinking each year will be better. That it will be less painful. And in some ways is. But then something happens or someone says something and I feel like it was just yesterday."

"I know what you mean," she said. "Tell me about your mom. What was she like?"

"My mom? She was smart and kind of reserved but she was also really, really funny. She could always make my dad laugh. But not like, goofy funny. She had this dry sense of humor, you know? Really witty. There was this one time she said something when my dad was drinking a beer and it made him laugh so hard beer came out of his nose."

"Oh no!" Beth laughed.

"Dad was laughing and choking and tears were running down his face. And we were all laughing at him. Except Mom. She just had this little smirk, kind of a 'who me?' face. I wish I could remember what she said. All I remember is her face. I asked Dad about it once, but he said he forgot. He doesn't like to talk about her much."

She couldn't imagine having had kids with Jeremy and then losing him. "Maybe it's too painful for him?"

"Yeah, I guess. I just think it makes it harder though. I feel better when I remember her and talk about her. It's like it keeps her alive. I'm not sure hiding from pain makes anything better."

"Maybe you're right. I don't talk about Jeremy much. I just got so tired of the pity people gave me. And if it wasn't pity, it was people saying stupid things like 'at least you're young, you can remarry,' as if that somehow made it better."

"Yeah, that's bullshit. Pain is pain." Todd took her hand in his and kissed it. "Beth, you can talk to me about Jeremy any time you want. You know that, right?"

She smiled, swallowed the lump in her throat, then told him about Jeremy.

26

She was 26 years old. And she was living at home. Again. *It's so hot. Why is it always so hot in Florida? It's December!* Beth was on her childhood bed staring up the tiny white ceiling fan covered in glow-in-the-dark stars. She turned her head and began to pick at the place on the wall where she had ripped down her old posters. Her cell phone rang but before she could even say hello, Jenna interrupted her.

"You have to come. I'm not going without you."

"But I don't care about seeing any of those people."

"What do you mean? They're our friends from high school."

Beth rolled her eyes as she peeled a large section of yellow paint satisfyingly away from the wall. "They're not my friends. I wasn't popular like you, Jenna."

"Stop it. Of course they're your friends."

"No really, I'm pretty sure most people we went to high school with only know me as Jenna's friend. And you know what happens when people see each other. It's all 'what do you do?' and 'who are you seeing?' What am I supposed to say to that? Uh, well, I did live in New York and work for a big publishing company but the economy took a dump and now I'm living with my mom and currently seeing Johnny Depp… on my posters from middle school."

"Who cares? The economy isn't your fault, Beth."

"That's easy for you to say, Jen. You live in LA with your *fee-AHN-say*."

"All of this is only temporary. Plus, if you don't care about those people, why do you care what they think?"

Beth ignored her point. "I shouldn't be spending any money on drinks anyway."

"I'll buy your drinks if you come."

Beth sighed. "Fine. But just one drink. And you have to tell my mom I'm not gonna be watching Jeopardy with her."

Crackers was the consummate dive bar. Like most dive bars in most small towns, it was full of locals and around the holidays, former locals. In the five minutes since she arrived, Beth had spotted at least a eight people she had gone to high school with, none of whom she had any interest in talking to.

She leaned on the bar which was covered in different kinds of crackers that had been shellacked over like prehistoric fossils trapped in amber. It just made the bar look like it was covered in soggy snack foods.

"Hey Lou," Beth said. "Can I get a beer?"

Lou was a lanky guy with long, thin hair who looked like he might have been a roadie for some long-forgotten rock band. He looked at her suspiciously, rubbing his goatee. "Sure. Can I see some ID?"

"Do you seriously not recognize me? I grew up three houses down from you."

Lou squinted at her, then began to smile. "Little Beth Brennan? Is that you? Damn girl, you have grown the hell up, haven't you?" He grinned appreciatively and leaned over the bar to give her an awkward hug.

Beth laughed and they talked for a bit about her mom and the other neighbors on their street. Then, beer in hand, she walked to the back of the bar and slid into a wooden booth to wait for Jenna. The table was sticky and scratched and the benches were covered in graffiti of familiar-sounding names. *Some things never change.* Beth slipped her phone out of her pocket to see if Jenna had texted her.

"Is this seat taken?" a male voice asked.

Without looking up from her phone, she said, "Yeah, I'm waiting for a friend."

"Jenna Duncan? I don't think she'll mind."

She glanced up, her gaze falling upon familiar brown eyes as he slid into the booth across from her. "Hi Beth." For a moment, she said nothing, waiting for her heart to start beating again. She hadn't seen him since graduation and his dark eyes and his easy smile brought her right back. That smile, his smile, was the one she had lived and breathed for every day of high school. She forced her face into something resembling indifference and looked him over. He looked good. His lanky frame had filled out a lot, his black hair was buzzed military short, and he had finally grown into his ears.

"Hi Jeremy," she said cooly in an effort to hide her agitation. Her stomach flip-flopped. It had been 8 years and she was furious with her body for responding to him like she had in high school. *It's just habit. Calm down.*

He held his beer out to toast hers. "To old friends?"

"I didn't realize we were," she said but picked up her beer and tapped his.

"Were what?"

"Old friends."

"Come on B.B., if it weren't for you, I wouldn't have passed English, like every single year of high school."

"Exactly," Beth said. When he had given her that nickname freshman year, it had cemented her feelings for him. It surprised her how much hearing it now still stung.

"What do you mean?"

She was so raw from losing her job and moving home that she couldn't help herself. His casual dismissal of what had happened, of eight years of silence irked her and before she could bite it back, she snapped, "I mean the only time we were friends was when you needed help with English."

He looked confused, his bright smile fading. "What are you talking about? You came over to my house all the time. My mom still asks about you."

"Never mind." Beth felt like an idiot for still being so mad at him. She willed herself to let it go and tried to get back to coolly detached. It was all so long ago, that night before graduation.

Beth had been at Jenna's hanging out, making lists of all the things they wanted to do now that they were done with high school. The piece of paper felt like a magic spell. She had folded it up and was holding it reverently as she walked out to her car when Jeremy called to her. He lived in the house across the street from Jenna's. When she told him what they had been doing, he grabbed the paper from her and stood holding her secrets over his head, teasing her like a little boy. Panicked that he would read them and know all her silly dreams, she came at him. Before she knew what was happening, he was kissing her. She had been waiting for that moment for four years. Her heart felt like it was going to explode from joy. That night, she drove home in a daze, plans swirling in her head. Maybe she should defer college for a semester. Then she could transfer to his school so they could be together. It was a childish fantasy really, but she couldn't help it. She had loved Jeremy Grant from the first moment she saw him. So the next night, at Denny Jefferson's graduation party when he pretended nothing had happened, even going to the point of avoiding her, it crushed her like nothing ever had before.

Jeremy sighed, looking down at the table before meeting her eyes. "Listen, I'm really sorry, Beth. I've felt bad about that night for years." She watched as he squirmed and fidgeted with the large Army ring on his left hand. Jenna had told Beth that he had joined the service after college. She pretended that she didn't really care but every night she prayed for him.

"I guess I just don't understand why you want to be seen with me now. I don't want to cramp your style." She said softly, her fiery temper already burning out but her heart still racing.

"Well," he sighed again. "It was really great to see you." As he got up from the booth, she put her hand out to stop him when they heard Jenna's voice cry out.

"Jeremy Grant! Oh my god! Look at your hair." Jenna squealed and jumped on him, her long blond hair swishing as he picked her up in a hug. When he finally put her down, she grabbed his hand. "You better not be leaving! I just got here so unless you're getting me a drink, you need to sit back down."

"Uh, I'm not sure." He glanced at Beth nervously. "I think Beth and I are all caught up."

Jenna glared at her. "Beth Brennan, are you still pissed about Denny Jefferson's graduation party? Don't you go scaring Jeremy off. No one has seen him in years!"

Beth blushed, feeling even more ridiculous for carrying such a grudge but heartbreak like that is hard to forget. "Of course he can stay," she said not meeting his eye. "I'm going to get another beer." As she slid out of the booth, Jeremy stopped her.

"If I buy you a beer, will you forgive me?" The grin was back but she could see he was still nervous and it gave her a little thrill.

Beth raised an eyebrow. She was going to milk this. "A beer?"

He laughed in relief. "Okay, I have your drinks for the rest of the night. How about that?"

"Fine," she shrugged. "Knock yourself out. But fair warning, I can hold my booze now."

"Bring it." Jeremy grinned down at her with that big bright smile and suddenly the tension was gone. "What can I get you, Jenna? The same?"

Jenna nodded and slid into the booth across from Beth. "Were you just trying to blow him off? What is wrong with you? It looks like I got here just in time."

"Whatever, Jenna. He tried to talk to me like we were old friends and nothing ever happened. I hate when people are so fake. That's why I never come here."

"Beth, it was high school. We all make mistakes in high school."

"I know." She sighed. "It just surprised the shit out of me how much it still hurt. But I'm fine. Really."

Jenna grabbed her hand. "I'm sorry. I shouldn't give you a hard time. I just love you both so much. I don't want there to be any hard feelings."

Jeremy came back from the bar and handed them beers then sat down next to Beth. They talked for hours, catching up, reminiscing, and ribbing each other like only old friends can. True to his word, Jeremy kept Beth in beer and she was racking up a pretty hefty buzz when the Karaoke started.

"Well, that's my cue to leave," Jenna said. They stood up, just as Jeremy came back to the table.

"You're not leaving are you?"

Jenna nodded, yawning. "Sorry, but I'm not drunk enough to listen to Karaoke."

"Yeah, I should probably go, too," Beth agreed.

"But I just got you another beer. You're not going to let me get off that cheaply are you?"

"Okay, one more. But I have to go to the bathroom."

"Good idea, I'll join you," Jenna said.

They sat in stalls next to each other in the cramped bathroom of Crackers. The plywood doors covered in graffiti hung askew on their frames.

"Blech! I never noticed how gross this bathroom was before."

"It's probably the first time you've been in here sober." Beth was smiling with her eyes closed as she peed, a sure sign she was a little drunk. As they washed their hands, Jenna watched Beth in the mirror.

"What?"

"I think Jeremy likes you," she said.

"Why? Because he's buying me beer? He's just doing that because I made him feel like a dick." Beth shook the water off her hands and added, a little slur in her voice, "Because he *was* a dick."

"He's been flirting with you all night."

"Psshha." Beth clumsily wiped her wet hands on her jeans.

Jenna shrugged. "I can see the two of you together."

"Psshha," Beth said again and pushed the bathroom door open with her butt.

"Ah, there you are! This song is for my dear friend BB." Beth looked up when she heard the nickname. "I've missed you!"

The music started and Beth's mouth dropped open. Jenna shouted over the music, "I told you."

Beth wrinkled her nose. "Kiss?" But she was too stunned to do anything except watch from the back of the bar as Jeremy finished the song. Most of the patrons knew Jeremy and they clapped and hooted their approval.

"What the hell?" She mouthed to Jenna but her friend was just laughing and shaking her head. Beth looked back at Jeremy who was still standing on the tiny raised platform that acted as a stage. "You're crazy!" She shouted at him over the noise.

Jenna left but when Lou announced that it was last call, Jeremy and Beth convinced him to illegally sell them a six-pack that they took down to the beach. Wrapped in a blanket from Jeremy's truck, they talked until the sun peaked up over the ocean. Then he took her hand and they walked to the diner for breakfast.

* * *

With both of them back at home for the holidays, they were like teenagers sneaking around, trying to find places to be alone together. There were more than a few awkward moments in his truck. One time, they were interrupted by a patrolling officer who turned out to be one of Jeremy's high school football teammates. Beth had blushed furiously trying to figure out how to surreptitiously button her pants while the guys reminisced about their glory days.

They spent most of his leave together. Being with him was better than she had even imagined as a hormone-soaked teenager. It was natural and magical, comfortable and exciting. It was everything. For Beth, it was like living the fantasy she had imagined her freshman year of high school. And because it felt so much like a fantasy, part of her didn't trust that it was real. So when on Christmas day he gave her a ring-shaped box, she flipped out and refused to open it.

"Jeremy, this is nuts. I can't accept this."

He laughed. "You don't even know what it is."

She shook her head stubbornly. "I don't want to know what it is. I just know it's too soon."

Unfazed, he kissed her. "Fine, I'll save it for when you are ready. Take your time BB, but you aren't getting rid of me."

"I don't want to get rid of you. But the only ring I want is a donut."

"Like ever?"

She shrugged. "It seems like such a waste of money. I'd rather use the money for something we can both enjoy. Like a boat or something."

Jeremy laughed. "You want an engagement boat?"

"Well, yeah. Or a downpayment on a boat. A small one."

"I'll get you an engagement boat. We can call it the SS BB."

* * *

On the second to last day of his leave, they lay side by side in the hammock in her backyard. Their intertwined hands looked as she always imagined they would, the darkness of his fingers making hers look all the more pale. His large thumb gently stroked hers.

"Come back to North Carolina with me. Move in with me," he whispered into her hair.

"What?!" She struggled to sit up and look at him causing the hammock to sway, then fell awkwardly back onto his chest, balancing her forearms on his torso.

"Why are you so surprised?" He looked up at her, his dark lashes nearly closed against the afternoon sun.

"You just asked me to move in with you!"

He tucked a stray strand of hair behind her ear. "BB, you know I got you a ring for Christmas. Did you think I wanted to marry you and *not* live with you?"

She opened her mouth and closed it. Then opened it again. "I guess I thought you were joking."

"Joking?" He sounded genuinely surprised. "Beth," he opened his eyes and stared into hers. "I really do want to marry you. I've never felt like this about anyone else."

She didn't know what to say. She had loved him all through

high school, but had written him off for good after graduation night. The last weeks, though. They had been really... *Is 'magical' too corny?* she wondered.

"I, uh. I don't know what to say."

He grinned. "Say yes." He pulled her toward him for a gentle kiss. "Please?"

"I can't," she sputtered, panic rising in her chest. "I can't just move in with you, Jeremy. We've been hanging out for what, two weeks? And now you want me to up and move with you to North Carolina? I can't do that. We barely even know each other."

"What do you mean we barely know each other?" His face had turned serious. "I've known you since you were fourteen. So what that we're missing a few years in the middle?"

"Jeremy, we aren't just missing a few years. We haven't seen each other for almost a decade! I'm not the same person I used to be. I'm not going to just follow you around like I did in high school. I have a life. I have a career." Beth stopped, horrified to realize that she no longer had either.

He shifted under her and dug a neatly folded piece of paper out of his pocket.

"What is that?" she asked, as he handed it to her. When she saw her own handwriting she gasped. "Oh my god, where did you get this?"

"I found it in the driveway the morning after I kissed you. I gotta be honest BB, it freaked me out. That's why I blew you off at the party."

Beth's eyes welled with tears as she read over the dreams of her 17 year old self.

"You've graduated from college, you've lived in New York," he said, reading down her list. "That leaves 'write a book' and..."

"Marry my soulmate," she whispered, tracing her finger

over the heart she had drawn around his name.

"I don't know how you knew it was me. But you were right. I'm sorry it's taken me so long to catch up."

The tears were spilling over her cheeks now. She was afraid if she tried to speak only a sob would come out.

"Just think about it," he said, wrapping his arms around her before she could bolt. "You could live with me while you write your book. We don't have to get married right away if it feels too soon. I just want to be with you."

Beth really had no idea what to do next. She figured she would just keep applying for jobs in publishing in New York until she got one. Then she would move back to the city and pick up where she left off. Now she wasn't sure that that life made sense anymore. Why go back now? Without a job and with Jenna in Los Angeles, what was there really to go back to?

They lay like that for a long time, Beth's head on Jeremy's chest, letting herself be soothed by the rhythm of his breath. After a while, he said softly, "Why don't you just come back with me for New Year's? You can see what you think. Like a trial run."

She planned to only stay through the holiday but with Jeremy, everything felt like home—the best, brightest, happiest version of home. On New Year's Eve, he made dinner and they ate on the floor in front of the tiny fireplace of his rental house. Cautiously, Jeremy brought up her staying. "BB just hear me out for a second. Maybe the whole reason you got laid off is because you're supposed to be writing. And what better place is there for you to write than here? There's nothing to distract you."

Beth grinned, "Except you."

He kissed her. "Except me. But even I have to go to work sometimes." The kissing got more intense until Jeremy pushed her away, still eager to make his point. "Come up here. Live with me. Write your book. Then when I get out next year, we can move wherever you want. Anywhere. *I'll* follow you."

She hadn't quite decided to move in with him, but she had no plans to go home either. "And how exactly would I contribute? I'm a proud, independent woman. I can't just take charity from you, Jeremy Grant."

He pulled her on top of him. "I can think of a few ways you can earn your keep, woman." There in front of the fire, they melted in to each other. Later, when he asked her again, "Will you stay?" she nodded. When she would think of him and remember his face, it would often be that night that would come to her. She had never seen him look happier.

A month later, he got his deployment orders.

"If something happens to me, I want to make sure that you're taken care of," he had said. "That you have insurance, that you have benefits. That you can make decisions on my behalf." She couldn't argue.

They were married by a justice of the peace four days before he shipped out to Afghanistan. They decided not to tell anyone, planning to get officially engaged and have a real wedding when he returned. After the three minute ceremony, they went to the donut shop and he bought her the only ring she'd ever wanted. Then they went to the local animal shelter and adopted a puppy to keep her company while he was gone. The puppy's first crime was stealing an unattended donut, which earned him the name Homer.

She didn't cry when he left. It was all too unreal. The shock of finding herself the wife of a deployed soldier less than three months after Jeremy Grant had walked back into her life took her weeks to adjust to. It wasn't until after hanging up at the end of their first phone call, that Beth sat down at their little, yellow kitchen table and allowed herself to cry.

At first, she tried to spend all of her time writing but the space without Jeremy was too big to fill. To stay busy, she took a part-time job at the community college. Teaching came naturally to her and she fell in love with it.

Nine months and a complete rough draft later, she anxiously stood with other military families at the arrivals gate. Many of them held signs. She held a bag of donuts. Her heart pounded so hard and fast that it felt like it was going to come right out of her chest. She hadn't known it was possible to miss someone the way she missed him. Some nights she felt a physical ache from his absence. But underneath her excitement lay a tiny kernel of doubt- *what if he's different? What if he thinks marrying me was a mistake? What if marrying him was a mistake?*

She saw him before he could find her face in the crowd. Any doubts she had about their reunion, their future, vanished when their eyes met. When Beth had imagined that moment, she had always thought she would run to him. That she would leap into his arms and he would swing her around like in the movies. But there he was, 30 feet from her and she was trembling so badly that she didn't trust herself to walk. As he made his way to her, she dropped the bag of donuts and opened her arms. Then he was holding her and she felt like she could breathe again for the first time since he left.

"Oh my god. Oh my god." She didn't know when she had started crying but Jeremy held her face in his hands and wiped her tears away. He kissed her and looked at her and kissed her again, like he wasn't sure which he wanted to do more. That made her cry even harder, all of her joy and relief spilling down her cheeks.

"Hey, it's okay. I'm back. I'm here." He pulled her to his chest, squeezing her tightly. "It's okay," he said again, his voice cracking as he lowered his head and pressed his face into her hair. Beth heard his breath catch, felt his body tremble, his tears on her neck. She held him even tighter.

When they both were finally still, she whispered, "I brought you donuts." And he began to laugh.

* * *

They drove home to Florida to tell their families they were engaged, then back to North Carolina to wait out the three months Jeremy had left before his discharge. He went back to work on base and Beth continued teaching at the community college. At night, they would make dinner together and sit at the little, yellow kitchen table planning their wedding and their future.

It was a cold Tuesday and Beth had put the kettle on to make tea when there was a knock at the door. Her first thought was that Jeremy had forgotten his keys. Looking back, she wasn't sure why she thought that. Jeremy never forgot anything. When she opened the front door and saw the two uniformed men on the steps, she shook her head.

"No," she said. "You have the wrong house. Jeremy is back from Afghanistan." She could hear Homer barking from the backyard.

"Mrs. Grant, may we come in?" One of them said.

"No," she said again. She was about to tell them that she wasn't Mrs. Grant when she remembered that she was. "I have to let the dog in."

She had turned from the door in a daze and walked to the back of the house. The two men followed her and after she let the dog in, they sat in the kitchen and told her what had happened. One of them said "training accident." The other said "helicopter crash." The kettle began to screech but she couldn't hear it over the screeching of her own heart. One of the men must have turned the kettle off because she couldn't.

If she could have stood up, she would have run from the room. But she couldn't. So she just sat there at the little, yellow kitchen table and watched her life fall apart.

27

Beth couldn't look away from her laptop screen. When the video was over, she pressed play and watched it again. She might have stayed there all afternoon, stuck in a loop, but there was a knock at the door.

Jenna breezed past her into the house. "What are you doing? Why aren't you ready? This Christmas shopping isn't going to do itself. Hi Homer." Then she saw Beth's face and she froze. "Uh-oh. What's going on?"

Beth didn't say anything, she just pointed to the laptop. Jenna dropped her purse onto the kitchen table and looked at the screen. The video showed Marian Cole sitting in a director's chair on a sparse stage. The décolletage of her white wrap dress gave her a sultry yet sophisticated air. Her auburn hair was perfectly styled, her make-up perfectly applied. It was hard to believe she was in her forties.

"We heard that you're currently working on a film with Todd Allman. Can you tell us about that?" an invisible voice asked.

"Certainly. He plays a college student and I play his professor... they have this steamy affair. I can't really tell you more but it's definitely a different type of film than any I have ever done before."

"What's it like working with He-Man?"

"Todd? He's a great guy! But I have to admit, when they cast him, I wasn't sure it was the best choice. I'd only seen him in the He-Man movies and I didn't know if he was up to anything as complicated as this role." She paused and smiled, leaning forward, playing to the camera, "Of course, this isn't anything I haven't told him." She laughed and a shiver ran down Beth's spine. "But he's really been putting his heart into this movie. He's even taking a college class to get into character."

"Oh yeah? Did he have torrid affair with his teacher like his character does?"

"Let's just say he's really dedicated to this film," She said with a calculated wink. "I think you're going to see a very different side of Todd Allman."

"And how much of the two of you do we get to see in this film?"

"Well, I don't want to give anything away but there's a scene in a pool that I'm very much looking forward to filming."

"We're definitely looking forward to watching that. Marian, thanks for sitting down with us at *Celebritating*, where we celebrate all things celebrity!"

Jenna gaped at the screen, her blue eyes wide with disbelief. Then she looked at Beth. "Oh my go..." She started but couldn't finish. "What the..."

"And guess how I found out about it," Beth said, crossing her arms over her chest.

"How?"

"Gene called me into his office to show it to me this afternoon."

"No fucking way?" The horror on Jenna's face mirrored what Beth had felt as she stood in Hy-gene's office. Watching the video, and in front of her boss no less, had felt like being in a car accident—time moving in slow motion, her chest constricting, her face hot like an airbag had just exploded into it.

"I guess she-Jean emailed him the link," Beth said, her face pale and drawn. "Apparently she's *keen* on celebrity gossip."

"Shit. So what did you say?"

"What could I say? That I'm having a fucking affair with Todd Allman?" She waved her hand angrily at the computer.

Jenna's eyes grew even wider. "So you told him?"

"No! Of course I didn't tell him. I lied to him instead." Beth winced, adding, "And you know how bad I am at that. I have no idea whether he believed me or not."

"What did he say?"

"It was so humiliating, Jen." The memory of her stammering to Gene, her face hot with shame made her stomach turn. "I think I'm going to be sick." She put her hand over her mouth and rushed down the hall to the bathroom. Standing in front of the toilet, she waited for something to happen. When nothing did, she bent over the sink and splashed cold water on her face. As she turned off the faucet, she could hear her cell phone ringing. Jenna was standing in the hallway holding up the phone.

"It's Todd." *Fucking Todd Allman!* "Do you want me to tell him to go to hell?"

The phone continued to ring. *Do I want to talk to him?* Her head felt thick but she took the phone from Jenna.

"Hey baby," his deep voice purred.

"Don't call me that," she said flatly.

Todd paused and she could hear the uncertainty in his silence. "Beth? What's going on?"

"I saw the interview. I know what you're doing."

"What interview? What are you talking about?" His voice was a mix of confusion and... *fear. He should be afraid.*

"Why don't you tell me exactly what your movie is about,

Todd?" she hissed. "Why don't you tell me exactly what you've been doing with me?"

He was silent for too long and it was all the admission she needed. "What. Interview," he finally said, too slowly.

She ignored him, the rage building. "The irony of the whole thing is that your sister actually thought *I* was using *you!* Please be sure to let her know that it was the other way around. And do you know what the best part was, Todd?" she spat his name into her phone. "I had to find out about the whole thing from my *fucking* boss!"

"I don't know…"

"Do you realize this could get me fired? Do you have any idea what this could do to me? All for some goddamn movie." Her voice was starting to quaver and there was a lump swelling in her throat but she absolutely refused to cry. "So no, you don't get to call me baby. You don't get to call me at all."

"Wait I… I…" She heard him stammer as she ended the call.

Jenna had shut the laptop but Beth still couldn't get Marion's sultry voice out of her head. *He's really dedicated to this film… a scene in a pool… looking forward to filming…* Beth hated Marion sitting there looking so glamorous and smug. Beth hated Todd for using her. Beth hated herself for being duped. Hot, angry tears burned in her eyes. "I can't believe this whole time he was just using me!"

Jenna put her arms around her. "I'm so sorry, hon," she said, letting her cry.

Beth wiped her eyes with the back of her hand. "God, I just don't get this. Why can't I stop crying?"

"Because someone you love hurt you." Jenna handed her a paper towel.

"Ha! It has nothing to do with love, Jen. It's my career, my reputation. I had to lie to Gene. I could lose my job. I trusted him and now everyone is going to know that I let a stupid kid, an *actor*," she spit the word out like it was dirty, "use me. I'm such an idiot! I should have known better." She blew her nose into the paper towel.

"You're not an idiot. Anyone would fall for Todd Allman."

"Yeah, but I am an idiot for not seeing that he couldn't possibly be falling for me. That it was all just an act."

Jenna began to speak but then clamped her mouth shut as if she thought better.

"What?" Beth demanded.

She opened her mouth again but then shook her head.

"Just tell me, Jen."

"I didn't think he was that good of an actor."

"I guess it didn't take much to fool me."

Jenna sighed. "It wasn't just you. I saw how he was with you at his birthday dinner. I guess he fooled me, too."

"This is so humiliating," Beth said, wiping her nose. "All of my students are going to know. And what about the people I work with? What am I going to say?"

"Well, you don't have to say anything right now. Isn't the semester over?" Jenna was right. Her classes were over, she just had to finish grading and she could do that from the house. "I'm sure by the time the spring semester starts, people will have forgotten all about it—if they ever knew in the first place. It's not like *Celebritating* is national news or anything."

Beth stared down at the little, yellow kitchen table. Before she could stop herself, she thought of Jeremy. And of how much her life had changed that day when she'd sat at that very same table. *This would have never happened if he hadn't left me*, she thought. *I wouldn't even be here.* She began to cry harder.

"Oh, honey," Jenna said, getting up and putting an arm around her again. Beth pushed her away, shaking her head.

"No, it's not that stupid kid," she gulped and swallowed hard. "I just miss, Jeremy."

Jenna nodded but didn't say anything.

"I'm sorry, I don't feel like Christmas shopping." Beth said.

"Of course you don't," she said. She was rummaging through Beth's fridge. "But you don't have any food in here and more importantly, you don't have any ice cream. I'm going to get us some take-out and I'll be right back."

Sometime after dinner the doorbell rang. Jenna answered it and returned to the kitchen with an enormous bouquet of roses. "Um…"

"You have got to be kidding me," Beth growled. She glared at the flowers until her eyes glazed over. She imagined yanking the vase out of Jenna's hands and throwing it to the ground with a satisfying crash. She could see the roses and glass and water littering her floor.

"Beth? What do you want me to do with these?"

Jenna's voice pulled her from her trance. Her eyes refocused on the giant bouquet. The impulse to destroy them subsided and her shoulders sagged. "Just throw them away," she sighed.

"Are you sure? I think this vase might be Waterford crystal."

Beth shrugged. "Okay, you keep the vase."

It wasn't until after she left that Beth noticed the card. Jenna had stuck it to the fridge, under a magnet. She reached for it, eager to throw it away. *Or burn it!* Yet with her guard down and no one to see, curiosity got the better of her. She opened the little, cream-colored envelope.

Beth, I'm so sorry. Please let me explain. -T

"What's there to explain?" she asked aloud. "What could you possibly say?"

28

Beth stood at baggage claim at LAX craning for a glimpse of her mother. She was excited and nervous and still a little sad. When she finally spotted Maggie, just past a large group of Japanese tourists, her heart soared. She cried out a strangled, "Mom!" before she could stop herself. They shared the same smile that lit their faces as they hurried toward each other. Tears pricked in Beth's eyes as she hugged her mother close.

"Oh Beth, honey. I've missed you." Maggie held her at arm's length and looked her up and down. "You look great!" Then she peered more closely at her daughter's face. "Well, your body looks great."

Beth laughed. "It's nice to see you too, Mom." More than anything, she wanted to tell her mother about what had happened with Todd. But she felt so stupid and unprofessional for ever hooking up with him in the first place that she decided to keep it to herself.

"What's going on? Is everything okay?"

"It's fine. I've just had a tough week."

At home, after cartons of take-out, Maggie yawned loudly.

"Mom, you must be exhausted. Don't feel like you have to stay up and talk to me."

"I know it's early but I can't keep my eyes open. I'll see you in the morning, sweetie." She bent over and kissed Beth on the forehead. As she walked past the front hall, there was a knock at the door.

Maggie turned and looked at her. "Who's that?"

"Um, I don't know." Beth's heart began to race and she jumped up from the table. "But I can get it Mom, you don't have to…"

Before she could finish, Maggie opened the front door.

"Uh, hello. Is Beth here?"

She heard him before she saw him. *Shit.* Maggie turned to Beth, her tired face a question mark. *Mom, meet He-Man. He-Man, this is my mom…* Homer had shot out the door and was spinning excitedly around Todd.

"Beth, someone is here to see you." Beth flushed, her stomach flip-flopping at the sight of him. "Are you going to intro…" But something in her daughter's face stopped her mid-sentence. Maggie looked from Beth to Todd and back. Then she turned to her daughter and said. "Well, don't stay up too late." Beth gave her a quizzical look and her mother began to laugh. "Oh dear, old habits die hard, don't they?" Despite herself, Beth laughed, too. Todd smiled tentatively and continued scratching the dog behind his ear. Giving him a last look, Maggie said, "Well, goodnight," and padded down the hallway.

When she was gone, Beth turned to him. "What are you doing here?" She had meant it to come out harshly but it sounded more weary than anything else.

"I need to talk to you and you won't call me back. I need to explain. I know you're angry and you have every right to be. But please, just hear me out."

Beth sighed. "Come in," she said. "We can go sit out back." He followed her through the house to the tiny back porch where they sank awkwardly into a pair of Adirondack chairs.

"So that's your mom?" he started.

She crossed her arms over her chest and stared at him. "Why are you here?" Beth never liked small talk and she certainly wasn't in the mood for it now.

Todd leaned forward and inhaled sharply. "Okay, yes, I'm making a movie about a student seducing his teacher. And I know how bad that sounds but... Here's the thing. I never meant to be an actor."

"What does that have to do with anything?" She hugged herself closer against the chilly night.

"When I got He-Man it was because they liked how I looked, it didn't really matter that I had no idea what I was doing. But it was fun. I really liked making movies so I decided I'd keep doing it. Then the two films I did after He-Man got really terrible reviews. They just blasted the shit out of me. I didn't know what to do. I felt like such a failure that I thought about quitting altogether. Then Danny got me in with this acting coach, Anton Bolinski. He's the best in the business. Practically everyone who has ever won an Oscar has worked with him."

Beth said nothing, so he kept going.

"Anyway, I met with Anton and he says that I have real potential. Then he hooks me up with the producers of this indie script that Marian Cole is attached to. So I sign on to do the movie under the condition that I keep working with Anton, which is a no brainer. And everyone is telling me that this is my big chance to prove I'm a real actor."

Beth sighed. "Where is this going, Todd?"

"Sorry, I'm getting there," Todd said, fidgeting with his hands. "Okay, so Anton's really into method acting and he tells me that I need to *live* the role and to really *become* the student. I swear to god, it was the very next day that you hit on me at the gas station. It seemed like it was, I don't know, a sign or something."

She cringed. "So, you *were* using me." Then added bitterly, "Just like you use all those groupies."

"I don't use them and I wasn't using you!"

"Of course you do! You said it yourself. You let them go down on you and then you send them on their way. I guess I should just feel lucky that I got to do more than give you a blow job."

"You know what? I don't use those girls," he said, anger flashing in his dark eyes. "They use me. Do you think they care about me at all? They just want a selfie with me and a story for their friends. They don't give a fuck about me. Or what I think or what I like. They don't make me laugh. They don't read my writing..."

"I got paid to read your writing," Beth snapped. "Well, at least that's what I thought I was getting paid for."

"Beth, please. It's not like that. Once I started your class, I knew it wasn't just about the movie anymore."

She glared at him. "Bullshit. You were trying to hook up with me from the beginning of the semester. You wrote that ridiculous story about me in the parking lot, then you hit on me at the Dolphins' game..."

"That's not because of the role," he interrupted. "That's because I was falling for you. I've never met a girl like you!"

"I'm not a girl."

"I know! Gah, I know, I know. You're a woman. That's why I love you. I wasn't lying when I told you that."

"Ha!" She angrily choked out the sound and before she could stop herself added. "You said that during sex. Everyone knows that doesn't count."

"Fine, then I'm saying it now. I love you, Beth." He put his hand hesitantly on her knee and she could feel the warmth of him radiating through her jeans. "I've loved you since I saw you splashing around the parking lot in the rain. I love everything about you—you're so smart and so real but you don't take yourself too seriously. I love that you smell like coconuts and that you always spill food on yourself. I love how you cover your mouth when you laugh and that your dimple only shows when you're really smiling. I even love your temper—you're so... so fierce. It scares me sometimes but I love it. I love you."

She finally met his sad, dark eyes. "Then how could you use me like this? I could lose my job, Todd. I had to lie to my boss. Do you know what people are going to say about me? What my students are going to think of me?"

"Beth, I tried to get out of the film. You have to believe me," he pleaded. "As soon as I saw Marian's interview, I called my lawyers but they said the contract is ironclad."

"Why didn't you just tell me what the movie was about?"

He dropped his head into his hands and rubbed his temples. "I should have told you. But I was scared you'd be mad."

"Yeah, I probably would have been mad." She shook her head sadly. "But I could have gotten over it. You didn't give me that chance. So now instead of mad, I feel used. And humiliated. And..." She stopped. There was a lump forming in her throat and she didn't want to cry.

Todd looked up at her, his eyes glistening. "Please, Beth. Don't end this."

"I didn't," she whispered. "You did."

* * *

The next morning, she found her mother in the kitchen, a cup of coffee and a magazine on the table in front of her.

Beth yawned. "Morning, Mom. How did you sleep?"

"Fine," her mother said, looking her over. "And how did you sleep?"

Beth grabbed a mug out of the cabinet, yawning again. "Fine, fine," she said. In truth, she had tossed and turned all night thinking of Todd.

Her mother waited until Beth had her coffee and was sitting at the table before she asked. "So, are you going to tell me why a movie star was at your door last night? Todd Allman is his name, right?"

She nearly dropped her mug in her lap. "What? Why are you… I mean what do you… " Maggie studied her as she set the coffee back on the table, dumbfounded. "Mom, how the hell do you even know who Todd Allman is?"

Her mother smiled and pushed the magazine toward her. It was a tabloid opened to a page with a picture of Todd and a picture of Marian Cole and a short article about their upcoming movie. In a block quote, there was a snippet from the interview Marian had given about Todd and his teacher. Beth read the blurb then looked at her mother. Her cheeks colored.

"Since when did you start reading the tabloids?" she asked, stalling.

"I picked it up at the airport. It seemed like a good idea since I was flying out to Hollywood. But don't change the subject, dear. What was he doing on your doorstep last night? Are *you* his teacher?"

So she told Maggie the general story of her time with Todd, downplaying her own feelings and leaving out the amazing sex. When she was done, Maggie said evenly, "I can understand why you'd be upset."

"Of course I'm upset. He used me as a guinea pig to get in character for his stupid movie. And what's worse is that he put my career in jeopardy. I can't believe I was so stupid."

"Well, what did he say when you asked him about it?"

"He told me that it started out as research for the role but that he really is in love with me now."

"And you don't believe him?"

"Why should I? Our whole relationship was a sham… just some kind of dress rehearsal."

"Does the fact that he took your class for the movie role mean that he can't be in love with you? Those two things are not mutually exclusive, Beth."

Beth had forgotten how much her mother loved to play devil's advocate. And how much it drove her crazy. She scowled. "But Mom, he didn't tell me that the movie was about an affair between a teacher and a student. He hit on me *while* I was his teacher. He could have gotten me fired. I could still get in trouble."

"I thought you said he dropped your class before the two of you began dating," her mother said.

"He did."

"So your career wasn't really in jeopardy?"

"Well, only because I wouldn't get involved with him while he was my student. But that's not the point, Mom," Beth was struggling to keep the whine out of her voice, feeling childishly desperate for her mother to take her side. "He humiliated me. Everyone knows that I was his teacher. They're all going to know that he used me for his stupid movie."

Her mother sighed. "Honey, I'm not trying to defend him. He screwed up. But didn't he only use you if he never actually cared?"

Beth frowned. Her mother had a point. But she also wasn't the one who had to return to school in January wondering what people were thinking, wondering what they were going to say about her.

29

Maggie hadn't said another word about Todd and Beth had pretended that there had been nothing more to say. But at Jenna's annual Christmas Eve party she had found Jenna and Maggie whispering in the kitchen only to change the subject when she came in. When they got home, amidst the usual mix of holiday cards and junk mail, there was a small, slim package with very familiar writing on it. She tucked it under her arm as her pajama-clad mother came into the kitchen.

"Anything good?" Maggie asked, filling up a glass with water.

"Um, there's a Christmas card from Aunt Ann," she said, holding the envelope out to her mom. Her mom took the envelope and when her back was turned, Beth slid the package into the drawer behind her.

In bed that night, she couldn't stop thinking about the package in the drawer. Quietly, she slipped out to the kitchen. The drawer squeaked as she slid it open and she froze to listen for sounds of her mother stirring. Then she pulled out the padded envelope and carefully opened it. Inside the mailer was a package, *obviously a book*, hand-wrapped in red paper covered in puppies wearing Santa hats. She turned the package over in her hands, staring at the wrapping. There was no note or label, so she slid a finger under one aggressively taped corner and ripped.

It was a slim book. And an old one. The hardback corners were worn. The pages were yellowed. On the front cover in blue script it said, Pablo Neruda *Veinte poemas de amor y una canción desesperada.* She took a deep breath and flipped open the cover. In perfect cursive was the name Maria Ruiz-Jaramillo. *Who is that?* Then she noticed a piece of paper marking a place toward the end. She flipped to the marker. It was a note in Todd's small, slanted script.

Beth,

> *This book of poems was my mother's favorite. She gave it to me years ago and I've always liked it but never really understood it. Until now. I want you to have it. I'm sorry. I love you. Merry Christmas.*

Todd

The note marked the twentieth poem in the book, *Puedo escribir los versos más tristes esta noche.* Her brain furiously translated. By the time she got to the lines—*Tonight I can write the saddest lines. To think that I do not have her. To feel that I have lost her.*—her eyes were burning. Not with tears but with anger. She closed the book. *How dare he send me a book of love poems? How dare he play the victim?* Briefly, she entertained the idea of striking a match and holding it to the fraying corner of Maria's favorite poetry book. But she could no sooner burn Todd's dead mother's book than she could kick one of the puppies on the wrapping paper. Instead, she stood on tip toes and slid it onto the top of her fridge where her own mother would never see it. She wadded up the packaging and the wrapping paper and buried it deep in the trash.

* * *

It was three days after Christmas when Beth put her mother on a plane back to Florida. It had been wonderful having Maggie visit. They had talked and eaten. They had watched movies and discussed books, except, of course, the one she had received from Todd. Beth wasn't sure why she hadn't told her mother about the package. After all, she had told her nearly everything else about Todd. Maybe it was the conversation they had the morning after Todd had shown up on her doorstep. It was clear that Maggie thought she should forgive him. But Beth was still far too angry to do that. The book of poems, so touching and personal, would just add to Maggie's argument that Todd really loved her. Though she wouldn't admit it to herself, let alone to her even-keeled mother, Beth didn't want to deal with what it meant if that were true.

Now, with Maggie gone and the new year fast approaching, Beth had one last thing she wanted to do on her winter break. She sat down at her little yellow kitchen table and, determined to keep her promise to herself, she opened the manuscript she had been working on when Jeremy died. She pulled up her music, put it on shuffle, and began to write. At first, the words came in fits and starts, sputtering and trickling onto the page. But soon she found her rhythm and got lost in the story, the music softly propelling her. It was the constricting of her heart, before anything conscious, that woke her from the writing. Something deep inside her was being pinched, being twisted and wrung. She gasped, shocked by the very real, very physical pain, unable to catch her breath. She had forgotten about downloading the Otis Redding album after the night in the pool with Todd.

She cried ugly and hard for a long time. When she was done, she had a throbbing headache but figured it was worth it if that meant Todd Allman was finally out of her system.

30

She stepped out of the yoga studio into the sunshine on the first day of the new year. Sandrine's early morning class had left her relaxed and happy. Beth loved Jenna's classes but if she was being honest, Sandrine was her favorite. Her warm open face and kinky grey hair gave her a maternal air and in her classes Beth almost always found a message that she needed to hear. Today, Sandrine had been talking about clearing out the baggage of the old year to be open to what the universe had to offer in the new year.

The roads were quiet, most late-night revelers still hours from waking. She cracked the window and let in a stream of chilly morning air, thinking about all that had happened over the previous year. Now she felt ready to put the strange events of the fall semester behind her. To move forward. *And welcome in the new year*, she thought with a smile. That was when she heard a *wham* and a crunch and felt the truck rock slightly forward.

What the? In the rearview mirror she saw the crumpled hood of a car. Startled and unsure of what to do, she got out of the car. There were no other cars around this early so Beth walked back to the injured vehicle. The nose of the Porsche had slid under her bumper, forcing the hood back and into the engine area. She was surprised how much damage there was for an accident she had barely felt. There wasn't a scratch on her truck.

"Are you okay?" she called out to the other driver, who had just opened the door and was hidden by the darkly tinted window.

It was the Dolphins' logo on his hat that she saw first. Her breath caught in her throat. "Not really," he said, standing to face her. He looked terrible. His eyes were bloodshot and he had a week's worth of scruff growing on his face. There was a fist-sized stain on his wrinkled shirt.

"Are you hurt?" she asked when she finally found her voice. Todd shook his head then pushed his hat up and rubbed his eyes. She took a step toward him. "What happened?"

His answer came out in a mudslide of words flying so quickly past her that Beth could barely follow. "I don't know. I saw you and I wanted to get your attention so I thought I would tap you but it's a stick and I pressed too hard or something and Danny's stupid fucking car just…" He gestured at the hood.

"You were *trying* to hit my truck?"

"Argh. Yes, but I just meant to tap it. I can't believe I just did that." He was rubbing his whole face now. Beth thought she smelled alcohol.

"Are you… drunk?"

Todd dropped his hands. "What? No! I mean, I was drinking last night but I'm fine. I was at Danny's and I couldn't sleep and I wanted… Uh, I don't even know what I wanted. I just wanted to get out of there. Then I saw you. And I thought maybe I could talk to you…" He stopped and shoved his hands into his pocket.

He really didn't seem drunk, just a little distraught. Beth

wondered if a police officer would feel the same way, given the look of him. And the smell. She watched a green sedan drive slowly past them.

"Well, we should probably move the cars. Will it start?"

Todd got back behind the wheel. A sad click-click sound came from under the hood. "Danny's going to kill me."

"Put the car in neutral and steer so I can push it out of the road," she said, going to the back of the car and putting her hands on the bumper.

"What? No. You get in. I'll push the car," Todd said.

They had managed to get the Porsche out of the road when Beth saw another green sedan drive slowly by going the opposite direction of the first. *Or is that the same car?* The driver appeared to be holding up their cell phone to the window. *Are they calling the cops?* Then, with a sinking feeling, Beth remembered the pictures outside the Meat Shed. Everyone with a cell phone was a paparazzo.

"Shit," she said. She watched the car pull up to the traffic light behind them and get in the left-turn lane, probably making a U-turn to take another pass. "I don't know what to do here but I think the person in that car is taking pictures."

"What?" Todd was rubbing his red eyes.

"Grab your stuff and get in my car." She was jogging back to her truck.

"I don't have any stuff." Todd called after her, confused, still leaning on the back of the Porsche.

"Then hurry up, Todd!" He hopped onto the passenger seat just as the traffic light behind them turned green. She had the truck in gear before he even closed the door, watching in her rearview mirror as the sedan made the U-turn and headed back toward them.

The traffic light in front of her was yellow but she gunned it and they lurched through the intersection before the green car could catch up. Beth wasn't sure what she was going to do with Todd. She looked at him out of the corner of her eye. He had turned around and was watching the sedan behind them, now stuck at the traffic light next to Danny's crumpled sports car. Her house was closer but the car might follow them. The Land Cruiser was neither quick nor inconspicuous. Plus she wasn't sure she wanted him at her house.

"I'm going to take you home," she said and made a quick left.

"But this isn't the way to my house."

"We're going the long way, just in case. Why don't you call Danny?"

"Nope, not a good idea." She glanced over and saw Todd shaking his head like a stubborn, little kid.

"What do you mean no? You have to call him. He needs to have his car towed."

"He's going to be so pissed. I'll just buy him a new one."

Beth rolled her eyes. "Dial his number and give me the phone." Todd pulled his phone out of his pocket, tapped on it and handed it to her. She put it between her shoulder and her ear as she down shifted and made another left.

"Todd, what the fuck? Where did you go?" Danny already sounded irritated.

"Danny, it's Beth Grant."

"Beth? What? Why are you calling me from Todd's phone?"

"Todd is with me. There was a little accident."

"Why? Wait, what?"

"He's fine but you need to send a tow truck for your car."

"My car? What does my car have to do with this?"

"Um." Beth bit her lip and glanced at Todd whose eyes were wide, the corner of his lips mischievously upturned. She heard Danny call out to someone in the background. "Is my car out front?" Wanting to get off the phone before the shit really hit the fan, Beth tried to get Danny's attention. "Danny, Danny! Listen to me. We're going to text you the address for the tow truck."

"Where the fuck is the Porsche, Todd!?!" Beth held the phone away from her ear as Danny bellowed. She handed it back to Todd who had his hand over his mouth, holding back a laugh as he ended the call. He texted Danny the address, then slipped the phone back in his pocket.

"Oh my god, you didn't tell me he had no idea you took his car!"

Todd laughed. "Yeah, I'm in big trouble. He freaking loves that car." When his phone started to ring again, he took it out and looked at. "It's Danny."

"You don't say."

"I don't think I'm going to answer this."

She tried not to laugh but couldn't help it. "Probably best to give him some time to cool off."

"Yeah." Todd turned his phone off and put it back in his pocket.

Beth continued to check her rearview mirror but there was no sign of the green sedan. She drove up Todd's winding driveway to the gate and rolled down her window. "What's the code?" she asked over her shoulder.

He didn't say anything and she turned to see a hurt expression on his blotchy face. "You don't remember?" he finally said. She sighed, shaking her head and punched in six digits. The gates swung open and she idled in front of his house, waiting for him to get out.

"You're not coming in?" He was still wearing the wounded expression.

"Um, I don't think that's a good idea."

"But… but… but I can't stand the thought of you hating me. I miss you so much, Beth."

Beth sighed. "I don't hate you, Todd."

"You don't?"

"No. I understand what you did and why. I even understand why you wouldn't want to tell me."

"You do?"

"Yeah." She nodded. *But it doesn't mean I like it.*

"I don't like not having you in my life," he said softly. She looked up to find him staring at her, his bloodshot eyes full of trademark Todd Allman intensity.

"Todd, we can be friends. I'm not going anywhere."

"Friends." He repeated, but not with disappointment.

"Oh, and thanks for the book but I really can't accept it. I'll bring it by sometime."

"You don't want it?" He was surprised.

"No, I mean, yes. I mean… I like it." She mentally crossed her fingers. The book was still sitting on top of her fridge. She had been waiting for Maggie to leave to take it down and had all but forgotten it until now. "I think I should give it back to you though. It seems like it should stay with your family."

"My friends are my family, Beth," he smiled at her, but it wasn't coy or cocky. It was just Todd. "Thank you for saving me today." He leaned in and kissed her on the cheek. Underneath the smell of alcohol was a familiar scent, the one that made her heart race and feel at home all at the same time.

31

Beth rushed up to the door of the yoga studio. When she flung it open, she saw Jenna behind the counter.

"Sorry, I'm late. The traffic... blech."

"You'll never guess who's here," Jenna whispered. She was grinning like the Cheshire cat.

When she raised an eyebrow and mouthed "who?" Jenna just gestured over her shoulder to the room behind her. Beth kicked off her shoes and shoved them into a cubby with her keys. "Who?" she asked again.

Jenna kept grinning. "Go see."

The room was packed and she was disappointed but not surprised to see the only open spot was in the front of the class, near the center. She unrolled her mat and sat down cross-legged. Then pretending to stretch, she twisted her body so she could see the back right corner of the room. She scanned the faces. No one stood out. *Who is Jenna talking about it? Is it some other celebrity I've never heard of?* She turned back around and twisted in the opposite direction. Still not recognizing anyone, she let out her breath and pushed into the twist a little further this time actually stretching. When she looked back up, she was face to face with the person directly behind her. His dark brown eyes locked with hers and he smiled. She smiled at him and mumbled a quick "hi" then turned back around. *Shit! What the hell is Todd doing here?*

Jenna had been nudging Beth toward Todd since Maggie's visit. It irritated Beth to no end that her mother and her best friend were colluding. Even though she knew it was childish, she felt like they were both somehow taking Todd's side. She didn't tell Jenna about the accident on New Year's day. But that had backfired because she ended up hearing about it from Danny.

Taking her seat at the front of the room, Jenna said, "Let's start in child's pose for a change." As she slid her bottom back toward her heels, Beth caught a mischievous look in her friend's eyes. A few moments later, Jenna had them on all fours doing spinal movements that went from traditional cat and cow to pretty much gyrating. Beth tried to concentrate but it was impossible to forget that Todd had a front row seat to her writhing sensually on the mat.

For the next hour, Jenna ignored the glares from her best friend and took them through every pose that required Beth to put her ass in the air. During what felt like the hundredth downward dog, she snuck a glance between her feet at the back of Todd's head, his blond hair hanging down toward the mat. Lost in thought, it wasn't until he shifted forward into updog, their eyes meeting, that Beth realized she hadn't been listening. She moved quickly to catch up with the group and for the rest of class, she refused to let herself look at him.

During savasana, the final resting pose of the class, Beth tried to relax but Todd's energy behind her was so strong that she felt waves of it radiating across her own mat. So she lay there wondering if he would say anything to her and how she should respond if he did. Even though she had told him they could be friends, she had never stopped to consider what that might mean.

When class was over, Beth turned to face him as she rolled up her mat. "Hello," she said, watching him wrangle his own mat, waiting for him to meet her eyes.

He looked up with uncharacteristic shyness. "Hi," he said. This Todd was completely different from the guy she had driven home the other day. Gone was the scruff and the blotchy face. His eyes were clear and the sheen of sweat on him only made him look better.

"I didn't expect to see you here."

He looked down at the uneven rolls of his mat. A strand of blond hair fell into his face and she raised her hand unconsciously to sweep it away. When his eyes met hers again, she stopped short. Her hand hung between them in the air until she yanked it back, awkwardly smoothing her own sweat-dampened hair instead. He smiled at her. *Does he know I was just about to touch him?* He pushed the hair behind his ear. "I remembered that Jenna taught yoga and Levi said she was really good so I thought I should try it."

"Yeah, she's great," Beth said, trying to hold his gaze as he studied her face. She waited for him to say something else, both of them oblivious to the woman who had walked up next to them.

"You're Todd Allman?" the woman said, a flirtatious grin parting her perfectly lip-sticked mouth, unaware or perhaps unconcerned, that she was interrupting. With only the briefest flicker of annoyance, he turned to the woman with full Hollywood Todd face.

Beth slipped away from them and out to the front of the studio. She grabbed her keys and shoes, then glanced back into the room just in time to see the woman giving Todd her card. *Where the hell did she get that? Does she keep them in her bra?* Her heart felt like it tripped on itself and her face colored. Jenna watched her from the front desk, an eyebrow raised but said nothing.

"Bye Jenna. Catch ya later," she said with a wave and walked out to her car. She sat in her truck for a minute feeling mad at herself for being mad at Todd for getting hit on. *This is so stupid. Of course he's going to get hit on.* With a deep breath, she started the engine but before she could back out of the space, she saw him jogging toward her car. She rolled down the window.

"Hey," he said. "Do you want to get a coffee or something?"

"Now?"

"Yeah." He looked so hopeful.

Why don't you get 'a coffee' with that woman who just hit on you? "Uh, I don't think so." She tried to hide her anger.

"Come on. You said we could be friends. Friends get coffee or a drink, or whatever. Don't they?"

She smiled despite herself and her heart did that weird tripping thing again. She really didn't want him to ask perfect lipstick woman for a drink but… "Classes start tomorrow and I've got some stuff to finish up. Another time?"

He looked defeated but stepped back from the truck. "Okay," he nodded.

Predictably, Jenna called her ten minutes later.

"What's up?"

"Don't 'what's up' me, Beth Brennan. I can't believe you just left without talking to me. What was Todd doing here? What did he say to you in the parking lot?"

"Nothing happened. He said he wanted to take your class because Levi said you're really good."

"He did?" Jenna was pleased and Beth was happy for her. For every celebrity that came to her studio the business grew exponentially. "Okay, but that's not what he ran out to the parking lot to say to you. What was that all about? Rhonda looked so disappointed. He must have stopped her mid-sentence."

Beth felt a nasty little thrill. "Is that the woman that gave him her card? At a yoga class? Who does that? Who just gives some rando their card?"

"Um," Jenna said, slowly. "I may know one other person who randomly gave her business card to a stranger."

"What, who? Oh…" And she began to giggle, the tension of the Todd encounter dissipating. "Okay, but at least I didn't know who he was. It wasn't like I was trolling a yoga class to pick up a movie star."

"Because a gas station is so much better."

Beth laughed even harder. "Okay, fair point."

32

A few days later, Beth sat in her car at the yoga studio swiping on some lip gloss, telling herself that it was just because her lips were dry. When she went inside, Jenna looked up from the desk. "Oh, I'm glad you're here. Can you lock up the studio for me after class? I just booked a private session but I don't think I'll make it in this traffic unless I leave as soon as class is over."

"Of course, no problem."

Beth took the spot in the back left corner of the room. She sat cross-legged with her eyes closed and tried to concentrate on her own breath, ignoring the sounds of the other students checking in and rolling out their mats. When she heard Jenna lock the studio door, she opened her eyes and scanned the room. There was no Todd. *It's just as well,* she told herself. But if she was being honest, she would have had to admit that she was disappointed he wasn't there.

Jenna settled onto a cushion at the front of the room. "Welcome," she said. Before she could say more, there was the unmistakable sound of a yank on a locked door. "Ah, they probably got stuck in that nasty traffic. Should we let them in?" The class murmured their approval.

The woman in front of Beth said, "They probably need yoga after driving out there."

Beth heard a deep, familiar voice apologize for being late and her heart leapt into her throat. Jenna came back into the room with He-Man himself and led him over to where Beth was sitting.

"Paula, would you mind sliding over a little so we can fit him in?" Jenna gestured to the woman next to Beth, who slid away so Todd could put his mat between them. Years of friendship had developed their telepathy and Beth knew exactly what Jenna was thinking as she smirked at her before returning to the front of the class. *"At least I didn't put him next to Rhonda."*

Again, she felt awkward and self-conscious from the nearness of him. For his part, Todd appeared too flustered at being late to notice her. She snuck a glance at him during the brief meditation and that was a mistake. Seeing the curve of his bottom lip, the muscles of his arms stretching his shirt, his face so earnest and serious, sent her body into a tailspin—as if her every cell was being pulled into his orbit.

She didn't have long to contemplate why he still had this effect on her or to even chastise herself for it. Jenna immediately began to put them through their paces and her pride took over. It demanded that she hold her planks longer, keep her arms straighter, stretch her legs further. By the time Jenna took them to the floor for a twist, she was sweaty and exhausted and had almost forgotten about Todd Allman.

"Now, make your way to savasana. Stretch your legs long, let your arms fall out to the side, and release any lingering tension." *Easier said than done.* As Beth spread her arms out, she accidentally brushed Todd's hand. The touch was like a shock and she yanked her hand away but just like that, she was spinning again.

"Sorry," she whispered with a quick glance at him. His head was turned to her. He was smiling. She smiled back and then closed her eyes and turned her face back to the ceiling. A moment later, she felt his hand against hers, just the side of his thumb touching the side of her thumb. Her heart raced but she didn't move away. For what felt like an eternity, she held perfectly still, pretending that where they were touching was not causing electric energy to flood through her.

As they rolled up their mats he said quietly, "Coffee?"

"I have to close the studio for Jenna." When she saw both the disappointment on his face and the approach of perfect-lipstick Rhonda, she hastily added, "But if you don't mind waiting…"

He grinned. "I don't mind at all."

For some reason—*Todd Allman*—it took the yoga students an extra long time to clear out of the studio. Beth waited patiently while Todd hung back in a corner talking to the few people bold enough to approach him. By the time they were gone, her stomach was rumbling.

Their class had been the last of the night and Todd leaned on the desk as she shut down the computer. He had changed his shirt. "So where should we go?"

Beth looked at the clock. "I know it's early but I'm starving. Do you want to just grab dinner?"

They walked two blocks down the street to Mambo, Beth's favorite pizza place. The owner greeted her by name and they grabbed a quiet booth in the back. He didn't seem to recognize Todd.

"Do you know everyone?" Todd was shaking his head and grinning at her.

"What do you mean?"

"Well, you know the guys at Pancho's and the people here know you by name. I guess you're pretty famous, huh?"

"Try not to be jealous," Beth laughed.

They ordered a pitcher of cheap beer and she poured them

both glasses.

"I'm guessing you know what's best here? Do you want to just order for us?"

She was surprised by how nice it felt to be with him, sharing one of her favorite meals, knowing he wasn't out somewhere else with someone else. They ordered the large version of her favorite pizza and when the waiter left Todd held up his beer glass. "To friends?" She nodded.

"So, what have you been up to? How was your Christmas?" Beth wondered if he was filming the movie yet. She wondered if, like he said, he really did care about her. She wondered if she had forgiven him for humiliating and using her.

"Remember when I told you about my dad's old records?"

"You mean how Duke ruined them all?"

"Yes, exactly. Well, telling you that story got me thinking I should try to find some of those old records for my dad. So I gave him a bunch of them for Christmas."

"That's so awesome! What did he think?"

Todd smiled. "He was so happy, he cried. It was like I gave him a piece of Mom back. I wanted to call you and tell you but..."

"It was a very cool gift." She cut him off, not wanting to venture into their break-up.

"Here, I took a picture," Todd got out his cell phone and pulled up the photo, then passed it to Beth. The screen showed a thicker, older version of Todd. His hair was more gray than blond and thinner than his son's but the joy in his smile was unmistakably Todd.

"Wow, he looks so much like you." Beth stared at the picture for longer than she meant to, then handed the phone back.

"Yeah, what about you? How was your time with your mom? I was sorry I didn't get to really meet her."

"Uh yeah..." Beth took another sip of beer. "That was a

little…"

Todd laughed. "Awkward?"

"Yes, awkward. I thought she would have no idea who you were but I guess she had just read some tabloid on the plane. I definitely had some explaining to do."

His eyes narrowed and he took a sip of his beer but before the conversation went further their pizza arrived.

On the walk back to the studio she felt full and warm and happy. As they strode next to each other, their hands touched but neither adjusted the space between them. She felt an overwhelming urge to hold his hand but *that's not what friends do…*

"Where are you parked?" she asked.

"I'm around back but I can walk with you."

At her truck, she turned to face him. "Well, it's been, uh, nice."

"Nice?" He looked down at her skeptically.

She laughed. "Really nice. Surprisingly so." Without thinking about it, she stood on tiptoes and gave him a hug. At first, he seemed thrown off by the gesture but when she tried to pull away, he was hugging her tightly back, their bodies pressed together. Beth felt a deep, constricting ache and a catch in her throat. *God, this is harder than I thought.*

"I should go," she said, finally pulling away and opening the door to the truck. "See you… later." It came out like a question and Todd nodded, watching her. He was still standing in the parking lot as she drove out onto the street. She took a deep breath trying to release the tightness in her chest. Her phone rang and when she saw that it was Todd, she scrambled to answer.

"Hello?"

"Hey, you're never going to believe this but I left my keys in the studio. Can you come back and let me in?" He was leaning against the door, arms crossed when she pulled back into the parking lot. Beth opened the door and he followed her in. She flicked the dimmer switch giving the studio a soft, warm glow.

"Hey, while we're here, do you think you could show me that pose we did today? I think it was called triangle? I don't think I got it right."

"Right now?" Beth said, her heart beginning to thump faster. *What is happening to me?*

"I mean, if you have time." Shy Todd was back and he was unbelievably cute.

"Um, sure, okay."

They went into the yoga room and he unrolled his mat. She showed him where to put his feet then stood in front of him. "The thing about this pose is that it's not really about the legs. It's more about trying to open up your chest. So pull this back," she said, placing a hand on his hip and gently pushing it back. "And stretch this arm up," she said, now running her fingers down his muscular bicep. Somewhere deep inside her there was a coil of tension that was getting tighter each time she touched him.

"Now, lower your arm to your leg. It doesn't matter how low you go, because it's more about stretching up here." As she ran her fingers down his side, the thin shirt crept away from his waistband exposing his firm stomach. When her fingers met his bare skin, he twitched and lost his balance a little, leaning into her.

"Sorry," she said, giggling. "But you should feel it right here." She tickled him again, this time on purpose.

"Hey!" Todd grabbed her, then fell back onto his mat, pulling her on top of him. She was still tickling his sides, laughing and breathless. Until he grabbed both her hands, causing her to lurch forward until they were practically nose to nose. Beth's heart was hammering and she was no longer laughing. She held her breath and without thinking, she kissed him. It felt like she had come home again.

He let go of her hands and kissed her back, wrapping his arms around her like he was afraid to let her go. He flipped her onto her back, each kiss fueling the heat between them. Soon, Beth was tugging at his shirt until his chest was bare. Then his shorts came off. The more skin she could touch of his, the more she couldn't stop herself.

He peeled off her yoga pants, then her shirt and sports bra and soon they were bare chest to bare chest and her nipples sang at the sensation of pressing against his warm, hard body. Everything between them was gone. Their lips met and their tongues met as she wrapped her legs around him and pulled him toward her. Todd pressed his forehead to hers and their eyes locked as they came together. He filled her and she moaned with each thrust, her body tuned to his in a way it had not been tuned to anyone. She tingled all over as they moved closer to climax. She arched her back as he thrust deeper and deeper. He kissed her as she came, moaning beneath him. And when she was done, she clung to him until he finished. Afterwards, he held her close, the floor hard beneath them. While she tried to catch her breath, he kissed her in his way. First on the forehead, then on each eyebrow. Then he kissed her nose, her chin and finally, gently on her mouth.

They didn't speak until after they crept guiltily out of the studio and stood at her truck. Todd had slipped his hand into hers but when she tried to pull it away to unlock the door, he wouldn't let it go. She turned to him, her face a question. He bent over her until their foreheads were touching. Goosebumps prickled her skin.

"Be with me," he whispered.

"I... I..."

He covered her stammering mouth with his and kissed her until she could hardly stand it. When she was about to yank him into the back of her truck, he broke away from her and said again, "Be with me, Beth. Please."

Her head was spinning. "I don't know," she said.

Hurt flashed in his eyes. "What do you mean you don't know? How can you do that with me and *not* want to be together? I know I screwed up but, Jesus, Beth, how can you doubt this?" His voice was strangled by emotion but he kept going. "Do you really think that what we have, that… that… you can get this somewhere else? I *know* I can't. There's no one else like you Beth. There's no one that fits with me the way you do." He rubbed his eyes with his hands.

She knew he was right. They fit together. It didn't make any sense but they did. But he had made her feel like such a fool. *My heart still hurts*, she thought. It wasn't her heart that really hurt, though. It was her pride.

"Yeah, maybe what I did was unforgivable. Or maybe you just don't want to forgive me." She looked at him dumbfounded. It was like he had just read her mind. "Maybe you'd just rather live in the past."

"That's not… that's not what I'm doing…" she stammered.

"You sure about that? That you aren't just convincing yourself that I'll never be good enough. That I'll never be Jeremy."

"This isn't about Jeremy. This is about you! You were the one who dicked me over!"

"Right. I did. And guess what? So did Jeremy. And you forgave him. And then you lost him. You don't think that has anything to do with why you won't forgive me? Why you're too much of a coward to give this a shot."

She was furious now, the skin on her face burning up. The energy between them was volatile. It took everything she had to stand her ground and face him. "Fuck you, Todd," she whispered.

"You just did." A frown twisted his beautiful face but she could barely see it through her angry tears. Beth turned away from him just as they began to fall.

Homer's greeting was extra crazy once he got a whiff of her clothes. Beth peeled them off and left them on the floor of her bedroom for the dog to examine more closely. She took a long shower, the water so warm that she couldn't feel the tears running down her face. Her body ached, her heart ached, she was exhausted. It was all she could do to brush her teeth and crawl into bed.

But sleep wouldn't come so she leaned out of bed, grabbed her shirt from the floor and held it tentatively to her nose. It smelled like Todd. Clutching the shirt, inhaling his scent, she finally drifted into a fitful sleep.

33

Beth stood at the front of the classroom waiting for the first students of the new semester to trickle in. Two nights before at Ladies' Poker, Janet and Tiana had asked her about the Marian Cole interview. At first she had started to deny it, to say that it didn't have anything to do with her but she was sad and weary and the night at the yoga studio with Todd had been so confusing that she ended up confessing almost everything. The women were surprisingly supportive. All of them but Allie thought that, consequences be damned, she should give him another chance. It had been a relief to tell them and to get some perspective. Now, in front of the steadily growing class, Beth realized that if the poker ladies, busy women that they were, had heard about the interview and put two and two together, surely some of her students would, too.

As she waited for the clock to hit the hour, Beth scanned the faces. *Is it my imagination or do some of them look more curious than usual?* Then it was time, so she stood up straight and introduced herself. During the class introductions, as the new crop of students described their favorite meals, Beth finally began to relax. *See,* she told herself. *Everything is going to be fine. Everyone has already forgotten about Todd Allman. Now, maybe you can.*

When they were done going over the syllabus, she asked the class if they had any questions. Several of the students exchanged glances. Finally, a girl in the middle of the class tentatively raised her hand. "Yes?" Beth nodded to her, noticing for the first time that she was wearing a He-Man T-shirt. Her heart started to beat just a little bit faster at the sight of Todd on the girl's chest.

"Is it true that you had Todd Allman in your class last semester?"

Forcing her face to remain immobile, something she'd never been good at, Beth stalled. "What did you say your name was again?"

"Abby."

"Well, Abby," Beth said slowly. "It is true that Todd Allman was in my class for part of last semester."

"What was he like?" the girl blurted out and then raised a hand to her mouth as if she had surprised herself.

Beth's mind flashed with image after image of Todd, his cocky grin, the intensity of his eyes, the way his muscular chest felt against her bare one, the tenderness with which he held her... Realizing the class was staring at her, she tapped her finger to her chin, hoping she looked like someone in careful thought for diplomatic phrasing, rather than someone with an aching heart.

"What was Todd Allman like?" She was stalling again as her mind raced for an appropriate answer. "Well, he was about what you'd expect I guess. Confident, a little cocky, but nice. And a surprisingly good writer."

Another girl in the front row asked, "Will you read us some of his writing?"

Beth laughed and shook her head—thinking of his piece about her in the parking lot in the rain. "No, I can't do that. Would you all like me to share your writing without your permission to my other classes?"

There was some murmur of agreement and Beth allowed herself a deep but surreptitious breath, pleased with how she had handled herself and glad that the first day was nearly over. Then, a deeper voice from the back of the class called out, "Did you see the interview with Marian Cole? The one where she talks about Todd and his teacher?"

Beth's heart dropped and she willed her face not to blush. "You know," she said, feeling more fierce than nervous. "I don't really pay attention to that kind of stuff."

"She said she thought Todd was doing…" He shifted in his seat as if he had to physically move to mentally change gears. "Um dating his teacher. Is that true?"

"I think," Beth said, staring him down, "that actors are in the business of selling movie tickets. And Marian Cole is very good at her job." Most of the students murmured their agreement, seeming satisfied. The frat boy in the back looked like he was going to say something else but Beth looked at her watch and said, "Okay, for next class please have your assignments typed and ready to turn in. See you then!"

She held her breath as the students filed out. When the last one was gone, her shoulders sagged, she leaned on the podium and let out a great, big sigh. It wasn't as overwhelming or embarrassing as she thought it was going to be but she was still relieved it was over. For days she had been playing out in her mind what might happen but had never come up with a good response. What she had feared most for that day had happened and she had dealt with it. She took a deep breath and stood straighter. Like so many times when she had to do things she dreaded, now that it had come and gone, she wondered why she had been so worried after all.

* * *

"How was your first day?" Jenna asked. "Did anyone ask you about Todd?"

Beth laughed. "Just cut right to the chase."

"Well, I know you were worried about it."

"Yeah, I really was." Beth told Jenna about the girl in the He-Man shirt and the guy in the back with the attitude.

"It sounds like you handled it really well."

"Thanks. I think maybe I did. It wasn't nearly as awkward as I thought it would be."

"Speaking of awkward, thanks for closing up the studio the other day. Was it super weird with Todd being there?"

Beth hesitated. She felt a little dirty and a little bad about what had happened at the studio and she wasn't sure exactly how to tell her, or if she should tell her at all. *What if Todd told Danny what happened and Danny told Jenna?*

"Yeah," she said, slowly. "About that..." When she was done confessing, Jenna was silent. "I'm sorry, Jen. Are you mad?"

"No," Jenna laughed. "I'm not mad. A little jealous maybe, I always thought I'd be the first to christen the studio, but I'm not mad."

"I promise, it won't happen again."

"Why? How did you two leave things?"

She told her about what Todd had said about Jeremy. And what she said back.

"Whoa," Jenna said. "That's intense."

"It was so intense, Jen. I cried all night." Beth could feel the hot tears filling her eyes and start to spill out in her voice. "I know he thinks I'm still in love with Jeremy but I don't think it's that. I think I don't know how to forgive him. I do love him but I'm still so angry. He humiliated me. And yes, maybe he fell in love with me, but what if he hadn't? I mean, his plan was to hook up with me and then dump me and make a movie about it? I don't want to be with someone who would do that to another person."

"Well, you won't technically be with that person because he's not the same person he was when you met him. And neither are you."

"It's not that simple. Sometimes I think about him and I miss him so badly. And other times, it's like I can't even imagine being in a relationship with someone like him. He's a pain in the ass. He's immature and has all this baggage and..." She paused to catch her breath, then blurted. "And everyone knows how he treated me. I feel like I'm an idiot for even wanting him back."

"Okay, maybe you're not supposed to be with him then. How does your heart feel about that?"

"I keep asking her but my brain drowns her out."

"What is your brain saying?"

"She says- get out there, date someone else, find someone who treats you well, avoid all the drama..."

"But..."

"But then my heart whispers, you can't even imagine being with anyone but him."

"What more do you need to know? He wants you, you want him, school went fine. What are you waiting for? Are you waiting for him to give up on you so you can go back to your quiet little boring life? Is that what you really want?"

"I don't know that he wants me. You should have seen his face, Jen. After I said it. He was so angry. I think it's really over."

"There's only one way to find out."

She sighed. "I know. But then I think about Jeremy. I gave everything to him and when he was gone, it was like I was gone, too. And Todd? Being with Todd would screw up my whole world. How long do you think we can hang out at my house and sneak around yoga studios? If we're seen together, what then? I have to confess to Gene? And maybe lose my job? What if it doesn't work out? What if I'm left with nothing? I just don't think I can do that again."

"You're not going to lose your job but you're right about the rest. A life with Todd is going to look very different from the one you have now. I know you like things as they are but nothing ever stays the same no matter how much you want it to. Life *is* change. You know that better than anyone. Date Todd or don't date him. Take the chance or don't. But isn't it better to be the one making the changes in your life instead of just sitting there and letting them happen to you?"

"I'm just not sure…"

"You'll know when you're ready. No decision is still a decision. If you aren't ready to decide, don't."

"I love you so much. Thank you for being my friend."

After they hung up, she opened the fridge and reached for a bottle of wine. *Hmmm… not wine. Not strong enough.* The good whiskey, which she rarely drank, was in the cabinet above the fridge. She dragged the step stool out of the pantry and stood on it. That's when she saw the book of poems. It was still sitting on her fridge resting on top of a faint layer of dust.

At the little, yellow, kitchen table she poured two fingers of whiskey and flipped to the twentieth poem, marked by Todd's note. She began to read Neruda's words from *Tonight I Can Write*. One line of the poem made her breath catch in her throat.

Love is so short, forgetting is so long.

Love is so short, forgetting is so long. Beth couldn't sit still. She paced. She looked at the clock. It was 10:47pm. She poured a second glass of whiskey. She stared at her phone. She paced some more. *Am I really going to do this?* Her heart hammered in her chest. She leaned against the counter and looked back down at her phone. Then she finally typed four words.

BETH: Is it too late?

She took a gulp of whiskey and stared at the message. Then, she hit send. Immediately she regretted it. *Why did I send a text? I should have just called. But I can't call now because I just sent a text!* She began to pace again when her phone pinged. She was so surprised, she nearly dropped it. The answer had come.

TODD: Never

34

She sat outside the dean's office trying not to fidget in her suit. At least she could look professional when she told Marcia Hatton about her less than professional behavior. Beth was mentally rehearsing her speech one last time when the office door opened and Dean Hatton waved at her hurriedly.

"Come on in, Beth," she said. "I hope this is going to be quick?"

"Uh, yes, it can be." Beth followed her into the office. Dean Hatton took a seat behind her enormous mahogany desk and gestured to the matching leather chairs across from her. The chair Beth sat in was deceptively deep and she sank much further than she anticipated. "Whoa," she said, grabbing onto the arms to keep from collapsing back into it. She righted herself as gracefully as possible and found herself looking up at Dean Hatton who was laughing.

"Don't you just love that chair?" Beth wasn't sure how to respond so she just smiled awkwardly. "I tried out a hundred chairs until I found that one. I like that it throws people off balance." She said, winking at Beth over her reading glasses. "You should see when Gene sits in it. He looks like a little, old lady trying to see over the steering wheel of a Cadillac." The mental image of the roly-poly Gene Walker trying to balance himself on the chair made Beth giggle and she felt her nerves start to dissipate.

"So?" Dean Hatton folded her hands on the desk. Her short, dark hair was slightly wild and her round eyes gave her an owl-like appearance. The way she peered down at Beth made her feel like a mouse. Suddenly the nerves were back. She cleared her throat.

"Thank you for meeting with me, Dean Hatton," Beth began.

"Marcia," she corrected her.

"Okay, Marcia. I wanted to talk to you about a student I had last semester. Well, sort of a student. Not really. I mean, he was in my class for part of the semester and then." Marcia was watching her with impatience. She took a deep breath and started again. "Do you remember Todd Allman, the actor that was in my class last semester?"

"Of course I do. Who could forget He-Man?"

"Well, he's asked me to accompany him to the Oscars." Beth said, skipping ahead in her rehearsed story.

"Ahh," Marcia leaned back in her chair. "Now we get to the heart of the matter. So Beth, are you asking permission or forgiveness?"

Before thinking it through Beth blurted, "Both!"

"So you were sleeping with him when he was your student?"

"What? No! Absolutely not!" Beth must have looked horrified but the dean just nodded.

"Okay, good. Well, Gene is your direct boss so we have to get him in on this conversation but I have no problem with this. It's never ideal when a faculty member has a relationship with a student but he's no longer a student so it's not technically against school policy." She pressed a button on her desk phone while Beth's head spun.

"Marcia, what can I do for you?" Gene Walker's smarmy voice came out of the speaker.

"Gene, I have Beth Grant here. She has been asked to the Oscars by He-mmm," Marcia grinned and mouthed *oops* at Beth. "Ahem, Todd Allman, the actor that was in her class last semester. I told her I have no problem with that but I wanted to run it by you."

There was a soft scratching noise and Beth realized unpleasantly that it was Gene rubbing his beard. "Well," he said slowly. "I'm not sure that is such a good idea. Are they having a relationship?"

"Yes, we are." Beth said defiantly, her face beginning to burn. She mentally crossed her fingers against the white lie she was about to tell. "But nothing happened while he was my student."

"I should hope not. You stood in my office last fall and told me that nothing was going on."

"Yes sir," she cringed. "And that's true. We met again recently at a yoga class and began dating. I don't have to go to the awards show if you all don't think it's appropriate but I imagine I will be seen with him at some point."

Gene made a harrumph sound. "This seems highly unethical. Especially given the nature of the movie he's working on."

"And what exactly is that?" Marcia asked.

Beth looked sheepishly at Marcia. "He's in a movie with Marian Cole and she plays his college professor. That's why he was taking my class, to get into character."

"Well, I don't really see any problem with…"

"A movie about the professor having an *affair* with her student," Gene interrupted.

"Oh, hmmm." Marcia took her reading glasses off and tapped them against her chin. "Well, there's a little life imitating art, huh?"

"Yes, but what will people say about our school when it becomes known that Mr. Allman is dating his teacher?"

You told me to give him special treatment.

"Former teacher," Marcia corrected. "And he wasn't really a matriculated student here, was he?" She looked skeptically at the phone.

"Well, no not technically. I believe he was auditing the class. But I still don't think the reputation of the school deserves to be impugned because of Ms. Grant's indiscretion."

Beth had been staring at the phone but she looked up just in time to see Marcia roll her eyes.

"On the contrary, Gene. I think this will be great publicity for the school. I wouldn't be surprised if our enrollment went up just out of curiosity. And since Beth will be the one who will have to deal with looky-loos because of who she's dating, I think the decision should be hers."

Beth hadn't given the "looky-loos" much consideration. She had only been concerned with getting through this meeting. Her heart began to pound but Gene's voice interrupted her panic.

"I suppose you have a point, Marcia. But I wonder, would you feel the same way if the genders were reversed? What if a much older male professor began dating his younger female student?"

Beth frowned. *I'm not that much older, you toad!*

"Come now, Gene. Beth isn't much older than Mr. Allman. And as far as gender is concerned, I like to take these things on a case by case basis." Marcia paused, a smirk crossing her face. "But I tell you what, Gene. You have my word that the next time a Hollywood starlet wants to take you to an awards show, I'll give you my blessing."

Gene was silent for a moment and Beth thought she could

actually hear him shifting his position, scrambling for moral high ground. "Marcia, of course I'll defer to whatever you think is best." The smarminess was back in his voice, with just a hint of defeat. "But should this all go awry, I'd like my objections on record."

Marcia smiled. "Noted." And she hung up.

"There you go. Anything else?" There was a twinkle in the dean's eyes as she watched Beth struggle to stand.

"Nope," Beth said. "Thank you so much for your time. Sorry to bother you with all this."

"No problem." She put her reading glasses back on and started looking over a paper on her desk. As Beth was about to slip out the door, Marcia stopped her. "Oh, one more thing. Do you think you could get me He-Man's autograph? My nephew is a big fan."

35

In the campus parking lot, she dialed Jenna's number. The phone hadn't even rung when she answered.

"Ohmygawdwhatdidshesay?" spewed from the phone like one word.

"They're fine with it," Beth said, still shocked by how quick the meeting was. "I mean, of course Hy-Gene tried to object but the dean shut him down." Nervous laughter that she'd been holding back since Marcia put Gene is his place began to bubble up and spill over. "I actually can't believe how well it went."

"I can! You're going to the Oscars!" Jenna shouted. "Now comes the fun part—figuring out what you're going to wear."

"Wow, oh… wow. I didn't even think of that." She had been so concerned about the meeting with the dean, that she hadn't even considered what she would do if they said yes. "I guess I need to borrow a dress from you."

"Ha!" Jenna scoffed. "Honey, I don't have anything Oscar-worthy hanging in my closet. I wish."

"Shit. What am I going to wear? Maybe Vintageous has something affordable?" Panic was slowly wrapping its icy fingers around her as she began to comprehend the enormity of the event.

"You're not going to Vintageous. That's fine for a Halloween party. It is not fine for the freaking Academy Awards!"

"But what am I going to do?"

"Relax, Beth. I can hear you freaking out already. You're not going to have to pay for your dress."

"What do you mean? I am *not* asking Todd for money…" Beth was horrified at the thought of needing charity just to go to an event with Todd.

"No silly," Jenna said. "But have you forgotten that we're friends with a fashion designer?"

"Oh my god, do you think Asha would make me a dress? Do you think she would give me a discount?"

"Um, I think she'd do it for free."

"I can't ask her to do that, Jen."

"Beth, any designer in the world would want to dress someone for the Oscars. You'll actually be doing Asha the favor."

"But I'm just a nobody. Are you sure she'll want to do it?"

"Todd Allman's date to the Oscars isn't a nobody. Especially since you'll be his first *real* date!"

"What do you mean real date?"

Jenna sighed dramatically. "The only person Todd has ever taken to an awards show is his mom, right before she died. You are the first woman he will have taken as a date. Do you realize how much publicity that is going to get? Whichever gown you pick is going to be photographed a million times."

Beth shrank down in her seat terrified by the thought of being in the spotlight. A flood of thoughts tormented her on the short drive home. *What was I thinking? I don't want to be in a tabloid. What have I gotten myself into? I can't do this. How am I going to get out of this? I'll just tell him the dean said no.* She pulled into her driveway without remembering how she got there.

Before she could put her key in the lock, the knob turned and the door opened. Beth screamed and Jenna laughed.

"You just scared the shit out of me! What are you doing here and where is your car?"

"I'm here to help you stop spazzing out. I just had lunch with Danny. He dropped me off."

"Lunch with Danny?" Beth raised a curious eyebrow, forgetting all about freaking out.

"Yeah, I kind of like him." Jenna couldn't suppress a grin. "But we'll talk about all that later. I called Asha and she's expecting us in half an hour."

Beth sobered. "No, no. I just can't do it, Jenna. I'm telling Todd that the dean said no."

"You'll do no such thing." Jenna grabbed Beth by the shoulders. "Look at me Elizabeth Brennan Grant. You. Are. Going. To. The. Oscars. With. Todd. Allman. And that's that!"

"I don't think I can handle this kind of pressure, Jenna." She thought about the students in her class knowing and what she would have to say to them. She thought about all of the awful students that would take her class just to try to find out more about him.

"Listen. You and Todd are together, right?"

"Yes, I guess so."

"So sometimes, in relationships, we have to compromise," she said slowly, like she was explaining things to a child. "To do things for our partner that we know are important to them, even if they make us a little uncomfortable at first. Can you imagine how Todd would feel if you bailed and he had to walk that red carpet alone?"

"But you just said that he never takes anyone to these events so what does it matter?"

"Because he wants you there."

"I'll just tell him the dean said no, that I don't have a choice.

He'll never have to know that I chickened out."

"Yes he would because I already told Danny you were going."

"What the fuck, Jenna?!"

"Beth, you can handle it."

"But what if I trip on the carpet?"

"You're not going to trip."

"What if I spill food on my dress?"

"They don't serve food."

"They don't?" Beth looked puzzled. "Then why would I go?"

"Because this man loves you so much he literally wants the whole world to know. How can you turn him down?"

She didn't say anything so Jenna continued with a smug smile. "Plus, if you don't go, Gene wins."

Beth thought about the Gene/Jeans watching the awards show. About their faces when they saw her with Todd Allman on the red carpet. "Hmmmm. I hadn't thought of it that way." Then she thought about Todd in a tuxedo. And the decision was made.

36

Jenna had picked Beth up early that morning for manicures, pedicures, and massages in the hotel spa. By the time they got upstairs to the room, the hair stylist was waiting for her. He swept her hair up into a simple but chic chignon, that was the perfect mix of messy curls, neatly corralled and pinned with a few artful strands framing her face. It had the effect of looking both elegant and effortless. When she had tried to pay him, he had refused to take her money, asking instead if he could post her picture to his Twitter and Instagram accounts. *It's a whole new world.*

Along with the dress, Asha had sent over a professional makeup artist who brought a completely unfamiliar combination of brushes, potions, and even an air hose. She had never had her make-up done before, not even at one of those department store counters. When the woman was finally finished, Beth had been transformed into a version of herself she had never seen before. She felt as if her face had been sprinkled with a little bit of pixie dust. Even standing in front of a full-length mirror in just her bra and panties, she was in awe of her transformation.

Jenna approached from behind, reverently carrying the dress with both hands. She stopped to watch Beth look at herself in the mirror. "It's so weird," Beth said. "I look like me but I don't look like me."

"You look great. Now let's get you into the dress." She gently unzipped the back of the gown and held it open while Beth stepped into it, still staring at herself.

"This must be what it feels like to put on your wedding dress," Beth said.

Jenna froze, studying Beth's reflection in the mirror. "Oh honey, are you okay?" Beth held her breath and considered the wedding that she had never had. She wondered if, wherever Jeremy was, he could see her all dressed up, this shiniest version of herself. She thought that just maybe he could. And that he was happy for her.

"Yes. I really am." Beth took a deep breath. "I'm actually starting to get more excited than nervous."

Jenna walked around to face her friend. "Good," she said, taking Beth's hands in her own. There was something in her face Jenna had missed when only looking at her reflection. The familiar spark that had too long been dulled by a quiet and persistent sadness brightened Beth's eyes. "You deserve this, Beth. You do." Jenna's eyes welled with tears and Beth squeezed her hands.

"Thanks," she smiled, her own eyes welling up. "I couldn't have done any of this without you. You're my rock and I love you so much."

"I love you, too, but I can't hug you! I don't want to mess you up." Jenna laughed and swiped at her eyes.

A knock at the door brought them back to the business of getting ready. As Jenna answered the door, Beth admired the emerald green gown. She didn't usually like strapless dresses, having spent several long nights as a bridesmaid tugging them up. But this one was elegant and so beautifully crafted that it felt like part of her.

"Your jewels have arrived!"

"Oh my God, Jenna. I feel like 'Pretty Woman.'"

"Except you're not a hooker. But here," she said opening the box that held a diamond necklace and earrings. "Put your fingers in the box. I totally want to snap it closed on them."

Beth did and then tossed her head back and cackled in her best Julia Roberts impersonation. "If I forget to tell you later, I had a really nice time tonight."

They continued to giggle as Jenna carefully fastened the necklace. "Good thing Todd already signed for these. Guess you're off the hook for a couple hundred thousand dollars."

"Holy shit!" Beth touched the necklace at her collar bone. "Maybe I shouldn't wear them." She had never been much of a jewelry person but something about the way these diamonds caught the light was dizzying and made her giddy. "They're gorgeous," she whispered.

"You'll be fine. The necklace has an extra safety clasp and the earrings are screw backs, so they're not going anywhere."

If the necklace was magnificent, the earrings were exquisite, with dainty diamonds and emeralds. She screwed them on until her ears hurt and then loosened them just a little.

"Here. Shoes. Put them on." Beth sighed as Jenna opened the Gucci box to the most lovely devices of torture she had ever seen. Though the shoes were platform they were also somehow delicate with tiny crystals that caught the light. They were so beautiful, it seemed a crime that they would be hiding under her dress all night but they would put her five inches closer to Todd's face, to his lips. And just maybe, in the dress and the shoes and the jewels, she could pass for more than the impostor that she felt like.

With the ensemble complete, Jenna and Beth stared in the mirror. "Holy crap," Jenna said, shaking her head. "I watched the whole thing and I still can't believe how good you look."

Beth giggled and moved her hand to cover her mouth. Watching herself move in the mirror gave her the impression that she was a puppeteer operating a marionette. She spun around and tried to see herself from behind.

"Asha is a magician! My butt looks awesome!"

"Yes it does!" Jenna said, handing her a fresh glass of champagne.

"I need this. It's making me forget about how I'm going to get down that red carpet without you."

"Well, you'll have Todd."

"Or how I'm going to go to the bathroom without you." Beth took another sip.

"Listen, once you make it in the doors, nobody cares what or who you're wearing. Just hike that bitch up and go!"

"Maybe I should stop drinking this. Oh look," Beth said as she downed the last of champagne. "It's all gone."

"You can do this."

"I can do this."

"You ARE doing this."

"I AM doing this."

There was a soft knock at the door and Todd's muffled voice asked, "Beth, are you ready?"

"Just a second!" Jenna yelled, then she fussed with Beth's dress one last time.

"I can't wait to get through this and see you at the after-party."

"You've got this. Keep your head up and smile." Then she opened the door.

Todd froze when he saw her, his eyes wide. She beamed at him. "Wow," he said when he found his voice. As he walked to her, she drank him in. *It's just a tuxedo, right?* But it was more than that. She thought that perhaps no man had ever worn such a perfectly fitted suit. It looked like it had been stitched on him by Cinderella's fairy godmother. Beth tried to look everywhere at once from his hair, to the French cuffs that peeked out from his dark coat, to his slightly shiny dress shoes. When he reached her, he kissed her cheek. "I knew you were going to look beautiful," he whispered in her ear. "You always look beautiful. But wow, Beth. You actually took my breath away." She smiled up at him, from a much closer distance than usual. Then she ran a hand across his smooth cheek and around to the back of his neck, pulling him in for a kiss.

"Hey—watch the lipstick," Jenna scolded.

Beth giggled. "Sorry, couldn't help it."

"You're taller," he said, staring at her. Jenna cleared her throat loudly and Todd turned to her. "Hi Jenna!"

"Hello, Todd. You're doing that tux justice. But you two better get your asses out to the limo before you're late and give Danny a heart attack."

Jenna air-hugged Beth and kissed each cheek, passing her a silver clutch that held the essentials.

"Oh wait, I didn't even get a picture yet."

Todd paused beside her, his Hollywood smile at the ready, while Jenna grabbed her phone off the table.

"Not you, Todd. I want one of just Beth. There are going to be a ton of you guys together. I want to post this and be the first person to ever hashtag BethGrant. Hashtag She-ra."

37

They sat side by side in the back of the limousine. Now that the fun of getting ready with Jenna was over, Beth's nerves were starting to get the better of her. Her heart was pounding and she tried to sit very still so as not to mess up the gown, her hair, or her make-up. Todd took her hand in his and brought it to his lips.

"Thank you for coming with me." She tried to smile at him but it must have come out as more of a grimace because he looked startled then laughed.

"Relax," he said and squeezed her hand. Then he leaned into her ear and whispered. "You look absolutely beautiful." His breath sent a shiver down her back and she squeezed his hand tighter. "Are you sure you don't want some champagne?"

She shook her head. "I better not. I'm already not sure I can walk in these shoes."

"Hey," he said. "You're going to do fine. I'll be right beside you the whole time. If you fall over, I'll catch you. And if you break your ankle, I'll carry you."

"Oh my god," Beth said. "I didn't even think about that. Now I'm really nervous. Todd, why don't you just go and I'll watch you on TV."

"Nope, I want to show the whole world that you're mine."

He squeezed her hand then whispered, "But maybe there's something I can do to help you relax." His free hand slipped under the gossamer folds of fabric and made its way across her thigh.

She giggled and pushed his hand away but it came back. His fingers slid between her thighs and instinctively she parted them. Todd kissed her ear and her neck and her bare shoulder while his fingers caressed her inner thighs.

She turned to him. "Todd, we can't. Not here."

He pressed a button and closed the divider between them and the driver. "Yes. We can." Then his lips were on hers. *My lipstick!* she thought. But his clever hand tugged aside her panties and his fingers began to work their magic. She closed her eyes, all thoughts escaping her.

Her breath caught in her throat and she held back a moan as her body shuddered. When she finally opened her eyes, he was smiling at her. She brought her hand to his face and kissed him. "Thanks," she whispered.

He grinned and pressed his forehead to hers. "Anytime." She looked down at the erection straining his tuxedo pants.

"Hmmm." She ran a hand up his thigh. "We may need to do something about this."

Todd checked his watch. "I don't think there's time."

As if on cue, the driver's voice came over the intercom. "Sir, we're nearly there. About five cars ahead of us." Beth looked out the window and saw throngs of people lined up with their phones and cameras facing the line of cars.

"What are we going to do? You can't get out like that. Can the driver circle the block or something?"

"Nah, if he circles we'll never get back and my publicist will kill me. But it's fine. They'll be so distracted by how beautiful you look, they won't even notice."

"I love you," she said. And the look he gave her almost

made her cry. He kissed her again, deeply.

"Well, that's not going to help the situation in your pants." She used her thumb to wipe a bit of her lipstick from his lips. "How's my make-up?" she asked, pulling a compact from her clutch. Her make-up was almost exactly as it was before their episode. *Wow, I wonder if this stuff will ever come off.*

She was touching up her lipstick when the driver announced, "We're next." Suddenly her heart was hammering in her chest again. Todd read the panic on her face and slid his hand back between her thighs. She laughed, feeling a little tension leave her.

Then the door opened. "This is it, baby," he said with a wink and stepped out of the car. Todd turned to her and held out his hand. After a deep breath, Beth took it. And then she stepped out into the light.

Acknowledgments

The authors would like to thank their family and friends for the love and support. We'd also like to thank all of our early readers for their time and feedback.

To anyone who has read, bought, shared, liked, or in any other way supported us as independent authors, we are so grateful. Y'all are priceless!

About the Authors

Kerry Love and Jill Cammack met in Girl Scouts when they were seven years old. They grew up in Florida, went to school together, and even sat next to each other at college graduation. Jill is the Queen of Branding and a small business owner in the promotional products industry. Kerry is an artist, teacher, and wanderer. Though they don't currently live in the same place, the pair remain (virtually) side by side. And no distance will ever keep them from being best friends forever. *By Chance* is their first novel.

kerrygretchenlove.com

Also by Kerry Love:
Not Fine
Fine Tuning
Finer

9 7 9 8 9 8 8 9 9 4 5 3 4